MIRRORED Reflections

Other books by JF Ridgley

Available on Amazon and Books2Read
Historical Fiction
<u>Red Fury ~ Agricola series</u>
Red Fury Revolt Book 1
Short story – The Chrysalis
Red Fury Rage Book 2
Short story – A Roman Affair

Vows of Revenge
Short story – Birth of A Bully
Threatened Loyalties
Short story – For the Family

Contemporary Romance
18-Wheeler
Love Backwards

Mirrored Reflections

Published by RPridePublishing

653 W 23rd St

Panama City Fl. 32405

Published 2022

First edition published 2022

Printed in the United States of America

ePub ISBN: 978-1-951269-25-8

Print ISBN 978-1-951269-26-5

"*I will never leave you nor forsake you.*"

Hebrews 13:5

Dedication to

God and Joe

My greatest supporters all the way through

Chapter 1

"Lemonade, Daddy," Lori begged. "I want lemonade. Can I pleeeease have lemonade?"

"Did you ask Mommy if you could have that?" Chad asked his six-year-old daughter who had his wife's brown hair and his blue eyes.

"Mommy, can I pleeeease?"

"Sure," Margery said, grinning.

"So, it's six tacos, two glasses of lemonade, and one Coke." Chad recited. Agreement brightened the two faces that he could never see enough.

The air was crisp and musky. The trees surrounding the Farmers' Market were busy changing colors in the suffocatingly hot, October day. Fragrances of the season of ripe produce and aromas of tacos, pizza, and barbeque drifted over the busy area. Instead of staying home to watch the Chiefs as he had wanted, Chad decided to give in to Margery's wishes to join this mayhem instead.

People greeted each other, laughing, asking questions on what to do next, buy this or buy that chattered everywhere. It seemed that all of Kansas City had agreed with Margery—the day was perfect to be outside and alive.

As he got in a long line at the taco vender, Chad glanced over at the two who had kept him sane while he was deployed in Afghanistan. It was a blessing from God that he returned home alive. Not a day had passed that he hadn't missed his wife and daughter during his two tours. Face Timing helped, but he wanted them in his arms. Now, just breathing the same air, hearing them laugh, basking in Margery's emerald gaze, and simply holding her hand meant everything. He was never leaving them again.

As he stood there watching the milling throng, like his buddies, he read every person that passed just as they had learned to do while on duty. He couldn't turn it off. Nor did he want to. Old habits die hard.

In Afghanistan, people weren't as lucky to gather in the open. Eyes watched every movement for any solitary person who didn't fit in. They clustered in their own private spaces, usually behind high walls, just to survive.

Chad looked over at his little family lost in an intense conversation over some animated story Lori was telling. Tears swelled in his eyes. *Thank you, Jesus, for bringing me home.* His new job with Southwest Airlines as a ramp agent started next month. Once his DD214 discharge papers came through, he was golden.

Margery felt his attention and turned. Smiling, she sent him a kiss airmail. He caught it in his palm and spread it over his heart. He stepped to the window. "Two lemonades, six …"

A loner suddenly appeared in the crowd, clutching the lapels of a winter coat. The odd man's gaze shifted nervously about the crowd. His movements were hesitant, indecisive, as if watching for that perfect moment.

The asshole bumped into Chad's shoulder as he scurried passed, firing a venomous glare at Chad. Their gazes locked. The guy scurried a distance away, looked around … and inhaled a deep breath.

The instant the stranger's hand disappeared beneath the coat lapels; Chad knew.

"GET DOWN! EVERYBODY! GET DOWN! GET DOWN!"

The blast exploded. A fist of heat slammed Chad backward into oblivion. His family's picture on his locker flashed before him, then … all went black.

"I love watching all your videos, Fantasy. You're good," the patient whispered.

Sierra winced at the sound of her porn name Colton had given her. Pretending she didn't hear him, she continued to hang another IV bag that was keeping this sleazeball alive in the burn unit of the hospital. His smart-ass grin was barely hidden by his facial bandages covering his burns. After pouring gasoline over his clothes and setting himself on fire, this creton was lucky to see or even remember anything at all.

"… watched you millions of times," he continued. "Tell you what. You come back tonight, and I won't tell the hospital about you."

Sierra pointed to her nametag hidden, of course, beneath her PPEs-the yellow protective covering that hid everything but her eyes. "I am not your fantasy. Sorry. That's not me" *any longer.*

Vitals taken, IVs hung, meds given, charting done, Sierra escaped the room and collapsed against the hallway wall. How did that asshole recognize her?

Nicki, the head nurse, stopped in front of her, concern blatant. "Sierra, you okay?"

No. "Yes. Fine." Faking a smile, Sierra nodded, "I … I just need something to eat. Long shift and I forgot to eat."

"Fresh cookies are in the staff lounge. Get a few. Okay?"

"Great. I will," Sierra assured.

The nurse patted Sierra's shoulder. "You have to take care of yourself, or this job will kill ya," Nicki said and departed into the next room.

Sierra headed for the nurses' station between the Burn ICU and the Burn Paradise, where the patients who were more stable could feel somewhat normal. The staff lounge next to the central desk presented a tray of warm, fresh, oatmeal cookies.

Grabbing two, Sierra dropped into the nearest chair. As she stared at the cookies in her hand, the long-buried memories resurfaced. Colton had given her the name *Fantasy* after being kidnapped when she was six years old. It was the only name she could remember.

After finally fleeing for her life, she had changed her name to *Sierra Smith*, hopefully putting the bastard Mario and that life as far behind her as possible. Apparently, not far enough.

Sierra threw the cookies back on the tray. Sure, she once was a hooker, an international courtesan, a porn star—whatever anyone wanted to call her. Then, when the opportunity—or nightmare—came, she had fled to the States.

After crossing the border, Carol had picked her up in San Antonio and let her ride with her on her 18-wheeler across the country. This gave Sierra time to sort through all possibilities for what she wanted to do with her life. She had decided to help people and not service them any longer. She hated that previous life. This one was clean and respected.

She knew she would always be in debt to Carol because not only giving her time to think, but she had also given her the keys to her apartment. It was near the hospital and only blocks away from a nursing college. "Stay as long as you want, Sierra. I just keep it for mail and for down time anyway." No apartment was better cared for.

With one semester left now, she would graduate as a nurse. A timid smile emerged on her lips and blossomed in her soul. This was her last rotation for her associate degree in nursing—the burn center, understandably the hellhole of the hospital. But she loved it.

Since burn patients couldn't regulate their own body heat, the temperature on that floor varied between 90 and 100 degrees. The first few weeks there, Sierra thought she had returned to Dubai. Only this time, her scrubs and protective gear were her daily attire, not string-thin bikinis on yachts.

She had no regrets for leaving her life behind in Guatemala. Now, she had the promise of a future of which she could only dream about. *If that creton doesn't ruin everything.*

An emergency sounded in the ICU. All available staff were expected to assist. Struggling into fresh PPEs and claiming a squirt of hand sanitizer, Sierra ran past a Code Blue cart waiting outside the door and bolted into the patient's room.

The monitors were going crazy. Blood pressure, skyrocketing—200/133. Heart rate, nearing 130. He was going to crash at any moment.

Jason, the staff nurse, and Dr. Kendrick, the head trauma surgeon, grappled to hold the patient down while Nicki kept the oxygen mask over the patient's face. Another floor nurse struggled to get a sedative into one of the IV lines as he thrashed.

Without a thought, Sierra clutched the patient's hand grappling for the IV line in his arm. "It's okay. It's okay," she whispered softly.

Immediately, the patient calmed. His breathing slowed. His blood pressure began to normalize. Yet, if Sierra attempted to pull free, everything started spiking again. She slipped her hand back into his and he settled ... again.

Where are they? Margery? Lori? I have to find them? Searing pain burned Chad's body like giant fire ants feasting on his flesh. *Leave me alone. Go away. Somebody! Please. Make them stop!* But they didn't. They kept biting, pushing, burning. He couldn't swallow. He couldn't breathe. *Just let me breathe. For God's sake, let me breathe.*

The torture kept prodding, poking, torturing him. Why were they shoving shards of glass through every nerve? Flashes of light kept streaking behind his eyelids. Hot yellow flashes. Blips on a screen.

Suddenly, like a gift from heaven, Margery's hand slipped into his. He heard her voice. "It's okay. It's okay."

Margery! Margery was there. She was with him. With him. His darkness wept relief until her hand started to withdraw. *No. No! NO! DON'T GO. DON'T* ... Her hand returned.

Chapter 2

Everyone stared at her as if she were some kind of magician. Then, Jason smirked from the other side of the hospital bed. "You aren't going anywhere, my dear."

"But … my patients …" Sierra gasped.

"One of us will *precept* for you," Jason assured.

"Stay put, Sierra," Dr Kendrick ordered also grinning. "This guy is the city's newest hero, so the mayor is watching our every move. He'll need constant monitoring. Think you can manage this for us, Sierra?"

Sierra shrugged. After all, she was a student nurse—single and available—so, "Sure. I can stay with him."

"Oh, and last I checked, his corneal abrasion is quite severe," Dr. Kendrick continued before he left. "Make sure his eyes remain bandaged until I say otherwise. No one touches that bandage."

"Consider it done." Sierra submitted to the comfort of the hospital chair to attend to her newest responsibility—to hold the unit's heroic train-wreck's hand for as long as needed. She glanced at his hospital band on his wrist. *Chad Michaels.* She may as well introduce herself since she had become part of his medical equipment.

"Hello, Chad," Sierra whispered softly. "I'm Sierra." *Not Fantasy.* "I'm your official hand holder, here to help you survive your train wreck."

The monitor maintained a steady beep; all the numbers held. The vent hissed softly and regularly. The patient now heavily sedated and wrapped like an Egyptian mummy, seemed to be resting well enough.

Curious to know her charge, she opened the drawer of the table beside his bed, Sierra saw a pocket Bible, a wallet, coins, key fob to an F-150, and his wedding ring in a plastic Ziplock bag.

Peeling back the black cover of the Bible, she read, *To Chad. I love you. God loves you. Margery Aug 2015.* His wife likely. Why wasn't she there holding his hand? The probable answer was not the one she wanted to consider.

Putting everything back, Sierra thought of the Bible Onyx had given her. It remained in Rio Dulce, Guatemala. There had been no chance of reclaiming much of anything when she fled Mario that horrid night.

Unexpectedly, Colton had died of a heart attack, and Mario had laid claim to Colton's stable. Everyone was his property now, and he had begun to 'break down' everyone. She had refused to be broken.

Months before, Onyx also refused and had escaped to a nearby convent where the true sparkle in her brown eyes returned. Her chocolate face glowed with joy. No fake happy. She had actually become radiant in that plain habit of a novitiate.

Onyx's new-found confidence haunted Sierra. How could Onyx say that after all they both had been through? However, she had toyed with the idea of becoming a nun like her friend. The idea didn't fit well. After all, Colton had made sure they all knew God hated prostitutes. And she had been a prostitute, whore, you name it.

Before fleeing, Sierra had warned Onyx not to set foot in the streets of Rio Dulce. Mario was watching for her and had eyes everywhere. She remembered Onyx's confident smile, *God will take care me, Sierra. I'll be fine no matter what Mario does now.*

Her patient lurched from some memory, some dream, but then settled just as quickly. Jolted back to the present, Sierra focused on Chad's vital signs. Other than his urine bag needing changed, he was holding.

As if she had X-ray vision, she studied the bandaged man beside her. Undoubtedly, beneath his dressings were burn wounds that would totally destroy what normalcy he ever thought he had. If he survived, the world would proceed to see him as a monster. Then, once people learned what happened to his body, they would see Chad as an innocent victim of life. He would then be received back into the fold of society with the full regalia of pity.

None of which would be allotted to her because no one could see her damage. It was buried in the dark depths of her soul. Even if those same scornful eyes could see her damage, they would never grant her the same pity or acceptance. Not even their God would.

Her cellphone and earplugs were back at the apartment. All that was left was a television with nothing to watch. The regular beeps were threatening to put her to sleep. Her limited entertainment included a lovely view of the parking garage, following clouds floating across the blue sky, and watching her day darken.

Nicki appeared in the room. "How is he doing?"

"Oh! Hi." Sierra grinned as if guilty. "Well enough, as long as I hold his hand."

Nicki opened Chad's chart. "FYI, everybody's jealous," she stated as she checked the chart and compared numbers.

"It's not what you think," Sierra assured sarcastically.

"Never is." Nicki jerked her attention outside the room's glass wall. "Oh, shit no. We have company."

Sierra followed the nurse's gaze to strangers who were likely Chad's parents standing outside the room as if waiting for an invitation. Tears flowed from a short, gray-haired woman—Chad's mother most likely. Beside her stood Chad's father holding an adorable little girl in his arms.

Nicki scurried from the room to stop them. "May I help you," she asked.

"We need to see Chad Michaels," his mother chirped. "We were told he's in this room? We are his parents, and this is his daughter. We need to see our son."

"I'm sorry. No visitors are allowed in the burn ICU. I'm really sorry. I understand, but you should never have been allowed up here. You need to leave."

Appalled, his mother puffed up. "You don't understand. We need to see him. Lori just lost her mother, and she needs to see that her father is still alive."

Sierra pitied Nicki at that moment. Even with two kids of her own, Nicki had the full responsibility of the floor, and had to stand up to any visitor regardless of how her heart bled for them. Outsiders brought germs, and patients' welfare came first.

However, Nicki wilted. "A few minutes outside the glass window. No more."

The wide-eyed gaze of innocent blue eyes stared at her daddy. "Gampa, daddy is a mummy."

"Those are just really big bandages, Lori," Gampa answered.

"Is daddy gonna be okay?"

"Of course, Lori. The doctors and nurses are doing everything possible to make sure." Chad's mother rested a hand on the girl's back. She turned to Nicki. "Why is she holding my son's hand?"

"So, we won't need to keep your son sedated any more than is necessary. Now, you need to leave."

The adorable little girl pleaded up at Nicki. "But I want to see him?"

"I'm sorry, sweetheart. You can't. But soon. When your daddy is all better you can. I promise," Nicki assured. "I know he misses you very much. Now everyone needs to leave."

Over the next few days, the only excitement granted Sierra were the cars moving in the parking garage. Storm clouds drifting in the blue sky. Stars moving across the night sky. The television presented yet another array of ridiculous ads and little else. She had all but memorized the outdated magazines that the nurses brought her.

Otherwise, the staff continued moving about the hall to attend patients. Soft talk, beeping, moving carts, various therapists and doctors coming and going, and cleaning crews continually stirring outside the room. And every one of them was covered in the same PPEs as she wore.

Chad had been weaned from the vent and was put on a full oxymask. His overall numbers were holding steady. Dr. Kendrick said Chad's eye movement wasn't acceptable yet. So, the ocular bandage had to remain. Jason was pleased with how well Chad's burns were improving. Debridement was now down to once a day instead of twice.

Sierra spent her time massaging Chad's hands open to keep them from locking into claws. If she was quick about switching hands, he remained quiet. Splints had also been applied to keep his arms from permanently curling in. His legs were constantly being lifted and lowered by the bed. If this weren't done, his body would have locked down by now, and he'd never be able to walk or work with his hands.

Boredom had prompted Sierra to memorize Chad's chart, which revealed that this Chad Michaels had 32% body surface burns: 10% second degree. 22% third. Bilateral corneal abrasion. Various fractures: skull fracture, multiple fractures to his ribs and to his left shoulder. Liver laceration and a ruptured eardrum-left side, damage to the right. He had also incurred a blast injury, over-pressure injury, inhalation/lung injury due to chemical toxins. Overall, he was one lucky man to be alive at all

The only other time Sierra remembered feeling this trapped was when she was nine. Colton had locked her in a broom closet as punishment for not doing what he expected—something she didn't want to recall. However, what had felt like forever had only been three days without food, three bottles of water, and a pee pan.

"All that is over. Behind me. I have a respectable future now," she whispered to herself.

Chad's food tray arrived, along with fragrances of more delicious food other than the infamous green Jell-O, straws for the orange juice, and bottles of Pedialyte. Fortunately, the staff snuck in enough to sustain her since she wasn't allowed to eat in a patient's room.

"Well, sweetheart, you finally get to eat something. So, I'm going to set you up." Sierra pressed the controls to raise Chad's head. As his head lifted, his blood pressure also rose. "Hey Darlin,' you have to work with me here," she cooed. "This isn't much, I know. But it is a start. Here."

As much as she hated doing it, Sierra fell into using the seductive tones she had perfected. Spoonful by spoonful, the food disappeared through the bandaged slit around Chad's mouth. Afterward, Chad drifted into a restless sleep.

Well into the night, his head started jerking about as his body flinched or attempted to strike out. He groaned, whined, sobbed. "Shhhh, sweetheart. I'm here." She called for more sedation.

Chapter 3

"Rise and shine, sweet cakes. You ready for this?"

Sierra jolted awake. In that same instant, pain shot through her neck as she jerked her head from Chad's shoulder. She had spent plenty of nights with a man, but never like this. "Ready? For what?"

"The *tank*," Jason stated as he proceeded to check Chad's vitals. "Looks like our train-wreck is doing great today." The breakfast tray arrived. "Once he's done eating, I'll take him for his morning walk. Then, you can get something to eat and then come join us. Ever helped with a debridement?"

Sierra shoved a straw through the plastic covering the orange juice cup. "No. Heard about it though."

Her hungry body thanked her for granting it some decent food. Since she had commingled with the public, no telling what germs she may have picked up in the cafeteria, so she showered and changed everything from scrubs to fresh PPEs. Tucking her ponytail under the paper cap, she headed in the direction of the *tank*. The hall there was long and lonely.

"No. Please. Don't do this again. Please. Don't ... NOOOOOO!"

The sound of torture greeted Sierra as she entered the dark chamber. The smell of antiseptic, putrid water, a humid dampness, and heat slapped her in the face like a tidal wave the instant she opened the door.

Jason was lifting Chad from a whirlpool that had washed the raw burns free of infection. Once his patient was secured on a rigid table, Jason picked up his torture device—a special washrag called a *fluff*—and began to gently remove damaged flesh from each burn.

Held down by the restraints, Chad fought him. "Stop it, you mother fucker. Stop or I'll kill you. Please stoooop."

Sierra remembered her class on burns. The dead skin had to be removed to prevent any chance of infection and lessen scarring. It was a necessary evil that had to be done.

Jason motioned to zip her mouth and whispered, "Hold his head, okay?" That was easier said than done.

The hours she had sat beside his bed, Chad had been bundled in bandages like his daughter's mummy. Now, he lay naked like a slab of butchered meat. The fresh washed, burn wounds started at the top of each foot and proceeded up the front of his body. The degrees of burn revealed either bare bone, or simply deep mutilated muscle and tissue.

Apparently, Chad had slightly turned at the blast because the burns ran fully up his left thigh but not the right. The damage bled out like a wave on a beach over his torso all the way up to his chin, to tip of his nose, face, and forehead, burning off one ear, singeing the other. Oddly enough, the fronts of his arms were not damaged because he had covered his eyes. But, the back of his arms looked like his legs.

"Don't do this. Please. Oh, God. Stop him. God. Make him stop!"

"Chad. We have to. It's for your own good. I'm sorry," Jason kept explaining over and over.

"Motherfucker! Stop. I swear. I will kill you if you don't stop!"

It took every ounce of Sierra's strength to hold Chad's head still. The cries, screams, pitiful moans were as endless as the foul threats. Oblivious to it all, Jason continued to *fluff* Chad's cheeks, jawline, ear, face.

Chad broke down into sobs, "Pleeeeease stop."

Eventually the sobs returned to threats. Yet, Jason quietly, steadily continued his task. "Sorry. I'm sorry, Chad." Over and over again, Jason's utterances fell on deaf ears.

The door behind Sierra opened and one of the fellow nurses appeared as a shadow. "Nate, so glad you could join us...finally," Jason quipped as he worked on abdominal burns.

"Car broke down. Sorry, I'm late."

Jason nodded at Sierra. "Go. Get a shower and we'll meet you in the room."

Sierra could not get the shower hot enough. Chad's hell, his torment, his anger echoed in her brain until she, too, sobbed. It was a hellhole, but a necessary hellhole. Dropping her forehead against the ceramic white tiles, she let tears fall with the water as if it could wash away Chad's suffering.

She'd seen beatings before. Mario was good at them. She couldn't remember how many girls came from the hospital after beatings by him or a john. But to watch a patient endure this had torn her soul in half. She needed to get back to Chad's room.

Sierra dried off, completely changed scrubs and PPEs again, and resumed her job as Chad's caregiver. Jason and Nate had Chad back in the room, freshly bandaged after slathering Silvadene, the magic ointment of any burn unit.

Chad was sitting up in what Jason called *the pink caddy*—a gray, overstuffed chair. "Well, he's yours, sweetheart. Lunch will be here soon. Want me to bring you something?"

She caught Jason's arm as he passed her. "You're a saint."

Jason smirked. "I had a preacher once. He had saved a kid in his burning church. Now, I know more names for Satan and how to use them than you can imagine. But, I'm hardly a saint."

Where was he? What happened? Why did they keep him blind? He needed to know why he was trapped in this demonic cocoon of darkness. Chad flinched from, fought, or cursed anything around him that made no sense. Why were they torturing him constantly?

All he wanted was to kill the son-of-a-bitch, whoever it was, who sank him into the water that scorched every inch of his body. Whoever it was that laid him on that cold slab and tore his flesh off, inch by horrid inch. There could never be enough curses, threats, or names he could call that bastard.

Once again, the flash of the yellow heat blasted behind his eyelids. Once again, he felt the fist of heat and his insides exploding. Flashbacks of Afghanistan returned along with the continual fear of being captured. Had they sent him back there? Were they the ones doing this to him?

No. He hadn't gone back. No. Margery was there, holding his hand. Please, make them stop, Margery. Please. Take me home. Pleeeeease.

Chapter 4

Even though Chad was getting stronger, Dr. Kendrick still wanted Chad's eyes protected. So, Chad had missed seeing the leaves whirl in small tornadoes outside the parking garage, the denuding of trees around the courtyards below, the first snowfall as well as the mix of Thanksgiving and Christmas decorations flooding about the hospital grounds and floors.

Chad had his lucid moments when he wanted her to read from his Bible. Learning quickly, Sierra read mostly from Leviticus for the Levite laws would put anyone to sleep. Then, there were other times when Chad would plunge into restless PTSD flashbacks. "Get down!" or "Noooo!" Or "Pleeeeease, dooooon't."

It was then that Sierra would slip into her seductive tones. "Shhhhh, darlin,' I'm here." Usually just touching his arm or tightening the grip on his hand broke the spell.

There was only one time during the day that she was free. That was when Jason took Chad to the tank, which happened every morning like clockwork. Then, she would shower, change into fresh scrubs, visit the nurses' station to simply chat and feel a part of the normal world.

She had learned that the creton was still there because someone had snuck him a peanut butter sandwich, not knowing he was allergic to peanuts. So, her past remained safe behind Benadryl.

"They are thinking of moving your guy over here to Paradise," Nicki stated as she closed a patient's file.

"Really? Then, does that means I'm back on the floor?" Sierra asked hopefully. She wanted back to the regular routine she only got to watch now. However, she also wanted to continue to help with Chad's recovery. After all, she had started this road with him and, in truth, wanted to see him walk out of the hospital holding his little girl in his arms. But, every nurse wanted to witness that with every patient.

Nicki smirked. "Not according to what I hear. Sorry. Big boss upstairs wants you to stay with him." She looked past Sierra and then closed her eyes in dread. "I'm talking to the front desk after this. "

Sierra turned to see Lori leading Gamma and Gampa down the hall. There was something very stalwart about all three. Chad's father appeared trapped. His mother was ready with fangs and fingernails. And Lori's blue gaze was already pleading.

"We need to see Chad," Gamma stated. "Where is he?"

"Your son is not allowed visitors," Nicki informed. "But they are thinking of moving him here soon and ..."

"Lori needs to see her father. Today."

"Mrs. Michaels ..."

Gamma's blue gaze lasered on both Nicki and Sierra. "She can't sleep. She has constant nightmares. She must see her father. Today."

"But ..."

"Nicki, what if his daughter wears a set of PPEs?" Sierra whispered. "And stays just for a short visit. It might do Chad some good."

Again, caught in the middle, Nicki melted. "Fine. But you are responsible."

Sierra saw the first hints of Jason appearing from the elevator with Chad laid out on a gurney. She turned desperately to his visitors, motioning to the nurse's staff lodge in hopes of them not seeing their son's approach.. "How about we can dress you all up like all the nurses. How's that, Lori."

Chad's daughter followed gleefully with grandparents in tow.

"Is daddy gonna be okay?" Lori asked as Sierra lifted the girl onto her lap beside her father's bed.

"Of course. He's already a lot better."

"He still looks like a mummy."

"Like your Gampa said, it's just a big Band-Aid."

For the first time, Chad's hand released Sierra's and rose toward the gauze covering his eyes. She gripped his wrist pulled it down to his daughter's little hand.

"I think he wants to hold your hand," Sierra whispered. Lori's tiny hand quickly became lost in his grip.

"I love you, Daddy. I miss you." Lori's huge gaze pleaded up to Sierra. "I kiss him? Pleeeeease."

"Be gentle. Okay, Lori?"

Sierra helped the little girl onto a small section of the hospital bed, close enough to kiss the bandages covering Chad's right cheek. "Love you to the moon and back, daddy."

"'ove 'ou, 'aby 'irl." slurred from the mouth slit. The monitor started beeping faster. All the numbers were rising.

"Sweetheart, your daddy really needs rest now."

"I wanna stay."

Concern was climbing into desperation. Pulling Lori's hand from his grip and inserting hers in its place, Sierra stated. "Lori, your daddy needs rest, and your grandparents are waiting for you."

As they left, Sierra focused on Chad. She had to be Margery again. "Lori is doing fine, sweetheart. You need to rest."

His grip on her hand tightened. The numbers began falling. The gauze over his eyes grew dark with tears. Something told her Chad now had something more to live for.

Evening slowly came. Chad had remained sedated, and Sierra remained, as usual, to watch his numbers in the event of another flashback or whatever. Four guys appeared outside the room, chatting like worried hens. Alas, the cute blond guy peeked around the door frame. "Uh, can we come in?"

A few visitors were acceptable since they had moved Chad away from the ICU. However, four pushed the limit. Nicki would have a heart attack, but she was at home. Sierra gave Chad a glance. His numbers were regular and normal. The sedative was still working. "Sure."

All adorned with gowns and masks, they all hustled in as one into the room to stand at the foot of Chad's bed. Obviously, they had been spared the realities of their friend's damages by the bandages now over Chad's face.

"Hi, I'm Charlie," the curly-haired, blonde guy said. The gleam in his eyes made her think of a sly fox, the boss of the outfit. "He going to be okay?"

"He's improving." *Physically, yes. Emotionally, not so sure.*

Charlie turned to the black-haired friend who was all Texan from his boots to the cowboy hat he carried at his side. "This is Hunter." The red head in military cargo pants was Axel. The black guy built like Rambo holding a large plant was introduced as Ryan.

They all said, "Hi."

Ryan placed the plant on the bedside table. That was another issue Nicki was adamant about. Actually, a few plants were okay on the paradise floor, but the number of them arriving wasn't. She could hear Nicki now, "We'd have a regular plant nursery here."

"Sorry," Sierra stated, "that has to go out to the nurses' station. You can leave the note. I'll see he gets it."

"How long will he be … like that?" Axel asked, worry buzzed in his gaze.

"Time will tell." She couldn't tell them anything beyond the obvious—hospital policy and government rules.

"And you are?" Hunter asked in his Texan drawl.

"His nurse."

"So, you the one holding his hand all this time?" he asked. "You know he is married? Or, well, was."

"Yes." Obviously, his mother had informed them about her. "It calms him."

Jason appeared in the door. Chad's grip "Time's up, fellas. Your buddy needs his beauty rest." Obediently, they left, and Jason smiled. "Thought I'd stop by before I left to see if you needed anything."

Chapter 5

Again, and again, and again, Chad remembered the bomber glaring at him, followed with what seemed instant—the blast. His mind flashed to Margery. Lori. Panic erupted. Then, Margery whispered to him, and her hand tightened over his. In that moment, everything calmed. All he needed, now, was to see her face and feel her in his arms.

The reality that he was in some hospital had slowly become apparent. The voices he heard were the doctors and nurses informing him in medical language that he had miraculously survived. "Can you hear me, Chad? Nod if you do."

It was the doctor. Chad nodded.

"That's good news. Now, are you ready for some of the bandages to come off so you can see?"

Please. "Yes." Yet, the instant hands touched his head, he flinched away.

"That's fine, Chad. There is no rush."

Slowly, carefully, the bandages unwound from his head. Hope

rose with each movement toward freedom. Little by little he felt the fresh air, lightness, and it didn't sear his flesh.

He clutched Margery's hand, excited to see her beautiful face. But what if ... what if he opened his eyes to darkness? *Please God, let me see. Don't take that from me!*

"Will I see?" he begged.

"We think so, Chad." The last bandage was removed, but a fragment of thick gauze remained over his eyes. "Don't open your eyes until we tell you. Okay?" He nodded.

The gauze lifted slowly.

"Okay. Anytime, Chad. You can open your eyes."

He could open his eyes and know. Know what? The answer. Did he want to know ... the answer? Tendrils of fear sliced through Chad's heart as his eyelids fluttered, leaking elements of light. He wasn't blind! He wasn't blind!

Forcing his eyelids open, he saw two blurry images beside the bed. Blinking in the darkened room, the faces cleared to two men, smiling proudly at him. The doctor had black hair and gleaming brown eyes and the other was a blond and blue-eyed guy with tears drizzling down his cheeks. Both beamed as if they had accomplished something.

Chad glanced around for Margery. Just the doctors and a nurse.

"Hello Chad. I'm. Dr. Kendrick and this is Jason, your nurse."

"Well, what do you see, Chad?" this Jason asked.

Chad immediately recognized that voice—his torturer, the one he had cussed with every threat he knew. But the fury instantly melted to joy of just being able to see him. "I'm not blind. Where's..."

"Then, how many fingers do you see?" Dr. Kendrick asked.

"Two. Now, three."

"What color is my tie?"

"Purple."

Joy exploded in the doctor's gaze. "Praise God. Yes, you can see. Chad. That is good news."

"It is."

Chad jerked his attention to Margery's voice, the vision he had pleaded to see ever since … That's not Margery!

"This is Sierra," the doctor said. "She's been with you through this entire process."

All Chad saw was the nurse covered completely by yellow, protective gear. Only her emerald gaze was visible, radiant, and simmering in tears. She wasn't Margery.

His gaze swept the room. The door. The hall. "My wife? Where is Margery? She was here."

"Chad, she's not here," Dr. Kendrick said gently.

"When … when will she be back? I mean, I know she's been here, holding my hand. I felt her. I heard her. Where is she?"

"I was holding your hand, Chad."

Chad jerked his attention to the nurse. "You? No. It was my wife."

The emerald gaze bravely rose to the doctor for that answer.

"Your wife did not make it, Chad. I am sorry."

"What do you mean. She didn't make it. She had to." They're lying. She was there. Chad looked to anyone to tell him the truth.

"Do you remember the blast?" Jason asked.

"Of course, I remember. Where…"

"Your daughter is alive," the doctor continued, "because your wife protected her from the shrapnel."

No. That can't be right. Chad's heart climbed into his throat as he heard his own voice yelling to get down. Didn't Margery hear him? God wouldn't let this happen. Not to Margery. He glared at the nurse. "Where is she?

Then he felt Margery's hand slip in his, only it was the nurse's hand. The familiarity struck like a flame. He jerked free. "Don't touch me."

The nurse let go and settled in the chair as he glared at the doctor who had kept him alive for this. "My daughter. Where is she?"

"With your parents, Chad," Dr. Kendrick stated.

"Not with my wife?"

"Not with your wife."

A scream of pain roared from his soul and filled through the room. Sobs followed, lacerating Chad's heart as he tried to draw his knees to his chest. They couldn't bend enough to close the hole exploding in his chest. Fists drew toward his face to hide his tears, but they were restrained to only inches from the bed.

He wanted out. Away from this hell. He fought the restraints, the tubes, the needles stuck in his arms, at whatever was holding him to the bed with every ounce of strength he had. He had to find Margery. Lori. Then something seeped into his body and slowly, ever so slowly. He calmed enough to breathe. Sleep swept over him.

Chapter 6

"You know you can go home now," Jason said, curiously.

She could, but she didn't want to. After all, she had spent the last weeks by Chad's bed. And even though he was healing physically, he wasn't emotionally. Maybe he still needed her.

Each day now, Chad had returned to his room, dressed in less and less layers of bandaging. The monitors beeped a normal rhythm. His numbers remained steady. Therapy was apparently going fantastically. Chad's arm splints had been discarded. Even though Jason continued to take Chad to the *tank*, his reports concerning the burns said they were closing normally. How much longer was the hospital going to let her remain as Chad's personal attendant?

Chad had made it perfectly clear to everyone that he didn't want Sierra near him. However, that wish was not granted because the staff had taken a hit with flu and was running short on nurses. And, since she wasn't on the floor, she wasn't exposed to the virus. So, she remained isolated in Chad's room whether he liked it or not.

"I want to see what I look like," Chad snarled.

Sierra bit her lips. Dr. Kendrick wasn't excited about that great reveal because of Chad's emotional reaction to her. "I'll let him know."

The usual silence followed. Lunch arrived. And as expected, Chad refused to eat. That worried her. "Chad, you must eat something. You have to stay strong for Lori."

"Don't you mention my daughter."

"Fine." Sierra sat the tray beside his chair. Did his wife realize just how much Chad genuinely loved her? Once, she and Onyx had talked about loyal husbands with Levi, one of the boys that Colton had rescued. Levi said some men treasured their wives so much that they would never seek another woman, which seemed more like a fairytale.

These hubbies had become their conquests. Like all the others in Colton's stable, she knew that all men wanted sex and would pay whatever to be pleasured. It was her job to see that they were, at any cost. The more the better.

There were many times she had been paid $5,000 to spend the night with her *john* who was married, with two kids in private schools, and lived in a country club. One john told her that he just did not like sleeping alone. But she bet his wifey didn't do the things she had done to service him. Even though her real dad didn't want her, Sierra wondered if he was one of those—faithful to her mother? What would it be like to be loved by a man who didn't see her as an object to fuck?

As Sierra starred window to the world, once again, she was drawn into her past. According to Colton, her mother had left her playing at the park so he could appear with a puppy. Sierra remembered glancing at her mom, who was lost in her cellphone again, and had ventured off to see the other puppies in his van. In a flash, her world changed.

First, she had fought them, Colton and Mario, who were keeping her in the van. She wanted to go home! Slowly, over time, they convinced her that everything went perfectly. They even showed her the money her parents had given them to take her away. A few days passed and no one came for her. Not her mother. Not her father. Not even the police. So, she never wanted anything to do with her real parents after that.

That was what Colton and Mario did, find children whose parents didn't want them any longer. Onyx. Levi. And the others. They all became her *other* family. And they all did what she learned to do—pleasure men, and sometimes women, for money. After all, they had to work if they were to eat, get riding lessons, pretty dresses, toys. Anything.

"Did you hear me?"

Sierra tore her gaze from the winter sky outside. "What?"

"You heard me. I want to see what I look like."

No, you don't, Chad. "I … I can't take the bandages off." And Sierra was glad she couldn't.

Everyone on the burn center looked at their patients as victims of an accident. They all knew each remained the same person inside, unblemished. But their patients rarely accepted that at first. They only saw damage, horror, what they would see every day for the rest of their life.

"I'm sorry, Chad. You'll have to wait for Dr. Kendrick."

"You sure you are ready for this, Chad?" Jason asked as he stood beside the gurney in the outer room of the *tank*. Chad knew the whirlpool loomed just beyond the side door where he, once again, had survived the living hell.

Obviously, the debridement was getting easier to endure because there was fewer threats and cusswords. Just pain. Even though Sierra had lied to him about Margery, Chad was glad she stood by the door. Even so, he wasn't sure he wanted to see what was about to be revealed.

"Chad, you're looking really good," Jason assured. "I mean it. Your burns are closing perfectly."

Chad glared up at the fool. "Perfectly?"

"Yes. Perfectly."

As Jason raised the bed upward, Chad witnessed the raw, torn, seeping wounds that stretched from the top of his feet all the way up his legs. His chest and belly were still raw. His underarms also fried and raw.

He stared at the destruction. This was the hell he had been enduring. The evident torture. And they say he is healing perfectly? Liars.

A dread, deeper than any well, loomed before him. All that was left was to see his face. "My face. Tell me what I'll see," Chad demanded.

Jason scrutinized him and came to a conclusion. "Well, I don't think you will ever have to shave. Certainly not your armpits. You're good to go there. And, you won't have to worry about hair getting in your eyes since your hairline has been pushed back."

"How far?"

Jason touched the top of his skull. "Maybe, if you grow the back side long enough, you can comb it over as a cover-up," he quipped. "And you may want an earring in this ear one day," he touched Chad's right ear. "I know a guy who makes some really cool guy earrings."

Chad reached for his left ear and felt a hole. "It's gone! The whole thing. It's gone!"

Jason bravely nodded. "But, the right ear is fine, at least. And, you aren't deaf."

"Give me a damn mirror."

Jason handed him a mirror, backside toward Chad. Chad studied the man. No reaction appeared—neither good nor bad. He looked at Sierra. Worry. Still, they waited. He waited. Finally, he turned the mirror around.

It was like the blast all over again. *That* was not Chad Michaels. He didn't know that freak. It had to be some Halloween costume of a monster from some horror movie staring back at him.

He thought of his high school senior picture. His black hair, dangling slightly over his forehead, his blue eyes gleaming so proud. His face beaming, smooth, fresh, real. That was Chad Michaels: football star; corporal in the Marines; Margery's husband.

But this freak in the mirror wore mishappened eyes and nostrils like a monster with mottled skin, raw, ginger-colored blotches, shriveled like a prune. Who would not run away in terror? He had become Freddy Krueger.

Oh, God, Lori? She would never let him close to her, hold her, be near her now. Ever again. Who would? Even he couldn't stand looking at … at … that thing.

Chad threw the mirror at Jason and heard it shatter on the floor.

He never could go outside in public unless he wore a mask. Sobs roared from his guts.

Sierra rushed toward him. "Chad, it's not as bad as you think."

He jerked his foot from her touch, wanting to kick her.

"Sierra is right, Chad. This is the worst of it. I promise you, it will get better. It will. The plastic surgeons are amazing," Jason said.

"I'm a freak. I'm glad Margery is dead. I wish I were as well."

"No, Chad," Sierra pleaded, "You are still you, the same man your daughter loves."

He didn't want to hear that … but needed to hear that. "How can she?"

"You're her daddy, and she loves you no matter what. I know that."

"She can't see me like this."

Sierra offered an encouraging smile. "Chad, you haven't changed. You are still you, regardless of what the blast did to you."

"Your real friends will see beyond this shit," Jason added. "Forget the others who don't."

He was ruined. Destroyed. A freak. A monster. At least Margery would never see him like this. "Get the damn bandages on me and get me back to my room."

"That's not my daddy!" When Chad heard his daughter's scream, it sliced through his soul.

"No. No Honey. He's … he's just …" His mother couldn't put it into words either.

Chad lay there in the bed in what was now called burn paradise, enduring his daughter's fear along with his mother and dad's brave expressions. This wasn't their son. He wasn't Lori's father. He said it for them. "I am a monster. A freak. Say it."

"No, Chad. You're no … uh … such thing," his mother assured. "Lori, that is your daddy. See. He's just …"

"Don't make her look at me." The words yanked every heart string in his body. "Leave. Just leave. Get her out of here!"

Sierra sat in the chair by his bed and motioned Lori, covered in a small PPE's, toward her. "Lori, come here, sit on my lap. Let me see. Humm. What happened to your knee?"

He couldn't help but listen.

Lori whimpered. "I fell down on the sidewalk and cut it."

"I bet that hurt, didn't it?"

"Uh-huh."

"Did scabs grow to protect your knee?"

"Uh-huh."

Tears drizzled into his missing ear as Chad listened to the gentle conversation.

"Oh! Is that a scab?"

"No. It's a scar."

"Oh, a scar. Do you have any more … scars?"

"Uh-huh," Lori's voice picked up a happy note. "Here. On my finger. I was cutting straberries and had to have nine stitches here."

Chad remembered that day. Margery was putting fresh strawberries up in the freezer and turned her back. Lori had claimed the knife and tried to cut a piece of the fruit. Instead, she sliced her finger and blood gushed everywhere.

The familiar sound of Sierra's voice drew him back. "My goodness. You had to be really brave to get nine stitches. Does it still hurt?"

"No."

"Lori, look at me," Sierra said softly. Chad also had to look as she continued.

"When the explosion happened, it hurt your daddy like when you fell and hurt your knee … like when you cut your finger. And, like you, he also has to heal."

"Uh, huh," Lori seemed to understand.

"Your mommy, daddy, and the doctors helped you fix your finger, didn't they?"

"Yeeees."

Lori's big gaze was focused eagerly on Sierra's face. She had pulled her mask down under her chin and, for the first time, Chad saw the person who had never left his side. She was breathtaking. What was even more stunning was how she looked at Lori, totally pouring her heart out to help his daughter. It was seeping about the room and into his heart as well.

"Mommy kissed my finger to make it all better."

"Did it help?"

Lori thought. "Kinda. If I kiss Daddy, will it help him too?"

"Oh, I think so."

He needed that more than air. Chad saw Lori's face turn brave like her mother. A smile appeared as did her arms. He felt the ribbons wrap his neck that put the pieces of his heart together. He soaked in the delicate kisses pecking at his cheek. Her tiny hand rested over his missing ear, blanketing that looming hole, soothing the loss.

"There. All better." His daughter pulled away, proudly. Her blue gaze feasted on him. "We get you all better, daddy. I promise. Okay?"

Sobs ripped through his soul as tears streamed on the faces of his parents.

"Lori," Sierra called, breaking the moment. "I could use some help putting on your daddy's bandages." She held out the fresh rolls. "Would you like to help?"

Excitement blossomed in the girl's face. "Can I?"

"I would really appreciate it, little nurse. Here. You hold this, and I'll do all the work."

Chapter 7

"Leave me the hell alone. Let me die."

"Sorry Chad, you gotta go to the tank," Jason ordered. "Get in the wheelchair."

Every inch of Chad wanted to lash out at the guy standing there like Hitler himself. But he had his little army of nurses who would simply sedate him. And the nightmares would return along with the image of that guy in a winter coat on a sweltering summer day. The blast. He would hear himself yelling, "Get Down! Get Down!"

Margery was dead because of him. Lori had a monster for a father now, and it was all his fault. He hadn't protected them. They should never have gone to the Market in the first place. He remembered that he hadn't wanted to go, but he had to please Margery. Now, he wished he hadn't.

That one question echoed constantly in his brain. Margery hadn't listened, and now she was dead. So, maybe it was her fault. If she had listened to him, their lives would never have been destroyed.

If he hadn't wanted to eat something, they would have been going back to his truck. So actually, it was his fault. Now, their lives were ruined beyond recognition.

Margery should be the one raising Lori. Not him. His daughter didn't deserve to be raised by some freak. Oh. He could see it now. Lori would come home from school, crying. Her friends had made fun of her for having Freddy Krueger for a dad. 'Your daddy should be in some circus.' And they would laugh and laugh as she ran away in tears.

"God, why did you let this happen?"

That was his second most asked question. However, God remained silent. His mother told him Pastor Pete was on some damn sabbatical, tour, or something. But Pete's answers would only placate him with Bible verses and platitudes anyway. None of which he wanted to hear.

"Dammit, God! Why? Tell me why?" he yelled. "Why did this happen to me? To Lori? To Margery? Why?"

The soothing surge of sedation trickled through him. But what the nurses didn't know was it only took him where he dreaded to go more than even the blast.

Home. Home where Margery was frying bacon for breakfast. They would be talking about the day, smiling, laughing. Lori would appear all sleepy-eyed, fist nuzzling her eye. She would climb onto his lap, and they would pray, thank God for the day, and eat breakfast. He would do the dishes while Margery got their daughter ready for school or church or a trip to the Farmer's Market.

Then he heard Lori again, "Lemonade, daddy. I want lemonade. Can I pleeeeease have lemonade?" The soft cocoon would melt. The blast would explode. The searing fist would strike. And he would be looking in the mirror at a monster while hearing Lori screaming, "That's not my daddy!"

"Chad, your lunch is here. Lasagna this time. It smells good, too," Sierra said as she placed the tray beside his chair.

He didn't remember returning to his room. Did he even go to the tank? Chad looked at the bandages on his legs. They were fresh. Beneath the cotton wraps, the burns breathed relief because they had been 'anointed with oil.'

"Take it away. I don't want it."

"No, not this time, Chad. You're eating this. Unless, of course, you really want us to feed you through another IV."

He glared up at the determined green gaze blazing down on him. "I don't care what the fuck you do."

Suddenly, his chair was wheeled from the window, and Sierra was dragging a chair closer. Fire burned in her green eyes. "Okay, let's start with this." She handed him the bottle of Pedialyte. "Drink."

Gazes locked. His cracked first because his stomach rebelled, and the damn shit really did smell good. It was the first bite of lasagna that did it. Images of Margery placing a steaming pan of the pasta on the dinner table like she had just conquered the world flashed before him.

Sierra jumped from her chair as he knocked the entire tray across the room. Nurses barged through his door. However, Sierra waved them away. Standing there, stalwart as any prison guard, she settled back into her chair.

"Chad, you have to stop this. If not for yourself, for Lori."

"You have no right to even say her name."

"Yes, I do. Lori is a sweet, adorable girl who loves you with every breath, and she is afraid she is losing her daddy. And she's right. Don't do this to her."

Chad wanted to stand. Fight her. Gripping the arms of his chair, he yelled, "She doesn't deserve to have a monster for a father!"

She settled back into her chair. "You are not a monster! Just a damaged person with scars."

A snarl mounted to his lips. "But why me? Why Margery? Tell me why?"

Tears loomed in the emerald gaze. Mask hugging beneath her chin, she shrugged. "I don't know, Chad. Shit happens." One tear ran down her cheek. She waved an arm across the room. "I think everyone in this hospital is asking that same damn question."

That one tear drizzling down her face burst the dam inside him. Sobs broke and flooded down the valley of his heart. "It doesn't make sense. I never wanted to go to that damn market. I tried to save them. But I failed. She is dead because of me."

Sierra's face shook as her gaze remained locked on his. "You did everything anyone could do. And right now, there are a lot of people asking themselves why they also went out that same day. But what you don't know, Chad, is … you saved a lot of people. You saved them from this hell."

"Why … not … Margery?"

Again, she shook her head and shrugged. "I don't know why shit like this happens. Seems life is full of it."

Chad looked into her eyes to depths far beyond just green. At her perfect face. "How the hell would you know anything about this shit? You sit there all perfect. I bet there isn't one scar on you anywhere."

Her gaze dried, met his with a heat that almost matched the bomb blast. "You don't know anything about my scars, Chad. But

I have them. And I've had to face them. Then deal with them the best I could.

"So, don't give me your pity about looking like a monster. At least, you have a family who loves you no matter what life has thrown at you. Whether you realize it or not, you are blessed … as your Bible says … beyond measure." She stood. "I'm going to order another tray. Now, if you think you can, I suggest cleaning up this mess."

Chapter 8

The next few days had been sticky. Still seething over Chad's remark, Sierra started into a new hospital room, to a new patient, to the familiar tasks of caring for someone harmed by burns.

How the hell would you know anything about this shit? You sit there all perfect. There isn't one scar on you anywhere.

How the hell could Chad know about her scars. He couldn't see them. No one could, but they were there. She faced them every day. She had asked herself why she had gone off on Chad like that. The answer: she was just sick and tired of his pity party. Like he was the only person who ever had their lives destroyed by a stupid fool with a bomb tied to his body, by a drunk, by an overwhelming spur of violent jealousy … by parents who didn't want their kid any longer.

Sierra jotted down the numbers, reports of the newest patient in paradise, closed the file, and left that room. Squirting hand sanitizer on her hands, she noticed her next destination. Rome 324. Chad Michaels. She glared at his doorframe.

Chad had so much to be grateful for. Every time Lori came to see him, she wanted to dress up like his nurse and help change her daddy's bandages. His parents were doing their best to assure their son that he was loved no matter what. His friends visited constantly, the black guy bringing another plant for the nurses. They brutally bantered with Chad until he finally started firing back.

Farther down the hall, the creton appeared in a wheelchair as he was escorted out of the 'paradise.' He saw her there by the nurses' station. His gaze settled on her as he was wheeled toward her. Recognition sparked. It was all she needed to escape into Chad's room.

Two therapists were leaving. "Great day. Keep up the good work Chad." That was a lie. Sierra could tell by the worried look on their faces as they left. One glance at the monitors, followed by checking his charts, proved that Chad was not getting better.

She walked to the *pink caddy* and started pumping the blood pressure cuff on his arm. It was higher than normal. Chad kept staring out at the garage as she tucked the cuff away. His breakfast food tray was half eaten, a bottle of the new protein drink unopened. Orange juice still unstabbed by a straw. His Bible lay sprawled open on the floor where he must have thrown it. If he didn't start drinking the water, he was facing another IV.

Chad was only half a mummy now. His chest, arms, and legs remained fully covered and would until he wore his future compression suits. However, his hands were exposed as they lay on the armrests, his fingers flexing into a loose fist. She remembered working them open, massaging them so they wouldn't curl into a permanent fist.

"Hey, How's the weather out there?"

Chad blinked at her question. He shrugged. For a long breath, Sierra gazed at the white linen covering the top of his head, knowing he remained lost in a self-imposed misery. She understood. It was hard to leave that port.

"Well, Chad, keep up the good work," Sierra lied as the therapists had said and started to leave.

"Sierra."

She came to an immediate halt at the sound of her name. The following silence left her gazing at the hole that should be his ear. Chad looked at her, his gaze intent. "I owe you an apology. I'm sorry."

She shrugged. "You don't need to apologize. I understand. When life kicks you, it can really hurt. I get it."

His eyes were a brilliant blue, blue like a perfect lake that invited you to swim in it. He continued, his words directed right into her soul. "No. About your scars. You are right. I don't know a damn thing about them."

Choking tears away, she forced a smile. "Don't worry. It's fine."

"I'm still sorry about what I said, Sierra."

That time her name rippled through her. She glanced out the window displaying a new wintery day. Heavy gray clouds loomed, wanting to release white snow on the frozen and cold world below.

Resting a hand on his shoulder, she forced a brave smile. "Chad, it's fine. Don't worry about it."

His hand rested on top of hers, capturing it ever so gently. "Tell me about them. Your scars."

Her heart smothered from the panic. Enough patients knew too much already. She didn't need to spread any more information about her past to anyone.

She eased her hand from his touch. "As I said, everyone has scars. We just have to keep moving ahead and try to get past them."

Carol's words. Reminding Sierra that Nicki had handed her a

letter from her friend. Why it came there, at the hospital, was odd. But rounds had intervened, and she forgot about it. It now offered her an escape to the nurses' station.

Hey Sierra. Sorry about this, but I sold the apartment and am moving to Miami. Gonna get me a new place on the beach and find out what it's like cooking under the summer sun. I left your stuff in the living room. Best come get it before November 10 when the new owners move in. Come see me. Keep on rolling Darlin'.

Carol

Sierra stared at the handwritten note. Carol was never one to text. The date on the envelope was two days earlier. "What is the date today?" she asked the nurse behind the desk.

"November 8. Why?"

"Nothing." Like hell … nothing. She had to find some place to live in two days. Shit. Where?

The sound of commotion at the elevators drew her attention. The president of the hospital, the city mayor with his little staff of butt-kissers, and Dr. Kendrick followed Jason down the hall. Everyone but Jason was busy chattering like chickens as they disappeared into Chad's room.

Sierra turned back to the nurse. "What's going on?"

"I guess the local news wants an update on their hero." The nurse stated as everyone's attention focused on Chad's doorway. Moments later, with the big wigs in tow, Jason wheeled Chad out of his room toward a gaggle of reporters and cameras gathering like vultures by the elevators.

"I don't think Chad needs to be doing this," Sierra muttered as she watched the distance shrink between armies. Clicking cameras were already sending shrapnel down the hall as the little red lights on the video cameras ticked off each step.

The usual barrage of questions erupted like popcorn. Dr. Kendrick fielded most of them. The mayor and hospital president stood by, gloating with success, answering benign questions as well.

"Oh, yes. He's healing very quickly."

"He's had much to deal with, but I believe the worst is behind him. Right, Chad?" Dr. Kendrick asked as another barrage of questions erupted.

"Yeah, I guess. No. Whatever. I'll leave that to God. WHAT!?" Chad sat straight up. "NO. I don't know what you are talking about."

Whatever was said, or asked, left the mayor, hospital president, even Dr. Kendrick in absolute shock. "There … there has to be a mistake," the president stuttered.

Chad glared up at Jason. "Get me back to my room. Now!" The look on Jason's face was livid as he drove Chad back into his room.

"Wonder what that was all about," the nurse smirked. "Not even a fire drill ever cleared that hall that fast before."

Sierra had a sinking feeling. She remembered the creton's smirk as he was rolled away. He finally said something.

Clutching a patient's file, Sierra departed to the appointed room, blocking her thoughts by the habitual routine of being a nurse. It was Jason who interrupted her attempt. "He needs to see you."

"Who?"

"Who do you think? Room 324."

"About?"

"Go find out. And do it now before it gets any worse," Jason warned.

Still sitting in the wheelchair, Chad wondered where they ever got the idea that Sierra was a porn star? One called *Fantasy*? Nothing about her was any of that. He'd certainly spent enough days watching porn, almost ruining his marriage over it. Sierra was no porn star. No way.

Through the glass wall, Chad saw Sierra approach his room and stop by his door. She squared her shoulders, bracing for a hit, and came into the room. "You need something?" Her words were contrite, short, pushing bitter.

"Did you hear what they asked me … about you?"

"No."

Chad rolled his wheelchair between her and the door. "They asked if you were some porn star named Fantasy."

Margery would have made a volcanic eruption look tame if he had asked her that question. Yet Sierra's reaction stunned him when her green gaze cut directly into his face.

"Yes. I was."

"So those are your scars?"

She shrugged. "I guess so."

The head nurse appeared in his doorway, concern blazing in her eyes. "Uh, Sierra. They want you in the waiting room. Now."

"Who?"

The nurse snarled at her. "Who do you think? The big boss and Dr. Kendrick,."

"Well, it's been fun Chad. I wish you the best. Hug Lori for me, will ya?" Sierra started to leave.

"Hey. God's got you," he assured. It felt like an automated remark. But maybe that much could be right...at least for her.

She stopped long enough to look incredulous at him. "Oh, sure. You, maybe. But not me."

Chad rolled the chair over to the window as an eternity struggled past. "God, don't let this happen to her. She's trying to get away from whatever is haunting her. Help her. Sierra doesn't deserve …"

Sierra burst into his room, drenched in tears, and grabbing what little she had in his closet. He wheeled into the doorway. "What happened?"

"Nothing." She started to go around him.

He blocked her escape. "Sierra, tell me. What's going on?"

A green laser cut at him. "What do you think? They fired me. That's what!"

He gripped her wrist. "No. That's not happening."

"Oh, and you think you can stop this?" She wheeled on him. "My whole life is ruined. It's all over the news. I will never get past my past. Now, let me go. I want out of here."

"No. You're staying."

Security guards appeared at his door. "Excuse me. Are you Sierra Smith? Are you ready?"

"Yes." Her voice was meek as if broken.

Chad wheeled toward the security escort. "She's not going anywhere. I need her."

They looked quizzically at him. "Ms. Smith is no longer employed here, sir. We are to escort her from the building."

"Then you will have to wait because I'm going with her."

Sierra melted into desperation. "Chad, you can't. You're not …"

"Let me and God worry about that, Sierra." He turned back to the guards. "Get the asshole in charge of this hospital in here. Now."

"Chad, they can't let me stay," Sierra blurted, "I am a stain on the entire staff. How many patients will now think they hire porn stars here and will want blow jobs, or anything else? 'It is an embarrassment to the reputation to the hospital. In fact, the city' … according to the mayor.

"Bull shit, Sierra. You and I know fully well it is."

The president suddenly appeared in the room. "Mr. Michaels, please. You must understand …"

Chad wheeled toward him. "My nurse does not deserve this humiliation or disrespect."

"I have to agree with you, Mr. Michaels, but I have the hospital's reputation to think about."

"Ms. Smith has been nothing but professional, a perfect nurse who has dedicated herself to my care. So, if you dismiss her, you dismiss me."

Dr. Kendrick appeared behind the president. "Chad, it's too soon. You aren't ready. We can't let you go."

"You dismiss her; you dismiss me. She goes; I go." He looked directly at the president.

Just then the television news came on the screen, *"News break! Patient and Porn Star …"* Sierra hid her face in her hands. The president nearly melted to the floor. Outside, by the desk, the nurses turned to each other in total disbelief, then focused on Chad's room.

Clicking the remote off, Chad glared at the men in his doorway. "Did I make myself clear?"

Dr. Kendrick's face paled. "Chad, I can't just let you walk out of here against medical advice. You must consider …"

His parents showed up at the blocked doorway. "What's going on?" his dad demanded.

Dr. Kendrick drew them aside and in less than a gasped breath, his mother scurried into the room. "Chad, you can't be serious. You can't go home now. You aren't ready. We have no one to take care of you. Nothing is arranged?"

Chad turned around to Sierra. "Would you continue as my nurse?"

"Oh, Chad. Not her," his mother begged. "I don't mean any disrespect," she said to Sierra, then turned back to him. "Chad. We need to find a professional caregiver. She's … just a student."

"She graduates nursing school this May," Jason piped in and endured the sudden threatening glares falling on him like boulders.

"That is May. This is now." His mother informed and wheeled back to Chad. "This is insane. Think about Lori. She needs her father."

Images of Lori dressed like Sierra danced before him. "Lori would love having Sierra there."

His mother glared at her husband as if for him to chime in. He didn't. "Well, you don't have the house prepared for … any kind of medical care."

"And we can't provide any of that for you," the president stated flatly.

"You can't or you won't?" Chad continued, "And what if the press learns my side of this story, that I'm leaving because the hospital's reputation matters more than your employees or students?"

"Chad, you know that isn't true," the president stuttered. "We … I mean, well …"

He'd had enough of their shit. "I'm going home." Chad looked at Sierra, standing by his bedside like a deer caught in the headlights of an oncoming car. "Will you continue as my nurse?"

Chapter 9

The question of how her picture got out became obvious. Apparently, during Chad's interview, someone had snapped a picture of her standing at the nurse's desk. That image had been blown up, googled, and published everywhere to reveal her to every pimp, john, and employer in the city. Once the news broke, every station in Kansas City and adjoining states fell on the hospital like locusts. News cameras, reporters, vans appeared until there was no escape. She and Chad had just become the latest press fodder.

Even though the president of the hospital fully explained to Chad that leaving without medical approval meant that they could not support him. It was ignored. Chad had no idea that this could mean his life. That he shouldn't do this for her.

Even so, Chad wouldn't listen even when Sierra lied and told him that she would make it. *Somehow.* That he was risking far too much for her. Hell, no man had ever gambled this much for her. Not ever. So, if he went through with this insanity, she had no choice but to see that Chad survived. He deserved that much.

His father eased his SUV through the quicksand of reporters

and stopped at the hospital entrance. The air was as electric as the sliding glass doors opened to allow Sierra to wheel Chad out to the car. He looked like a bundle of thick blankets piled in the wheelchair with various parts of a human peeking from it. She wore her PPEs to hide her own identity under her thick, flannel shirt as the frigid winter air hit.

"Get him in the car as fast as possible," she ordered Axel and Charlie who were handling Chad like precious glass. "He can't chill."

As soon as the car door shut, she climbed in the back with Chad's mother, her glare searing at Sierra. Her fury was palatable. After all, her son was taking home a prostitute … not a nurse.

Again, his father eased through the bodies bludgeoning the car with microphones and questions that fell like hail. Once on the I-70, the car phone rang, and his dad answered it. "One of the church members has a hospital bed. It's on the way to the house now," the caller assured.

"Thanks, Rosie, you're a doll. Thank the rest of the church and keep the prayers coming." Chad's father said as he drove. "Chad needs them."

"Will do. I'm keeping Pastor Pete informed. All the other churches are praying, too."

Another call sounded. "Gotta let ya go, Rosie."

"Furniture is moved, and the bed is in place," the Texas drawl assured. "May be needin' some better arrangement of the furniture, but the dinin' room is clear. Anything else?" Hunter asked.

"Sierra? Anything else?" Mr. Michaels asked as he drove.

"It has to be as sterile as possible."

"Figured," Hunter assured. "Ryan did the floor while we waited for the bed to get here. Says, while he was at it, he washed everything he could. Guess his momma taught him well."

"She did," sounded in the background.

"Good. Turn the heat up as high as you can. Make it like Dubai in there," Sierra ordered.

Settling back for the rest of the ride to Chad's house in Lees Summit, Sierra breathed some relief. A smile drifted over her lips. Jason had filled Chad's personal bag with as many jars of Silvadene cream as he could steal. He also left a note to let him know if there was anything else he could tell Dr. Kendrick. At least, they were on her side.

Nicki had been able to get Chad sedated before leaving. Even though the car's heater was blowing full blast, Sierra kept her hand on Chad's shoulder to check how his temperature was holding. He needed the heat shield packed away in his baggage.

Security lights on the garage burst to life as they pulled into the driveway of Chad's two-story house. It was set in a typical suburban area cushioned with massive trees and shrubbery, all looking like winter skeletons. Along the way there, pumpkins, scarecrows, and ornaments of early Christmas decorated the yards and windows of the neighborhood's sleeping houses.

The garage door opened to a dark green Honda CRV and a Ram truck. "I should have moved Margery's car before we left. Let me out," his mother instructed. As Chad's father drew to a stop, Charlie appeared at her door. "I'll get it, Mom. You stay put."

Out in the street, cars and vans were gathering like cavalry in front of Chad's house. Reporters and camera operators climbed out like an invasion.

Chad's dad called Ryan and Hunter. "Stop their asses from stepping one foot on the grass. They stay in the street, or I own them."

"Got it, Dad." Soon both men appeared from the front door: Ryan with an AR-15 and Hunter striding out like a five-star General toward the media. They flocked around Hunter and then backed into the street as if stung.

Once inside the garage, Charlie and Axel gently removed Chad from the car, carrying him into the house like he was the Ark of the Covenant. Sierra followed, scanning everything around her. She had been well-trained to know her escapes, who was around her, and what options she had for anything: pleasure or protection.

The garage was organized with shelves that lined both sides. Nothing unusual for garages: hoses, gardening stuff, chain saw, more guy stuff. The kitchen greeted her: white shelves with glass fronts, clean cabinet tops, cooking island in the center. Green curtains covered the patio doors to a wood deck.

In the center of the dining area was a round wooden table with small pumpkins in a reed bowl placed in the center of four orange plaid placemats resting before each chair. A sitting area beyond the table had been turned into a hospital room filled with a hospital bed.

Instantly, his mother became the head nurse—more dominatrix to Sierra's mind. "Put him there. Be careful. Axel, the heating blanket. I knew Chad should never have left the hospital."

"I agree, Mrs. Michaels," Sierra stated. "I told him he should stay there."

His mother turned on Sierra. "It's because of you, he did this. I just hope and pray that you know what you are doing."

"I hope so, too." Sierra stepped into the living room overflowing with couches, upholstered chairs, table lamps all fighting for a proper existence.

"You have the guest room upstairs beside Lori's room," his mother ordered, waving her to leave. "I'm sure you will find it."

Chad was quiet, resting. So, as ordered, Sierra climbed the stairs and stepped into Lori's play area that stretched between bedrooms. Barbies, doll houses, Legos, a small table and two chairs lined the back wall between two windows offering a view to the backyard.

She peeked into the master bedroom to her right. A massive, king-sized bed blanketed with a blue bedspread with matching curtains. Its bath was just off the bedroom, as was the walk-in closet. She ventured into the master bathroom, only steps from the bed. Two-sinks in the cabinet faced a large whirlpool. At the end, was a large glass walk-in shower and the toilet area.

It was perfect for his debridement. But how was she going to get him up there?

Lori's bedroom was directly across the play area from her parents' room. It was cotton-candy pink with matching curtains and bedspread covering a single bed surrounded with a mass of girl toys. Sierra walked through the adjoining bath that she would have to share and entered what was to be *her room*.

A double bed dressed in the usual white bedspread filled most of the lavender room. White curtains hung over the single window. Typical nightstands with lamps guarded the bed pillows. A single upholstered reading chair sat in the corner.

No way in hell was she staying up there. She plopped a hospital bag full of scrubs on the bed. Claiming the bedspread and a pillow, Sierra returned to the downstairs.

"It may be best for me to sleep down here in case Chad needs attention," Sierra announced. Under everyone's shocked gazes, she dropped the bed stuff on the black leather couch and began arranging it as if she owned it.

Once done, she began her inspection of Chad's area. The house was working on the Dubai temperatures well enough. She pulled out her stethoscope and blood pressure cuff from a bag that Jason had absconded and went to work checking Chad's vitals. Everything was steady. His mother had to step aside as she opened the iPad tablet to record a report for Dr. Kendrick.

That done, his meds came next. Sierra dug into Chad's personal things for the plastic bag the hospital had allowed her to take. After all, they were paid for. Setting Chad's meds, Silvadene, and water bottle on the side table, she scanned the area. She turned to her audience

"He's resting well enough. I have things under control for now." She waited expectantly for them to read her mind. *Now's the time to leave, folks.*

It took a few moments.

"I think we should check on Lori," Mr. Michaels said, motioning toward the garage.

"Uh, we'll be downstairs if you need us … anything. This way, guys." It was Charlie who led the parade to the basement. "No pool tonight. Rack time."

As soon as everyone left, everything got quiet. Chad was asleep. Sierra remembered her things in Carol's apartment. Shit! Tomorrow the new owners took possession!

Just then, Hunter strode into view, heading to the kitchen. "You're Hunter, right?"

He halted. "That's me. You needin' somethin'?"

"Well, yes. I don't have anyone else to ask. But my things, I mean, … I can't leave Chad and get them."

Interested, Hunter walked closer. "Want us to go get them? All I have is my truck though."

She wanted to laugh. "Your truck is more than enough, and I would really appreciate it." She dug Carol's apartment keys from her purse laying on the kitchen island and handed them to Hunter.

Barely two hours later, Axel, Ryan, and Hunter appeared through the front door with the one box of her books and her belongings stuffed in a large hiking backpack.

"This is all we found," Hunter stated, concern written all over his angular face that the *Marlboro Man* would envy.

"That's all I have. That's it."

All three guys looked at each other, astounded. Ryan gazed at her. "You're sure. Nothing hidden in storage?"

"I'm sure. Guess you can say I travel light."

Axel huffed. "Shit. Lighter than any girl I've ever moved."

"Where do you want all this stuff," Ryan asked, offering the book box toward her.

"Upstairs, I guess, in the guest room."

Chapter 10

A loner in a winter trench coat. Hands clutching the coat. Too hot. Too hot. "NOOOO! GET DOWN! GET DOWN!" Bacon's ready! Can I pleeeeease? Lemonade, Daddy … I want lemonade … Sounds right to me … Six tacos, two glasses of… Sounds right to me. I swear I'll kill you if you don't stop! Lemonade, Daddy … I want lemonade. Can I pleeeeease? Sounds right to me. Sounds right to me. Sounds right to me.

The hot, bright flash. Something thick, black. Moaning. Chad heard moaning. Someone was moaning.

"Chad, you are safe. Chad!"

As his mind cleared, he realized he was the one moaning. Gasping, Chad searched his surroundings. Where was …? He looked up at very worried gazes. Sierra. The other … it was Charlie. Charlie, wearing some stupid red Chief's ballcap backwards like he always wore.

"Hey, bro," Charlie stated chirpily. "You're back. You had us scared there for a minute."

The hands withdrew. Chad nodded "Yeah. I guess so. Where am I?"

"Home, bro. Home," Charlie stated. "And I better get back to the bacon before it burns."

Like a million times, Sierra put the cold end of a stethoscope on his neck and looked at her watch, counting. Finished, she smiled. "Welcome back."

"Yeah," was all he could say. His brain was still whirling from the flashback. The familiar smells of bacon floated over him, threatening another onslaught. Margery was always frying him bacon. Every morning. Margery ...

He broke the memory by studying Sierra, wearing the usual hospital PPEs. The sheets were white. He was still wearing the cocoon of bandages. Then he saw Margery's dining room table. The patio doors to the outside deck. Kitchen. Behind Sierra was the living room clotted with furniture. Margery would never leave furniture arranged like that.

"Where's Margery?"

"Not here right now," Sierra answered.

"When is she coming back?"

Sierra shrugged. "Not sure."

"Didn't she tell you?"

"Uh, no. No, she didn't ... tell me." She looked at Charlie. "She say anything to you?"

"Nope."

The familiar sound of the garage door rising greeted his ears. *Margery.* "She's home. She's home," he whispered happily even though Sierra and Charlie gazed dubiously at each other.

He couldn't wait to see her. He needed to feel her arms around him. He needed to see her face, her beaming green eyes. No doubt her hair was pulled back in a ponytail like she always wore. Excitement shivered through him, lifting his heart to his throat. She was home. She was …

His mother and father stepped through the garage door. "Daddy! Daddy!" exploded from Lori. The patter of running feet started across the kitchen.

"Wait. The PPEs. Put those on first," Sierra ordered. Like good soldiers dressing for battle, they obeyed and finally his parents and Lori were allowed to come to the bed.

"Daddy, I draw this for you." A picture of some sort of fat turkey dancing on some kind of corn stalks was shoved at him. "You like it?"

"I … love it." With a brave smile Chad hoped would convince his daughter. Something ticked in his brain. Something he was told in the hospital. Margery wasn't coming with Lori. She …

No. He couldn't deal with that right now. His brain was shutting down with a reality he did not want. Tears blurred his gaze. Scalding tears. Desperate tears. No. He did not want to know … she … she …

Chad again faked a brave smile for his daughter. "Lori, it's beautiful. That's the fattest turkey I've ever seen."

"How are you this morning?" his father asked as he took Sierra's place beside the bed. The gleam in his gaze darkened to worry.

"Fine. At least, she says I am." He motioned to Sierra standing by the table with Charlie.

"You do seem much better. Doesn't he, Lori?" his mother asked.

"Uh-huh. Sierra, can we put my picture on the wall over there?" Lori pointed to the family picture of the three of them that Margery had hung in the small family room. He couldn't see the fireplace because the bed was set in front of it.

"Of course," Sierra assured. "Charlie, can you find the scotch tape?"

"Sure enough." Chad saw his friend escape into the kitchen area to dig in the junk drawer. "Found it."

Chad watched as Lori's picture was stuck just below the family portrait of who he had been. A Marine in uniform, wearing a full head of black hair, smooth skin, wearing a proud smile. He had the perfect wife there beside him, and his perfect daughter joyfully in his arms. The perfect picture of a perfect family.

But there he lay, bandaged in destruction. He wasn't that man now. "Where's Margery? When is she coming home?" he demanded.

The room seemed to freeze. No one breathed. "She's in heaven, Daddy," Lori whimpered. Tears trickled down her beautiful cheeks.

No. No. No. His insides caved as he remembered them telling him that in the hospital. Closing his eyes, he saw Margery's green eyes and forever brown ponytail etched behind his eyelids. Smiling. She was always smiling.

Sounds right to me. The flash exploded again. Her face floated before him. *Sounds right to me.* The words kept floating around him until he was dizzy. *Sounds right to me.* Margery was gone and it was his fault. Tears flooded down his cheeks as something deep inside him ripped open. *His fault. I didn't save her. I didn't protect her.*

"Daddy! Please. Daddy, please." Silken hands clasped both of his cheeks. "Daddy?"

He opened his eyes to his daughter, blue eyes, brown hair, little image of Margery. She was worried. Both of his arms swept around her, pulling her over his shredding heart. 'I'm sorry, Lori. I'm sorry. I should have saved her. I should have …"

"It's okay, Daddy. It's okay. She's in heaven."

No, it wasn't. She's supposed to be here. Chad wanted to continue holding his daughter, but she was telling him lies that he didn't want to hear.

"Lori, look what uncle Charlie has," his mother said as if he held up a new Dollar Store toy. "I bet he has another one in the basement to show you."

"Uh, sure," Charlie stammered. "Yeah, come on. I bet we can find it."

Chad stared at the picture on the wall as his daughter left with his friend. He couldn't make it without Margery. He couldn't. He didn't want to. He wanted Lori to have her mother.

His mother's hand touched his shoulder. "Chad. Honey, we must talk."

He jerked from the touch. "What?"

His father got that stern look on his face when a serious discussion had to happen. "Uh, Son, we have to. It's about Margery."

Chad turned to his father standing beside his mother, both wearing those damn yellow gowns and caps. "Don't tell me she's in heaven. Or that she's dead. I don't want to hear it."

Pain shot in his parent's gazes as they looked at each other as if to let the other continue. His father heaved the submissive sigh. "Chad, the funeral home that has held Margery's body needs to know when to plan for her funeral."

Sierra stepped away from the table. "They have waited this long. Can't they wait a bit longer?"

His father turned to her and shrugged. "They are running out of room."

"It's too soon," Sierra was flustering like a mothering hen. "Chad isn't ready to go outside. It's too cold. He …"

He didn't believe them. This was all an act. Margery wasn't dead. "This weekend."

It was as if Sierra were about to melt. "No. No. That's too soon, Chad. There is a chance of snow. Your body can't keep warm enough. It's …"

They were lying. Hiding something from him. Margery was on one of her church missions that she loved going to. "This weekend."

"Chad, maybe you should listen to Sierra." His father looked toward the dining room. "You think in a few weeks maybe?"

"Maybe. I don't know," Sierra answered, worry blazed in her eyes.

Yes, he was being stubborn and, when he was, Margery's eyes would flash like that too. He smiled in anticipation for when he saw the real ones again.

Chad just sat there, staring at the back of the gray driver's seat of the funeral limo. Images of Margery in that casket, covered with roses. Red, White. A few pink … her favorite. All around her were more flowers, wreaths, plants, ribboned with love, sympathy—Rest in Peace, Beloved Mother, Beloved Daughter, Beloved Wife.

Faces. An ocean of sad faces, sympathetic faces, tearful faces, forced smiles still hovered around him. Music. Words. Hands full of tissues had touched him as if to comfort.

None of it reached him. He just had sat there, staring at the profile of Margery's face, frozen in death. But she could not be as dead as he was now.

Why God? Why?

The answer remained as silent as death itself.

A freezing wind blustered into the limo as Charlie and the others climbed in like rats seeking the warmth. Sierra turned from the seat across from him. "Charlie, you have to tell the minister to keep it short. Chad cannot be out there that long. The snow suit is not enough to keep him warm. He can't …"

"Whoa, there, darlin'," Hunter stated. "Got it covered. We already talked to him."

"If I see him shiver once, we go home. Clear?"

"Yes, ma'am."

All four guys manhandled Chad into the wheelchair. The red, full body snowsuit—complete with Artic fur hood and boots—filled the chair to overflow. The ride over the frozen ground jostled his body in unfamiliar ways, shooting pain through him.

Alas the convoy halted inside the funeral tent where Margery's casket, now closed, blanketed with the flower wreaths and surrounded with a thick carpet of flowers, stretched before him.

Space heaters on both sides of the wheelchair blared warmth and drowned the assistant pastor's monologue. Bodies huddled for warmth. He was supposed to know them. But, he didn't. And he didn't care that he didn't know them. All he could see beyond the yellow plastic goggles was the looming hole below Margery and the iron rails tied to each other with green bands that held her above its depths.

Pity suffocated him, chilling him to his soul. In that instant, something yanked him away. He was being taken from the misery looming before him and back to the limo.

Chapter 11

"I knew it was too soon. I knew it," Sierra spewed as she tucked blankets surrounded Chad's snowsuit. He was losing body heat. His temp had dropped to 92. She had to get him home and into the whirlpool in his bathroom.

"You all have to get him upstairs as fast as possible. I'll get the water running in the tub. One of you, get the house temp up to full blast."

Her mind was racing. They had to get Chad into the water as hot as he could stand it. Then he had to be taken out and rebandaged. The room must remain the same as the water. Hot. But How?

"Is there a camping cot anywhere," she asked.

"In the garage," Axel stated. "I'll find it."

"Clean it and then bring it up to the bathroom. It's gotta be clean. Towels. We need hot towels. And hot bandages."

"Got it," Charlie assured.

Oh, God, where was the Silvadene? She had to grab that on her way upstairs. 91 degrees. Chad was still shivering even though everyone else in the limo were sweating like sunbathers.

Everyone went into action the second the garage door closed. Sierra bolted into the house, found the antiseptic ointment by the hospital bed, and bolted upstairs to the shower. She turned the hot water of the whirlpool on full blast. She had to cook Chad like a lobster, cool at first, then raise the temperature as quickly as possible.

The guys managed to carry Chad into the narrow space as Axel appeared with the wheelchair. Once Chad was placed in the swirling water, busy hands began unzipping every part of the snow suit, revealing the Chief's sweats beneath. Chad slid down into its depths like a wet rag.

Sierra dove in beside him, keeping his head above the water. He was still shivering. She had to do something. *Now.* The area became her command post.

"Open the drain and turn the hot up. Get a cot in here and keep the bandages warm. We need clean sheets on his bed."

Sweat poured off the guys' faces as they impersonated any trauma unit in a hospital. Grabbing one of the ornamental washcloths from the towel bar, Sierra began warming Chad's face, continuously plunging the rag beneath the scalding water.

"I need my bag from downstairs," she said. Ryan bolted toward the stairs.

Cradling Chad's head in her arm and swabbing it with the scalding water, she whispered, "Well, now you know, Chad. Margery is not here. All you have is me and your friends. I'm sorry. I really am sorry." She pressed the thermometer to his forehead. 95. He wasn't shivering. "Just a bit more Chad. You've about got it. Hang in there."

Axel appeared with the camping cot and stretched it alongside the tub. Immediately, Charlie draped it with the sheets and then two quilts. They both looked at her for approval.

The thermometer read 98. "He's normal. I gotta get out and change. Don't let him drown."

Charlie knelt by the tub as she relinquished Chad to his care.

"You know you have this place hotter than Dubai, don't ya?" Axel smirked by the tub.

Like she didn't know how hot that place could be. She just looked at him. He then realized his mistake. "Sorry. I got him," he said as he handed her a towel.

Stripping down to her undies and proceeding to wrap a towel around herself, Sierra continued her tirade of orders. "I will need help ..." She noticed their gazes hotter than the bathroom. Glaring, she snarled, "Strip his bed?"

"Uh, yeah," Ryan said and, again, disappeared through the door as all attention poured back into the whirlpool.

Finally, Chad's heartrate was normal as well. The sedative was working. Enjoying the fresh scrubs, Sierra checked through a list of what Chad needed as he lay in his own bed. She had decided that taking Chad back downstairs would be too stressful. He had to stay there for the night.

Settling in a chair in the corner of his bedroom, Sierra recalled the burns she had just cleaned and bandaged—still open to infection, yet truly little to debride. Jason would like that.

She missed his happy face. She also wanted to report to Dr. Kendrick that they had successfully dodged a bullet, and that the patient's numbers remained steady. She wanted him to smile, say she was doing an excellent job. Right now, she needed all the encouragement available.

She missed the hospital's routine too. The classes. She missed everything. She missed the nurses, the chatter, the concern that followed each like a worried pup. She missed the surprise goodies someone would bring from home.

What her future held was a million years away, at least for now. But she had long ago learned to adjust to whatever came her way. *Deal with it.* Mario's famous words pounded in her brain.

Chad's parents had come upstairs last night when she was checking their son. His mother almost fainted at seeing the naked burn wounds. His father had to take her home. They suddenly needed to see to Lori. Yes. Lori who had been with Margery's parents after the funeral.

"How is he?" his mother asked, suddenly appearing into the room early the next morning.

Startled, Sierra glanced at Chad. He was sufficiently covered with blankets. "Fine."

His mother studied her son sleeping like a babe now. "I had no idea how bad he was until I ..." she couldn't finish it.

"He really had me worried," Sierra said. "He should have stayed in the hospital."

His mother tugged the comforter closer around Chad's neck as if he were still five years old. "I agree. But he always was stubborn."

Sierra glanced up at her. "You think he will change his mind?"

His mother shook her head. "Knowing him. No." She looked at Sierra. "Were you really a ..."

"Yes, I was Fantasy. It was a life I want no part of ever again." Tears swelled in the shadows of the bedroom. "I'm no risk to Lori. I promise."

"I'm sorry I reacted like I did." His mother smiled bravely. "I judged you. I apologize."

Sierra smiled at the sincerity in the woman's face. "You aren't the first. Nor likely the last."

"Just know, my dear. God loves you. I also think God is up to something in all this. I just don't know what, but maybe we will find out before we all go insane." Pressing a hand on Sierra's shoulder, Chad's mother left the room.

God loves you. Sure. Maybe everyone else, but not prostitutes. Read the Bible, Sierra thought.

He could smell her. She wasn't gone. But images flashed of Margery laying over some looming black hole. No. He could smell her. She was there. He tried to reach for her, but his arms wouldn't bend. He couldn't turn over.

"Chad. Chad. Wake up."

He didn't want to wake up. He knew, opening his eyes, he would expect to see Margery. Instead, he saw Sierra, worried as usual.

"You need to get up. Time to move."

"What do you mean time to move," Chad didn't understand. He glanced around. Where was he? Not in the dining room. He was … "How'd I get up here?"

Sierra smirked. "The guys carried you. After the funeral, we had to get you in the whirlpool to get your temps back up. Do you remember the funeral?"

Chad glanced about at the familiar walls. The familiar bed. And remembered the funeral and feeling cold. Margery's fragrance floated to him from her pillow.

"I remember." Even though he wanted to forget. Disappointment set in.

"Time for PT and then another whirlpool. Might as well use it while you are up here." Sierra whipped the blankets off and offered a hand.

No part of him wanted to leave that bed, leave all that remained of Margery. But he accepted the offer. He needed to pee. Sierra handed him the plastic urinal as he sat up on the side of the bed.

Axel showed up with breakfast. "Hey, you made it. Had us hopping through hoops last night. Brought you some eggs."

It felt ridiculous sitting on the side of the bed with two people whom he didn't want in that room just then. One disappeared in the bathroom to flush his pee and the other remained standing there holding a food tray.

Every moment of Margery's funeral flashed in his brain. She was gone. Chad felt his body melt. He started to lay back into the sheets, to hug her pillow, smell her there with him.

"Oh, no, no, no," Sierra commanded. "Help me. He has to get up."

"Leave me the hell alone." Trying to jerk from their grasps was impossible.

"Come on buddy, PT time. No excuses," Axel ordered. "Don't make me get the other guys up here."

Like it or not, he was forced into the walker and directed out into Lori's play area between his bedroom and the other rooms. The windows presented a brilliant winter day with sunny blue skies. He somehow ambled past Lori's Barbie house, Barbie things, bean bag, small table with an array of her scribblings or, as Margery would say, artwork.

He turned at Lori's doorway and started back toward his and

Margery's bedroom. He could hear the guys coming up from the basement, their ruckus pouring out into the living room below. It flooded over the open railing. He did notice Sierra's backpack on the guest bed before he turned to make another circuit.

The moment he lay back on the bed and Sierra began removing the bandages, the doorbell rang. Chad recognized the voices of his doctor and nurse from the hospital. Charlie directed them up the stairs.

"Looks like we got here just in time," Jason said chirpily. He hurried toward the bed to do an inspection. "Looking good, Sierra. What do you think, doc?"

Dr. Kendrick came closer to observe "The burns are looking good. Do you have anything like a chart?" he asked. Sierra immediately handed him the iPad. "Looks like you had a bad night last night."

"The funeral was yesterday," Sierra informed, "And, as I thought, he got chilled. That's why he's up here. There's a whirlpool, and we used it."

"Oh, yes. I see. Good thinking." Dr. Kendrick smiled as he scanned Sierra's notes. "You think you are strong enough to do stairs now?" he asked Chad.

He wasn't up to much of anything. "I doubt it. But I don't want to go back downstairs." Margery was there with him. "I thought you guys weren't allowed to come by."

Jason smirked at him. "Last we heard was we could do whatever we want on our own time."

The doctor nodded. "We wanted to stop by earlier, but the press was still lingering outside. Apparently, they got bored." He looked seriously at Chad. "If you want to stay up here, don't go down those stairs until the physical therapists say you can. Got that? We don't need you falling."

"Roger," Chad assured, relishing his small victory.

"Well, the media is gone, finally," Sierra stated by the bathroom door.

"What happened to them?" Chad asked. He remembered the first week at home. The street looked fuller than Chief's stadium on game day.

All interest turned on Sierra for the rest of the story. "Well, your dad threatened them to not step foot on your yard. Then your friends began taking their guns out of the trucks and bringing them inside. I think Axel posted guard at the picture window while carrying his assault rifle. It was mentioned in the news, so, the local police started driving by more often, I guess, making them even more uncomfortable."

"Well, apparently, they're gone and getting out of the house now will be easier," Dr. Kendrick remarked.

"I think so," Sierra assured.

"Good. Then I would like to set up visits to my office to proceed with Chad's care." He looked at Chad. "Is that okay with you?"

"Sure."

As Dr. Kendrick started checking Chad's vitals, Jason looked to Sierra and nodded toward the door. They both walked from the bedroom to the railing. "You doin' okay? Need any Silvadene? Well anyway, I brought you some."

"No, but great."

"Need anything more, text me. I'll see what I can do." He motioned toward clamor downstairs. "Weren't they at the hospital?"

"Yes. One of his friends is here all the time. They've worked it out with their jobs. His parents find whatever I need and bring it. And their church is keeping the fridge stocked with food."

"Sounds better than the hospital," Jason quipped. "So, you know, we miss you."

"I miss everyone, too."

Dr. Kendrick left Chad's bedroom. "I'll have my office call you. Is PT coming by?"

"They start tomorrow," Sierra answered, breaking away from the railing.

"Seems you have everything under control then." Dr. Kendrick smiled. "Let us know if we can help."

Chapter 12

Thanksgiving came and went—uncelebrated. Sierra endured the family's excuses that the holiday would be too much for Chad anyway, too complicated with everything that happened now. And well, Chad didn't want to celebrate much of anything either. The family's repertoire was endless, and all reasoning was accepted as truths.

Chad had chosen to remain upstairs, in his bedroom, because he said he was unable to manage the stairs without help. That he didn't want anyone's help. In fact, he wasn't wanting anything, other than to be left alone, which was something Sierra could not allow.

The camping cot had become her bed, put nightly at the foot of his, so she was present if Chad had a flashback or reaction to meds. Some nights he slept fine, muttering Margery's name. Some nights he screamed and moaned, thrashed like he was wrestling with some demon. A text to whoever was sleeping in the basement would bring them racing up the stairs to help hold Chad until he calmed, either medically or naturally.

Usually each morning, one of the guys would wake her by making breakfast downstairs and bringing the food upstairs. By then the cot was folded and she would talk a sullen Chad into eating, help him relieve himself, and assist in brushing his teeth there by the bedside.

The fit-filled routine proceeded to PT: breathing exercises; stretching; walking circuits in Lori's play area. Chad was fully irritated by then, the whirlpool providing some respite. Then, she proceeded to inspect his healing body, debriding where needed, which was less and less, and rebandaging the sullen male. Chad had no idea he was almost to the point of needing compression suits. But that was Dr. Kendrick's call.

Different therapists would arrive and take charge of dealing with Chad at various times of the day, usually afternoons. Meals were adjusted accordingly. Liquids pushed constantly.

Appointments to Dr. Kendrick's office were set up for a weekly visit, driven by his parents, accompanied, but uninvited, by her. There was no way his parents could relay to Dr. Kendrick what he needed to know, nor could they explain to her what the doctor wanted done. Which necessitated her being there regardless of what anyone wanted.

Sierra's greatest concern was Chad in all of this, which was simply that he was present...living, breathing, growling, grumbling, doing as he was told. With little interest that he was improving far faster than was normal.

Nearly every day, his parents brought Lori after school. The little urchin drew more reactions from him than anyone. Chad would brighten at her drawings now plastering the bedroom walls. He would listen intently to her chatter, even playing any game she wanted to play. It all seemed sincere until Lori went home with his parents. Then Chad would retreat into his robotic shell.

Sierra was considering talking to his mother about letting Lori return home. One of the guys could drive her to school and his parents could pick her up, giving them the option to stop by whenever, hoping not to have to endure their son's sudden wrath. Which was continuous.

"I'm fine," he would snap. "You don't have to constantly check on me." Or he would yell, "Just leave me the hell alone."

Distracting herself, Sierra retreated to the laundry room to change the loads of laundry. Charlie appeared in the doorway. "Hey. Can I help?" he asked and then proceeded to pluck a warm towel from the pile and started folding.

"You guys are a Godsend. Thank you for being here," Sierra stated with a smile as she folded Chad's sweatpants.

"We figured you may need help. Chad would do this for us. How you holding up?" he asked, rolling yet another strip of bandages.

"Fine." Sierra grabbed a tangled bandaged strip that had self-tied around pieces of laundry and began rolling it. "I don't know where I'd be otherwise if Chad hadn't decided to leave the hospital on my account. Which he should not have done."

Charlie smirked. "Well, that's Chad, but I think he wanted out of there anyway. He can't stand being helpless." One roll done, he grabbed another. "Any idea of what you are going to do after this?"

"No."

The pile diminished slowly and quietly. "How'd you get into that skin game anyway?" Charlie asked as he folded.

"I was raised in the game, I guess," she stated with some fake element of humor.

Charlie stopped and stared at her. "Come on. Your father was a pimp?"

Sierra saw the beagle puppy that led her to Colton's van. "He wasn't my real father."

"You were kidnapped?"

"Not exactly. My real parents didn't want me." *Oh God, it hurt saying that.* Sierra loaded the laundry basket quickly. "Gotta get these put away. Thanks for the help."

She escaped the shrinking room and headed to Chad's master bath, to put the towels and the wash rags in their place. To put everything else away to avoid reliving everything that was assaulting her.

Bracing on the vanity with both arms, Sierra's mind exploded with reality. She didn't want to think about what she was going to do after Chad didn't need her anymore. She couldn't stay there as his pet. Move? Where? Return to 'the life'? What other choice did she have? No one would hire her now.

Patient & Pornstar. That headline still reverberated in her brain, so where the hell could she go? Europe? Italy? Too many memories. And the press there would be worse than in the States. As tears flooded from her heart, she laughed. There was nowhere to go that would free her from servicing men.

"Sierrrrra?"

Sierra looked up at a little shadow standing in the bathroom doorway. "Lori?"

The shadow approached. "Are you okay?"

Stiffening upright and swiping at tears, "Uh-huh. I … I, uh, got something in my eyes. What's wrong?"

"Can I go potty here? Uncle Charlie is in the other one."

"Of course, you can."

Helping her, Sierra sat down by the whirlpool. Once done the little urchin climbed in her lap. Something precious immediately seeped into her. Something new. Something delicate. Something innocent. Sierra lingered in it.

The delicious moments passed, and Lori pulled back. "Is it gone?"

"What?"

"That thing in your eyes?"

"Oh. Yes. It is gone."

"Is daddy going to be all right?" Lori's gaze was deeper than the oceans.

"Yes. We will make sure your daddy will be all new again. He's working with his therapist right now."

"He says he's a monster."

Sierra pulled back to look seriously into Lori's face. "Do you agree?"

"No. I don't care what he looks like. He is still my daddy."

"I bet he would like to hear you tell him that."

"I did." The blue eyes filled with tears. "He doesn't believe me," she sobbed.

"Oh, honey, I'm sure he believes you." The lie was easy enough. To change the subject, Sierra asked, "What do you want Santa to bring you for Christmas?"

Lori brightened instantly. "A dog. I want my own dog. Gama and Gampa says I can't have one. Daddy and Mommy …" there was a hitch in her voice …, "said I could have one when I'm older. So, I asked God. And he said I could have one right now."

Colton wouldn't let anyone have a dog or any pet because they were always flying to some country on his black, private jet. "Pets are too much trouble to get through customs."

"Sierra, what do you want Santa to bring you for Christmas?"

Sierra jerked her thoughts back to Lori. "Oh, Lori. I have no idea. What do you think Santa should bring me?"

"I don't want God to bring you a new home, because I want you to stay here. Daddy needs you. So, maybe a teddy bear."

I want you to stay here. Lori's words sank deep into Sierra's heart. But that was impossible. "Well, I will be here as long as your daddy wants me to stay." A few more months. That would give her time to figure things out. "A teddy bear sounds really nice. Lori, do you think you could tell Santa what kind? I'm not good at picking out teddy bears."

Lori's eyes lit like stars. "Yes. I can do that. Daddy!!!" She bolted away from Sierra's lap. "Daddy! Gamma!"

Watching the girl race out of the bathroom with her heart, Sierra sank back into tears. *I don't want God to bring you a new home, because I want you to stay here. Daddy needs you.*

If you only knew why I can't. If you only knew.

Chapter 13

From the leather recliner reset in the dining room, Chad's gaze fell on to the tree twinkling as if their lives had never changed. It had gone up on December 1st like Margery always said. Halloween. Thanksgiving. *Then* Christmas.

That weekend, everyone decorated the damn thing as he just sat there, watching them act as if everything was holiday perfect. Carols played on Charlie's laptop. The first batch of eggnog was passed around. He recalled just sitting in the wheelchair, handing perfect little ornaments to eager hands to put it into its perfect little place. He had endured every perfect moment of his fucking appointed job.

Then, like always, his father got out *The Christmas Story*, plucked Lori into his lap, and read it aloud to everyone. Again, he endured, while staring at Margery's nativity set on the end table.

He had sent that to her from Germany on his first deployment to Afghanistan. He remembered their FaceTime when she showed him where she and Lori had decided to put it. Between the lamp beside the sofa and the Christmas tree. Right where it was now. "And I won't put it away until you return home."

Now it was back on the same damn table. Parts of him wanted to demolish it.

Staring at the fire in the fireplace, all he could think about was why. Why did God let this happen to them? Why? Of all people, Margery was the most faithful person he knew. She loved Jesus even more than she loved him. She always said that God was first in her life, but he was a close second.

All he cared about was keeping his little family happy and providing his girls with the best life he could. He could live in a shack. But not his girls.

He had gotten into porn once on deployment. They all had. But when he came home, Margery caught him watching it on his phone. She was beyond furious. "You promise me, you will never watch that filth again because if you do, I'm leaving. I will not be loved like that."

Margery not only got on his case, but Charlie and the others too, holding them responsible for his new addiction. After he and the guys talked about it, yeah, well, prostitutes were used as objects, appreciated maybe for the moment, but that was usually it. Like a mosquito bite, scratched and ignored. Ultimately, women had started treating the guys like objects, too, expecting a romance novel encounter that would never happen.

After realizing how porn had twisted his brain, he began to see Margery as the only person that he wanted to be with. Pleasing her had become far more important than what he wanted So, yeah, things got interesting after that. He had never been happier in his life.

So why, God? Why did you take her from me? Still no answer.

Simmering in the silence, Chad realized he had no presents for Lori under the tree and Christmas was a few weeks away. He had to get something for her … from her mother. No matter what, he could never let Lori forget Margery.

After Lori was in bed and everyone left, he blurted, "I need to get something for Lori for Christmas."

Sierra turned from doing dishes in the kitchen. "I'll tell Charlie and the others. They can get whatever you want." She started toward him with a tall glass of OJ.

Even with her blonde hair pulled back into the usual ponytail, not an ounce of makeup, wearing the simple scrubs covered with only a protective gown now, Sierra was stunning. It wasn't the first time he noticed that. And well, he now knew he was still a normal man who could still appreciate a beautiful woman.

No. He wasn't going … there. His heart belonged to Margery. Only Margery.

Yet, he couldn't pull his gaze away. After all these years and his share of hospitals either coming to see his buddies or them coming to see him, he realized that Sierra was more of a nurse than all of them put together. She had a sincere kindness about her.

"What?" Sierra looked around for whatever he was staring at.

"Thank you," he stated as he took the glass. Again, the sunlight radiated on her flawless face. "Thank you, Sierra. My mother would never put up with all of this."

A tiny blush deliciously tinted her cheeks. "Thank you for wanting my help or I would be out on the streets."

"Who was the rat in the hospital?" he asked.

She stared through the patio doors at the velvet darkness beyond. "Someone who watched a lot of porn."

"You actually did porn?"

She looked over at him. "What do you think? Not because I liked it."

"That's not who you are, Sierra. The world needs more nurses like you. Don't give up on your dream."

"Hey. How's he doing?" Charlie joined Sierra by the patio door. The next day, snow was falling, making the backyard into a wonderland. Sierra glanced at Chad's friend. He was cute, blond, curly hair, brown eyes, and about the same height as she was. Very likeable but something said, clever like a fox. Possibly the officer of their little band of brothers.

"Sleeping," she answered. A glance proved Chad was actually resting in his lounger. No flashbacks. "Did he say anything to you guys about getting presents for his parents? And Lori?" she asked.

"Yeah, we can manage that. What about you?" Charlie asked.

Sierra's gaze turned to the backyard thickening with snow, allowing her thoughts to go back to Guatemala and the presents everyone had gotten for each other.

Back then, it was a game to see who could outdo each other with glitz and glamor—who got the greatest "ooos" and "ahhhs"? But no one was content until Colton smiled with satisfaction. It was then that everyone could breathe. She shrugged the memory off. "I don't have the money."

"You can pay me back after you graduate."

She hadn't told anyone about the letter she had received from the school, dismissing her from her last semester. Her final semester. So, she was never going to graduate ... so she would never be a nurse.

Once the background check was done, no nursing school was going to admit her now. How was she ever going to pay back her student loans, much less Charlie?

Charlie kept pressing. "Lori? Chad? What? Just tell me."

He wasn't going to give up. She could see it in his eyes. Lori? What would she want? A sex cartoon series? Skimpy, sheer pj's like she had at her age? Dodging the assault of every pornographic gift ever given to her in her past, Sierra offered, "Uh, you know what his parents like better than I do. Lori likes Barbies? Chad … Pajamas? Christmas pj's. How's that?"

An impish twinkle lit in Charlie's eyes. "Consider it done."

The rest of that day moved normally. Therapists came and went. She helped Chad to the half bath off the kitchen area, knowing he would avoid his reflection in the small mirror. He ate. Slept. Stared outside at the blue evening.

She checked his bandages, administered and logged his meds, pushed water, and searched the refrigerator for something for dinner. Then Charlie texted that he and the guys were bringing pizza.

"Daddy! Daddy, guess what? Daddy?" burst through the garage door.

A chocolate lab bolted across the living room along with his daughter, startling Chad awake. Before Sierra could stop it, the dog bound into the dining room like a tornado but came to a halt by Chad's chair, sitting beside it like he had found the prize.

"Daddy, God gave me an early Christmas present. His name is Owen." Lori said as she got on the floor to hug the dog.

"A dog?" Chad asked his father as his dad sheepishly trailed into the room.

"Guess so," his father said as mother appeared with yet another bundle of presents. "Just showed up this morning," she continued, as she deposited everything under the tree like a good Christmas elf. "No collar. No nothing. Vet said no chip either. But the dog seems reasonably cared for."

"Owen. Gamma, his name is Owen," Lori announced. "Can I keep him, Daddy. Pleeeeease?"

Chad's dad looked at Sierra. "We got him bathed, and his nails are trimmed."

Sierra saw a flashback ignite behind Chad's eyes. No clue what it was about, but the dog glanced up at Chad, worried. This Owen stood up and started nuzzling his snout under Chad's arm as if it were a service dog. Impossible.

"Lori, I bet Owen likes snow," Sierra announced. "Would like you to show him the backyard?" A desperate glance at Chad's father put him in action.

Sierra immediately touched Chad's shoulder, which was starting to jerk. "Chad? Chad? It's me. Chad?" Stroking a cold cloth that she kept by the chair across his forehead eased whatever was going off in his brain. "It's okay. Chad? Talk to me. Chad?"

His eyes fluttered open with a desperate gaze. His breathing came in gasps. He was through it. She, too, was back to normal. However, his mother wasn't. She stood in the dining room doorway dumbstruck.

"It's over," Sierra whispered and returned to her patient. "Chad, are you okay?"

He nodded.

Sierra glanced back at his mother who was back with the living and continued to explain the sudden appearance of the dog. "It, I mean Owen, showed up at the door this morning. We think someone dumped it on our road. Of course, Lori immediately laid claim to ... Owen. After all she's been through, how could we say no?"

Sierra wasn't sure she could manage a dog. She had enough on her plate with Chad. Plus, she knew nothing about dogs.

"You're right, Mom," Chad mocked. "You're so right. Lori's been through *so* much. No. I haven't lost my wife. I'm a freak now because of a stupid fool's death wish. Yes, Mom, she's been through a lot lately. So, why not a damn dog?"

"Chad, I didn't mean it that way." Tears swelled in his mother's gaze. "I mean ..."

"Just leave it alone, Mother."

"Uh, Mrs. Michaels," Sierra said, trying to redirect what everyone at the house had been dealing with lately. Chad's snarky attitude. "The guys are bringing pizza. Want to help me with a salad. Is there any Ranch dressing?"

Accepting the offer of an escape, Chad's mother went to work in the kitchen. "I didn't mean it that way," she whispered as she dug into the refrigerator door.

"Mrs. Michaels, he didn't either. Your son is struggling. But he's right, your lives have all been torn up. It's going to take time."

His mother tried to smile as she dumped the bag of lettuce into a bowl "You're right, Sierra. Thank you for understanding."

The guys appeared from the garage door bearing three, huge boxes of pizza, placing them on the small island counter. The fragrance drew everyone from the basement. When everyone gathered to argue over which piece they wanted, Owen had found Chad's chair and sat proudly beside it.

Chad's hand rested on the dog's head like a reward. She watched to see if it triggered another flashback. Instead, Chad's eyes closed as he drifted asleep.

"Lori, we best be gettin' Owen cleaned up for dinner," Hunter offered with a broad smile. All three headed toward the kitchen bathroom.

"Oh, not that one," Sierra ordered in a panic. "Downstairs. Downstairs." She had to keep Chad's rooms as clean as possible. That was her responsibility, and no dog was going to mess that up.

Sierra was starting to put fresh bandages around Chad's legs when the doorbell rang from downstairs. Ryan answered it. Sierra knew no one was coming through that door with his black frame blocking it. Even Jesus.

"Hey, "Dr. Kendrick. Here to check on Chad?"

"Well, yes. Jason and I thought we might stop by."

"How's your friend doing?" Jason asked as the three climbed the stairs to the bedroom.

"I'll let Sierra answer that. But I think he's doing better. He's back to his rude self."

Sierra looked up from Chad's charts. "Hi. Didn't expect to see you … here."

"With the snow, we thought we'd come here instead of Chad coming to the office," said Dr. Kendrick. "How's he doing?"

"Resting."

Sierra handed over the iPad. As the doctor pursued her reports, Jason asked, "How you doin?"

"Okay." Her hesitation was noted.

"Looks good," Dr. Kendrick assured with a smile. Sierra's worry melted like the snow. "Mind if I look at his burns?" he asked.

When Chad stirred awake, the conversation shifted to doctor and patient, "Hey, Chad, how are you?"

Once again, Jason nodded toward the play area and started out of the room. Sierra followed him downstairs to living room. "Seriously, Sierra. How are you?" he asked again.

"Like I said, okay. Just grateful Chad wanted me here, or I'd be on the streets."

"Well, you are missed, and by orders from the floor, I brought you this." He handed her an envelope full of dollar bills. "All the nurses went together to give you this. Merry Christmas."

Sierra sat in one of the chairs and burst into tears. She would be able to pay Charlie back for the gifts and make a payment on her overdue loans. "Thank you," sobbed from her lips.

"And may it be a Happy New Year." Jason sat beside her. "Dr. Kendrick and I talked about that while driving over. He's speaking to the school about you finishing when you are done here. So, keep praying. We want you back, Darlin.' You are a damn good nurse."

"I needed to hear that."

"Aww, shit," Ryan snarled. "They're here again." He thundered down the stairs to stare outside at a gaggle of cameras and reporters on alert for any tidbit in the window.

"Son of a bitch," Jason growled. "They must have followed us."

"I'll take care of this." Ryan stated and disappeared down the stairs. Almost as quickly, he reappeared with his AR-15.

"Ryan, no!" Sierra stopped him before he made it to the front door. "That will be on tonight's news in some form or other. We don't need that." She turned to Jason. "Can you please just tell them to leave.

"Oh, yeah, I would like to do that, but when has that ever worked," Jason retorted.

Chad appeared at the top of the stairs. Everyone panicked as he started to come down. Shoving the weapon into Jason's stunned hands, Ryan bolted up the stairs to catch their patient should he start to fall. Soon enough, Chad was peering out the window.

Snarling, Chad glanced at everyone. "Let one of them in. I'll talk to him. Then, they all better leave."

They watched behind curtains as Jason strolled out to the vulturous reporters, garnering one reporter to the fury of the others. Appearing like a gold medalist, the reporter came in the house, stomping snow on the rug and scanning the living room for any meat. Before he could find her, Sierra escaped into the kitchen.

Watching the reflection off the picture glass over the couch, Sierra watched as Jason directed everyone to the two chairs on the other side of the dividing wall, allowing her to hear every word from behind the dining room wall.

In the reflection in the glass, she saw Ryan standing guard with his weapon by the staircase, adequately intimidating the reporter. Dr. Kendrick sat across from Chad, leaving the reporter to stand or sit on the floor, which ever he chose to do. He stood. Chad's answers to his questions were terse. "Yes … No … Ask him." Chad pointed to Dr. Kendrick.

Dr. Kendrick's responses were laced with encyclopedic medical terminology that only Sierra could understand and enjoy. The questions quickly sputtered to a dead halt. "Well, I guess that is about it," the reporter hesitated. "Is Fantasy still caring for you?"

"There is no fantasy here except you," Chad informed.

As the reporter started to leave, Ryan stepped toward him, backing the poor man up to the staircase. "Now, get the hell outta here and never come back, you or all your other buddies out there. Got it?"

"Sure. Merry Christmas to you too."

Once the door closed, Jason smirked up at Ryan as Sierra joined them in the living room. "You really think they will listen?"

"No. But it's a good try. News tonight should be interesting though."

Chapter 14

Almost immediately after the reporter left, his parents drove up with Lori and Owen. Like the Pied Piper, Ryan drew the dog and Lori to the basement while Sierra headed to the kitchen to start dinner. The moment she rounded the dining room doorway, she overheard his mother's statement, "It's Lori's Christmas play at the church tomorrow, Chad. We, especially you, need to be there for her."

Sierra returned to the living room. "It's too soon." She looked to Chad, hoping he didn't want to go. Not because of being exposed to everything out there, but because of how everyone would be staring at him. And Chad wasn't ready to face that reality.

His mother continued, "We don't have to stay for the whole thing. We just need to be there for Lori's part in the nativity. Then we can leave."

Sierra noticed something stir in Chad's face. And it wasn't what she expected.

"I want out of this house. I'm sick of just going to doctors' offices and looking at these damn walls."

"Oh. You look fine, Sierra," His mother shrugged. "No one dresses up for church anymore. Not like they used to. Even Pastor Pete wears jeans that look more holy than his sermon."

"The dog," Sierra said, "I mean, what about Owen? I can stay to make sure he doesn't disappear while you're gone."

Charlie came through the door. "We put him downstairs. He'll be fine."

Shit. They weren't letting her out of going to church where girls like her were consider demonic. So, there she was, trailing into the church lobby behind their little group. The night air was sharp and clean. Stars sparkled in the black sky. The smell of cinnamon and coffee greeted everyone as they came into the warmth of the church, which was not some elaborate cathedral but a refurbished movie theater.

The only thing missing were the sheep and camels, Sierra thought as Hunter pushed Chad's wheelchair into the lobby full of people milling about as if they had just stepped from the original stable, too busy laughing and chatting with others to notice Chad's entrance.

Colton had lectured about how judgmental, pompous, and overbearing *Bible thumpers* were. And she had been with enough Christian men who proved they were sinners, coming "short of the glory of God" by a long way.

She and Onyx used to make fun of them. The next thing she knew, Onyx was spouting this "Jesus loves you" bullshit to her, right before she ran off to the States. And this Jesus may well love people, but not her, not after all she had done throughout her entire life.

Lori saw them and raced toward her daddy, her angel wings

bobbling about as her halo slipped over her left ear. "Excuse me, I have to go to the restroom," Sierra said, hoping to escape.

The instant Sierra stepped from the bathroom stall and began washing her hands, two young teenage girls dressed in angelic gowns passed her on their way back to the pageant. With a sneer, one asked, "Are you Chad Michael's caregiver?"

"Uh, yes. I am," Sierra answered, stunned to be asked.

"We thought so, by your scrubs."

The other girl snickered. "We're sure he is very glad you are … taking such *good* care of his every need." They glanced at each other and giggled their way out the door.

Clinching her fists, Sierra just stood there, hearing Colton's condemning diatribe all over again. Another stall door opened, and a regal black woman appeared at the other sink.

"I heard that, Sugar. Just let it go. Those girls are just starting into their valleys of death, while we have already made our trips through more than once." Rinsing her hands, the woman moved to the paper towels.

Sierra wasn't sure she understood what 'valley of death' this woman meant. But whatever, she wasn't ready to confront another such attitude in a church bathroom.

The woman's face lit up with humor. "That's from Psalm 23. "Yea though I walk through the valley of the shadow of death, I will fear no evil." Oh, never mind all that … Hi. My name is Rosie. Yours?"

Something about this woman reminded Sierra of Onyx, and it wasn't just that she was black. It was her warm, chocolate gaze. "Uh, Sierra. And yes, I am Chad's caregiver."

"I got that. Kids, today. Seriously. They really can be rude. Come with me. I want to show you something."

Sierra followed Rosie out of the restroom and stopped by the double wide doorway looking out at people still milling about in the lobby. "You see all those people. Well, every day I ask Father God to help me forgive them for they know not what they do." Resting a hand on Sierra's forearm, Rosie looked down at her. "Because, Sugar, just like those girls, they really don't know what the hell they are doing most of the time."

Before she could thank Rosie, Charlie came rushing at her. "Sierra. There you are," he gasped. "It's Chad. He's having a panic attack or something." He motioned to the front doors of the church. "Hunter went for his truck. Come on. We need to get him home."

Once back in the night, Sierra saw Chad gasping for air, sweat pouring into the bandages surrounding his face. His eyes darted like bullets everywhere. "Get me home. Get me home."

"Chad. Chad. I'm here. It's okay. Breathe, Darlin.'" She looked up at Charlie and Ryan, coiled, ready to help. "Get him up. He needs to walk." She saw Hunter's truck approaching and waved it to halt. Confusion exploded from Hunter's face behind the windshield, but he stopped.

She walked with Chad along the handicapped ramp. "Breathe deep, sweetheart." Her seductive tones continued to work. Chad responded. "Keep walking, sweetie."

"Take me home."

"We will. We will. When Hunter finds his truck. Okay?"

Chad was shooting glances everywhere, jerking his body each time. The sweat-soaked bandages on his face dripped onto his Royals sweat suit. His gaze slowed.

Counting each breath, Sierra noted his panic attack was melting like snow. "Hey babe, there's Hunter. We can go home now." She waved for Hunter to join them.

Tears swelled in Chad's frantic gaze as he gripped her hand on his shoulder. She performed a soft, assuring smile. "You're okay, sweetheart. It's all good. All good." She looked to Charlie, "Tell his parents they are responsible for Lori. Okay?"

"Done."

Chad's hand locked on hers the entire trip home; his gaze lost outside the truck's window. The instant they were home, Ryan and Hunter helped him into the dining room and into his stuffed leather chair. Sierra plucked her stethoscope and a bottle of sedatives as she followed.

The guys disappeared downstairs as Sierra checked Chad's pulse and blood pressure. His heart rate was good. However, his gaze stared ahead, lost somewhere. But no longer frantic. She put the bottle of sedatives aside and sat in front of him on the leather footstool, resting her hand on his knee. "Hey, what happened back there?"

"I don't know. I don't know. The crowd. The noise. I … I just couldn't …."

"It's okay. I was afraid this would happen. But it's okay," Sierra whispered. "You're home now."

His blue gaze settled on her like a morning breeze desperate for a place to go. "When will it go away? How long? Will it ever?"

How would she know? After all, her past followed her like a putrid stink. Like her, he saw his damage every time he looked into the mirror of life. She looked directly into his eyes and lied, "It will eventually, Chad. It will get better. You just can't rush it. I promise."

"Sierra? Why did God do this to me? Take Margery?" He looked up at their picture still on the wall. "She's gone. Why?"

"I don't know. I don't understand this God of yours. This Jesus. I really don't. He's not ever been a friend of mine."

If there was a God, He would not have let her parents sell her off like a pet dog to a life that sucked the spirit out of her soul. Then, even when she tried to leave her past behind, this so-called God allowed the torment to continue. If He "so loved the world," then why did he let bad things like this happen anyway?

Chad's blue gaze darkened like a storm. "Once, I thought Jesus was my friend. Not anymore. Not anymore."

Christmas lights flicked on, shedding light through the shadows of the dining room.

Chapter 15

For the next few days, Chad stared at his phone, whisking through pictures … pictures of Margery. He was like a robot. He continued to participate with therapies, whirlpool, bandaging. Ate. Slept. Not seeing anything or anyone except Margery's pictures and the next and the next.

Sierra sat down beside him, hopefully to get him to talk. "Is that Margery?" she asked.

"Yes."

"She's beautiful."

Chad nodded.

"Where was that taken?"

"Hawaii. Our honeymoon."

"And that one?"

"At Pearl Harbor."

Little by little, he told her more about each shot. "She was miss-goody-two-shoes. I was Mr. Jock. We hated each other." His laugh sounded strange. "I loved the way she smiled. I just wanted to be her guy." He laughed with a lurking sadness. "When she would get mad at me, she would glare, like you. I miss her."

Another picture flipped by of a sunset over Diamondhead. "I guess I finally won her over."

"You certainly did."

"And lost her." Tears budded in his eyes. "Why didn't she listen to me?"

"She's like all of us … stubborn."

"Very stubborn." A tear escaped and sank into his chin bandage.

Each photo earned another pause that revealed what Chad and Margery once had, and what he lost. Sierra saw so much love. It was obvious in every picture.

He turned the phone toward Sierra. "She was carrying Lori, here. Just before I had to leave for … for …"

"The first time you had to leave on deployment?" Sierra asked.

"Yes. The first time."

"And that one … was when?" she asked, to move past that moment.

"When I came home. Yes. Came home."

It was a beautiful picture of Margery draped around Chad's neck while he held a toddler in his arms—a perfect family picture.

Onward, Chad took her though what seemed a thousand pictures and started over again with the first one. Fortunately, Hunter appeared from the garage, carrying bags of hamburgers and fries. Chad never noticed the worried look filling his friend's gaze.

She stood up and went to the kitchen island.

"How is he?" Hunter asked.

"Second time around for me," Sierra said as she emptied the food bags. "They really were in love."

"More than you know," Hunter assured, stealing a fry. "Margery was an amazing wife and mother, that's for sure. Chad had what we all want."

Sierra remembered the looks she got in the hospital when the guys saw her holding Chad's hand. "I can see that. I wish I could have known her."

The December sun was unusually bright and warm on the patio that overlooked the expanse of the backyard dressed in snow for the holidays. Closing the bag of birdseed, Sierra started back into the house. The winter chill submitted to the warmth as Sierra closed the patio door and started toward the coffee maker.

"Chad, do you want some coffee? I'm fixing." She looked at the dining room where he sat like a stuffed pillow staring at his phone. No answer.

She was at a loss with helping Chad through this invisible shell he had wrapped around himself. Chad needed to get out of this fog, for Lori, if for nothing else. After all, the girl had moved back home after the Christmas program, dog and all.

If there is this God in this heaven, do something for once? Sierra thought.

Owen was all dog, playful and protective with Lori. However, there were moments when suddenly, the dog would halt and look at Chad as if trying to read him. Invariably, Chad would be sinking into another flashback. Then, Owen would trot over and sit beside him. Chad would rest a hand on the dog's head and, magically, the moment would just melt away.

Everyone noticed. All would glance at each other with questions.

How did the dog know? Was he trained? Was it natural to Owen? And, of course, Sierra overheard his mother say that God must have sent them Owen.

Normally, after someone brought Lori home from school, Chad would venture out of his misery long enough to tell her about the pictures that had absorbed his present life. The delight in the girl's face would vaporize his pity parties.

Since school was out for the holidays, Lori was all over the house with Owen on her heels. "Come on, Owen. Get this, Owen." The chocolate lab was, at the moment, prancing around the living room wearing a pink tutu around its midsection.

Owen charged after a ball rolling into the dining room. Lori was right behind him. "I got it. I got it." Nope. To Lori's delight, Owen won yet again. "Mommy, can I ..."

Chad burst to his feet like a volcano. "She. Is. NOT! Your. Mommy," he yelled and took two steps toward the girl.

Lori froze, like a deer caught in headlights.

"Sierra is nothing but my nurse. You got that! She is not and never will be your mommy. Is that clear?"

Lori burst into tears and ran toward her room. Chad's fury shifted to the dog. "You. Get out of here you filthy mutt. Get OUT!" Owen bolted after Lori.

Nothing but his nurse? Sierra leaned against the kitchen island, arms crossed. Waiting. Just waiting for Chad to see her.

His gaze seemed frozen on the staircase. Slowly, like snow, he began to melt. Sucking in a deep breath, he turned around, lifted his phone, and glanced at it. Then, threw it across his chair, smashing it against the dining room wall. Finally, Chad's gaze found her. "What?"

Frigid as a piece of ice, Sierra pulled off the island and walked toward him. "Like Lori does not know that I am *not* her mommy," seethed from her lips as she passed her patient standing there like a snarling fury.

Chad watched Sierra disappear up the staircase. *Like Lori does not know that I am not her mommy.* No one was replacing Margery. No one. She will not be replaced by anyone. Anyone!

He looked down at his empty palm. His phone was gone! Margery was not there. She was gone. All that he had of her … was gone! Then he remembered hurling Margery's pictures against the dining room wall. Panic flooded through him. He had destroyed her. Like he had that day in the Farmer's Market. No. He had to save her!

Stumbling around his chair he saw his phone shattered into pieces laying below their family picture. Fractures on the screen cut through her beautiful face. "No. I'm sorry, Margery. I'm sorry. I didn't mean to. I should have been there for you. I'm sorry."

He gathered the precious fragments of the cell phone into his palm, punching the button to bring it back to life. Nothing moved on the fractured screen. He put the phone to his ear, pleading to hear her voice. Dead. Dead as Margery was dead. He had killed the phone like he had killed her. Chad drew back to fling the object from his life and froze like a statue.

Lori? She was all he had left … of Margery. *My God, what have I done?* Dropping the phone onto the footstool, Chad hobbled through the living room and struggled up the stairs, using the railing like a rope. He stopped on the top step, hearing Sierra soothing his sobbing daughter.

"He didn't mean it, Lori. Listen to me. He didn't mean it."

"I want ... my daddy ... back."

"Honey, we call it lashing out. He was just lashing out with his anger. Nothing else."

"But ... it ... hurt."

The sound of his daughter's sobs seared over every burn on his body.

"Yes, sweetie, it did hurt. And it was scary. I've never seen your daddy blow up like that."

"Me ... neither. It scared ... me."

He heard Sierra sigh.

"Me, too, Lori. But he didn't mean to. Do you know what, I think? He scared himself."

Tears burned in his eyes as he crept toward one of the windows by the Barbie house, listening.

"You think ... he did?"

"Yes, I think he did, Lori. He is missing your mommy as much as you are. Doesn't that hurt sometimes?"

"Uh, huh... It hurts a lot." Silence. "I see Mommy in my dreams, but when I wake up,... she's not there. I miss her, Sierra. I want her baaack."

"I want her back, too," whined from Chad's throat. Every night. Every day. Every moment. He wanted Margery back. He needed to see her. The photos helped him remember every moment they had. Their wedding. Their honeymoon in Hawaii. Her pregnant. Both holding their daughter when she was just born.

Images of Margery floated to him, after she had just given birth, all sweaty, hair laying in sweat locks, flushed with giving birth to their daughter. Yet, Margery was never so beautiful than in that moment.

He remembered handing Lori to her and Margery reaching for

her like a grand prize. And the way she had gazed up at him in that moment as if thanking him for something priceless. The memory cut him at the knees.

Chad collapsed to the carpet below the frigid window. Tears sobbed from his soul. His hands curled and went to his forehead as tears dripped onto his knees. She was gone. Margery was gone. He had destroyed her. He had destroyed everything.

Owen appeared before him, whining, and then started to lick his tears coming from deep in his soul, ripping at his heart. He shoved the stupid dog away, but the damn dog refused to leave and kept licking his face, sopping up the endless flow of tears.

Chad slumped back against the wall and grabbed the dog to his chest like a lifeline.

"Lori? Maybe you can forgive your daddy for hurting you. Can you do that?"

"Uh, huh. Jesus said we have to."

"You think this Jesus is right?"

"I dunno. I don't want Daddy to do that again. He's scary like a monster."

"But we both know he's not … a monster. He's …"

"I don't like that monster either," Chad pleaded as he stepped into the pink bedroom. "And I'm sorry. I'm really sorry," He shouldered the pouring tears. "I am sorry to both of you. I am so sorry. I should never have said any of that."

Lori raced toward him, arms reaching skyward. "Daddy. Daddy. You're back." He lifted her into his arms as hers swept around his neck in a stranglehold. Chad clung to her, soaking in all the life his little precious daughter offered. She was all he had left now of Margery.

Chapter 16

"Don't tell me this is another pair of ugly pajamas," Chad begged as he ripped at the wrapping paper. A long, miserable groan crawled from his throat while Hunter grinned like the cat that ate the mouse.

"That was our mission," Hunter assured. "Find the ugliest pj's possible, just your size."

"Like in Goldilocks," Lori chimed in, "just your size, daddy."

Everyone laughed as Chad's father handed Hunter another gift from the tree. "I do believe this has your name on it."

The tall lanky Texan dug into the tissue-filled bag and pulled out a shirt that Blake Shelton would envy. It was long-sleeved, denim, with all the perfect snaps and flaps that come on cowboy apparel. It even merited Hunter taking off his black cowboy hat to unfold it. Everyone watched as if he were unwrapping baby Jesus.

Sierra laughed as she watched the process taking place—everyone, waiting for that magic moment when the object is revealed, then witnessing the reaction of the receiver. She remembered how Onyx had gasped at the six-inch-rhinestone-studded heels she had given her. The girl could not have been more overwhelmed. Both shoes went instantly onto her feet and Onyx strutted around the room, sapping up the envy of all.

More images returned of everyone drowning in tissue paper and bags full of gifts, expensive Versace track suits like the one Onyx had given her, tailored shirts, name brand blouses of pure silk, ruby-like rings, and matching bracelets. Long gold necklaces. And rhinestone-studded six-inch heels.

Sierra looked down at her hand, absent of the emerald ring Levi had given her one year for Christmas. It had been surrounded with diamond chips. She also remembered hocking it to get across the border. Little by little, piece by piece she had sold nearly everything to get to the States.

The image of Colton's face arose in her mind. His gaze hard; his expression sour, not pleased. Oh, how that face had ruled her life for so many years. In fact, everyone's lives. Joy survived only on Colton's utterance. Everyone silently read his every expression as he sat in the large, over-stuffed chair like a god. If Colton was happy, then, they all could breathe.

Suddenly Lori strangled her. "Thank you, Sierra. Thank you. I am going to name her Sara. Okay?"

"Yes. Sure." Sierra glanced down at the Barbie box that Lori was clutching. She looked at Charlie and mouthed, "Thank you." He nodded with a grin.

Everyone knew she had not had any time to go shopping for presents, but obviously, they had taken care of that for her. Most of the presents she had given out were an equal surprise to her. Even Chad had received a pair of pajamas sporting Rudolf with a blinking red nose on the pocket.

The room settled quietly as Chad's mother handed Sierra the last gift from under the tree. "This is for you, my dear."

Scrunches, a fat Santa bear, Christmas scrubs, scented soaps, even pink fingernail polish from Lori lay beside Sierra's chair. This time, however, everyone seemed intent on this one last gift.

Under their watchful gazes, Sierra pulled the ribbon surrounding the narrow, rectangular box. One sweeping glace, she noted that no one appeared worried about anything. Anticipation gleamed in their eyes. She eased the box lid off to a white Bible, gold engraved with her name. *Sierra Smith.*

"Open it," his mother whispered. Stars would challenge the gleam in her gaze.

Sierra glanced at Chad. His gaze was tentative as he watched. Opening the front cover revealed a list of signatures: Mom, Dad, Hunter, Axel, Charlie, Ryan, Chad, and Lori in her own huge, personal script.

Thank you and God bless you and may His angels always surround you with His love.

That would have brought Colton from his throne. He would have snatched that gift from her hands and flung it in the blazing fireplace. However, Sierra's hands grazed over the silky pages, the names. Blinking at tears, she closed the book and hugged it to her chest. Regardless of whether she believed what the book said or not, they obviously had given it to her with their hearts. Whispering, she said, "Thank you so much."

"Thumb through it," Chad ordered, grinning.

Her audience continued watching as she obediently thumbed

through the pages that dropped open to a white envelope. She felt the eagerness mount as she revealed a check with her name on it, dated just days ago for five-thousand dollars. Her school loan payment.

"I don't know what to say but thank you." Words clogged Sierra's throat. "I will never forget this."

His mother's hand rested on Sierra's arm. "And you have earned every penny."

"Well, I say, let's get this place cleaned up," huffed Chad's father. "I'm getting hungry."

The entire room burst into action, smashing through tissue paper for gifts hiding in the piles. Gift bags, once again, overflowed from the bounty. Garbage bags were stuffed with torn shreds of wrapping paper. Moments later, his mother was vacuuming the floor.

Charlie was in the kitchen rummaging something from the fridge as the others disappeared downstairs. In front of another of huge Barbie house, Owen lay, chewing on his gift—a rawhide bone. Meanwhile a naked Barbie danced in Lori's hands.

In that same moment, Ryan's huge frame burst through the front door like a black Santa bearing more gifts. His mother and sisters followed, carrying boxes full of food dishes that were immediately sucked up by the kitchen.

Ryan began handing out his gifts, "Ho-ho-hoing" with each presentation. He handed Sierra a small bag that displayed a small velvet box that opened to a gold chain wearing a gold cross. "It's what God's angels wear," he said. "You need one."

Lori peeked over Sierra's arm. "I want one."

Ryan studied her. "And your birthday is when, little girl?"

"May 15th."

"Hmm. I will remember that," he assured.

Happy and content, Lori looked expectantly at Sierra. "Put it on."

Ryan retrieved the chain and did the honors, settling the cross around Sierra's neck. Choking her.

"Honey, that looks gorgeous on you," Ryan's mother said. "It's perfect. Don't you all agree?"

Sierra fought yanking it off because she wasn't one of them. She was something God hated. Just like Colton said, girls like her were His filth. They were man's destruction.

Enduring the golden noose bearing the cross, Sierra set her bag of bounty on the steps upstairs and walked back to the kitchen. "How can I help."

Sitting in one of the leather chairs, Chad rested a hand on her wrist as she started past him. The soft touch trickled deeper than it should have. She halted and looked down at him. "I agree with Mom, you deserved every penny. I mean that, Sierra. But can we skip the whirlpool routine tonight?

"I'll think about it." She grinned down at the small patches of scaring that puckered the corners of his mouth, at his hairline sprouting hair strands like random weeds. "But I will let you choose which pair of Christmas pj's you want to wear."

Chad snarled at her. However, the new sparkle in his gaze ruined it. "This won't be forgotten. I promise," he said.

"Mom, where's the table extensions?" Axel asked from the living room.

"In the closet by the front door," Chad's mother yelled from the kitchen.

Sierra refocused her attention to the nest of cooks stirring about the small kitchen like a perfect pot of stew.

"Here, let me get that." Ryan ordered his sister to relinquish the huge pot of boiled potatoes to him. Once drained in the kitchen sink, five sticks of butter were dropped in, and Ryan began smashing the potatoes like sinful sacrifices. Along with Chad's mom, Ryan's mother was investigating the oven for the success of the forthcoming dishes.

Chad had gone outside with his father, sending up smoke signals to the neighbors that the turkey was almost done. Charlie was playing with Owen, Lori, and Barbie in the living room. Hunter was reaching for a dish on the top cabinet shelf for Chad's mom.

"Excuse me. Meat comin' through." Everyone backed up as Chad's dad carried a golden turkey toward the kitchen island.

This was nothing like any Christmas that Sierra could ever remember, since all this mayhem normally took place behind closed doors. Dressed in gowns or tuxedo, she, and everyone else were in Colton's massive living room, raising toasts of expensive champagne in fine crystal glasses to the man himself, in celebration of yet another year of success.

"Sierra, can you get the silverware?" Chad's mother asked as she bustled about the extended table being surrounded by any chair Hunter and Charlie managed to find. "Oh, and the Christmas napkins are in that drawer."

Sierra sprang into action, placing the everyday forks, knives, and spoons in their proper place. No silver dessert spoons sat above the plate because there were no dessert spoons. Nor were any silver salad forks placed beside China plates. Just a common-day fork, knife, and spoon. Plastic glasses or plastic cups sat just above the triangular, poinsettia-covered paper napkins beside the mismatch of everyday plates.

Food began to fill all remaining space on the table. Turkey was sliced. Dressing, gravy, a mountain of potatoes dripping in butter, fresh homemade dinner rolls, more dishes than Sierra could name were paraded to the table where everyone claimed the nearest chair. Sierra waited for everyone to sit and took the lone chair left beside Lori.

Every person around the table were oblivious to any propriety as anticipation mixed with the fragrances of food like a "greedy, hand-rubbing, can't-wait-to-dig-in" moment. Dressed in ordinary jeans, shirts, T-shirts, everyone seemed lost in some joke told with a stolen morsel of food. Chad's dad radiated happiness as he laughed at some comment from Axel. His eyes held the joy of a child anticipating every forthcoming tidbit.

The excited hunger silenced as Ryan's mother offered a prayer. Then, everyone's attention shifted to the closest bowl. After claiming a scoop, the dish was passed to the next person, and they eagerly turned for the next proffered bowl.

Sierra never dared to eat this much but, somehow, her plate filled to absurd proportions. "Lookin' like a pig these days … look, she's gaining weight on her ass … turning into a real fatty are we …" rang in her memory.

Every Christmas Sierra could remember, Colton sat like a god at the head of the table, directly across from Mario. Everyone had to stand and wait behind their assigned chairs—assigned according to the earned profits for that year—waiting for Colton to nod; then everyone sat and ate under their watchful gazes.

Servers presented various selections of food displayed in silver bowls or platers. A submissive nod was granted, and the proffered spoonful was placed onto each China plate. Fine wine flowed into the crystal glassware. All around the table, everyone modestly feasted under Mario and Colton's attentive gazes, gloating as if they were responsible for every crumb.

"Sierra, I want some 'tatoes, please?"

"Oh, yes. Here." Suddenly, Sierra was back. Home? No, she wasn't home. She had no home. However, as her training once again set in, she submitted to what was before her.

Chapter 17

"Nite, Mr. and Mrs. M. Thanks for everything," Charlie yelled as he disappeared down the stairs behind the other guys already setting up for a game of pool. From the dining room doorway, Sierra watched as Chad's parents hugged everyone and waved as they, too, left. Then, everything suddenly went quiet to the point of empty. Even the twinkling Christmas tree, devoid of presents, appeared lonely.

The kitchen was immaculate as if nothing had ever happened within its confines. The dining table had shrunk to normal size, and the wreath holding a burning vanilla candle had returned, as had the holiday tablemats.

Sierra sat in the leather chair that matched Chad's. He was putting Lori to bed. Between the chairs, stretched, once again, the loveseat and a wooden coffee table.

Chad was improving faster than most burn victims, she thought, which meant her time with him was eroding like sand. The reality that Kansas City would not let her remain loomed like the shadows. So, everyone she had met since the suicide bomber would become history. She would have to find another town in which to start over. Dallas. San Francisco. Seattle. Europe, once again, offered its services.

But no part of her wanted go through all the covering up of her past again, only to have it find her. As it would. After all, the *Patient and Pornstar* had made international news thanks to Google. However, in a few more months, she would have to find some way to survive.

She remembered, as a young girl, escaping to St. Felipe's Castle ale Lara with its lace of palm trees. She felt its strong stone walls that not only protected the castle but also her, at least for a time. She had loved going there every chance she could, to hide in Guatemala's Champey Natural Park and rainforest to escape the world she didn't want to be in.

Noise behind her interrupted her thoughts. Sierra turned to watch Chad easing down the stairs and making his way across the living room. Owen followed faithfully at his side. The day had obviously taken its toll on him.

"How about some eggnog?" Chad asked as he walked toward the fireplace to add a log to the simmering coals.

"Sure. I'll get it." Sierra stated and rose obediently to serve. By the time she returned with two glasses and a plate of leftover cookies, the fire had relit with a happy, busy flame.

She handed one glass to Chad and returned to her chair. Propping her feet on the coffee table, Sierra looked over at Chad lost somewhere in the flames. "You ready for your compression suits? They should arrive any time."

He motioned to the compression mask now covering most of his face like a Halloween mask that velcroid over the crown of his head. "No. Wearing this thing is dreadful. Do I really have to wear this all day?"

"All day … minus one hour. And guess what that hour is."

"The whirlpool."

"Correct."

"When will this hell end?" he asked.

"When it's over."

He snarled at her. "I'm due for my first plastic surgery next week. What's that going to entail?"

"More itching."

"More scars where I don't have any now. What's this ballooning thing?"

"Oh, something more to add to your fun," Sierra assured and returned to watch the flames casting a glow to the holiday shadows that remained. Owen had settled on the hearth, creating a Thomas Kincade effect to the room. "I bet you sat here with Margery drinking eggnog every night after Christmas."

"Not just Christmas. We would almost every night. Summers, we would go out to the swing in the backyard," he said, letting the flames reflect the memories.

"If the mosquitoes let you."

Casting an impatient glance at her, Chad huffed. "They ran us back inside many times."

Sierra studied her patient. Images of him in the hospital surfaced, covered with white sheets, thrashing in the hospital bed and then in the dining room. Now he sat, facing the fire, wearing his new compression mask, and his new Royal's sweats. Like her, Chade He propped his Christmas house sandals on the table, appearing almost normal.

"I miss Margery," Chad said to the flames. "I couldn't stop thinking all day that she should be here. And not me."

"I think everyone did," Sierra answered. "And they would miss you as well."

He shrugged. A solid silence followed, then, "I know they did. But, like the plague, they avoided saying anything."

"No one wanted to dampen the happiness."

"Still, nothing feels right without her." Chad got up abruptly and started poking at the burning log. He returned to his chair. "Do you ever miss your parents?" he asked.

That was a nuclear blast she didn't want. "No. I don't miss them. Colton is dead."

"I meant your real parents."

"No." They were a subject she kept buried as deeply as possible. Faking a yawn, Sierra smiled across the fire glow. "So, are you ready to wear those pajamas?"

"You are not letting me out of the whirlpool."

"Nope. And I washed the Rudolf pair just so you can wear them before you must deal with your new attire arriving tomorrow."

"Wonderful. Just wonderful."

"I'll go get things started."

Chad stared at the fireplace as the flame burned down. Sierra had disappeared upstairs. He could hear the water filling the whirlpool that started the daily routine.

Alone with Margery's hole in his heart, he sipped the last of the eggnog. She really wasn't there and never would be again. All he had now was their daughter. Every time he looked at Lori, he saw bits of Margery. But he knew Lori could never fill that hole that had truly been his better half.

Chad swiped open his new phone that his parents had given him for Christmas. The guys had downloaded everything he'd lost. He set the picture that Margery had taken of him and Lori at the KC Zoo as his cover page. It was him and Lori, with Margery shadow as she took the picture—the invisible part of his life. Staring at the pictures now left an uncomfortable vacancy instead of, how before, just seeing that memory had soothed his pain.

He remembered the panic attack at the church. He was a fool to think that going there would help him deal with being without Margery. After all, it was their church. Their people. Their friends. What made him think that Jesus would perform some miracle and bring her back, or at least, heal the monster he was now?

No matter what everyone said, he was the reason she was dead. He was the reason Lori no longer had a mother. Again, he heard Lori calling Sierra "mommy," and seeing Margery's face cracked across his old screen. It was like looking at his life … cracked and broken.

Itching ignited beneath the bandages as sweat beaded where he still had normal flesh. His throat started closing. Tears emerged. Owen instantly appeared at the chair, his head propped on the fat leather armrest.

Chad's hand rested on the dog's head. Just feeling that warm fur permeate up through his arm, calmed him. In that same moment, Rudolf with his flickering nose on the pocket of the pajamas dropped across his lap. "It's time." He looked back up at Sierra's taunting gleam in her eyes.

The night resisted sleep. Flipping the lights on revealed the quilted bed set that Margery had created just for him. Chad stared at her handiwork, once again seeing her plying the needle along each piece. She said it was like putting together a fabric jigsaw puzzle.

Pulling the quilt to his nose as if to smell her hands, his gaze drifted to their walk-in closet. It was open, revealing his shirts, trousers, and jeans on one side, and her dresses, blouses and slacks across from his. He felt the memories crashing into him. Thoughts of what he needed to do—but couldn't—flooded over him. Tears burned behind his gaze as he strangled the fabric in his hands.

Chad made for the bathroom to escape. Normally, he avoided looking in the mirror. But this time he halted over Margery's sink, still surrounded by her makeup, her perfume, her things. He looked up as if expecting to see her reflection. But it was him. Wearing a mask.

Sprigs of black hair pointed skyward around the Velcro closing over his skull. His gaze was hard. Angry. The tip of his nose peeked out from beneath the compression cloth. Pulling the Velcro apart, hearing its scratching as it released, he let the mask fall into the sink.

Pink, white, brown marbled flesh presented the same stranger down to his jaw line, no longer sharp and smooth. Again, he studied the one-eared man who had destroyed their lives. He opened his mouth as far as he could, enduring the strange pull that spread across both cheeks that mirrored Margery's quilts.

He knew his neck was just the beginning of a horror that lay beneath the cotton bandages covering the rest of his body. Slowly, he unwrapped each bandage as if he were a Christmas present, revealing what damage that bastard had done to him. Each strip fell to the floor at his feet. He opened the door to the linen closet and stood before the full-length mirror and saw the raw, full-meal deal.

From his chest with misplaced nipples, he studied the red, mottled scars. The damage continued over his stomach, which once was a proud six-pack. Normal skin appeared around his groin, but not to the tops of his thighs—also a patchwork of scars. He turned as he had that day in the market, slightly to the left, somewhat protecting his right thigh. But not his left, which explained why he could pee pretty much normally.

Fully turning revealed his backside, smooth, untouched from his shoulders all the way down to his butt and down the back of his legs. But Dr. Kendrick said that skin was needed for harvesting. Pieces of it would be sliced off to put over the burns, marring even that flesh with scars.

Lori didn't have a mother because of that monster in the market that day, but he did deserve that reflection in the mirror.

Daddy, I don't want to. Please.

Fantasy, he paid $500,000 for this night with you. You must do this. It's for all of us. We've talked about this.

Daddy, I don't want to. Please. Don't make me do this.

We've talked about this.

Daddy, I don't want to. Please. I don't want to. Don't make me.

Sierra remembered struggling in Colton's arms, pleading. She didn't want to go in there with that man. She didn't care how nice he was. He was going to hurt her.

Only this time, Fantasy. Only this time. Only this time … We've talked about this.

Daddy, I don't want to. Please.

"Sierra. Sierra."

"Daddy, I don't want to," Sierra pleaded to the stranger. "Please. I don't …"

"Sierra, wake up. You don't have to. You don't have to. Wake up."

Gasping, Sierra opened her eyes but not to the john. It was a worried face. It was Chad. It was Chad!

"Sierra, are you … are you okay? What?"

"I'm fine. I'm fine." Blinking from the lights that were now on, Sierra struggled to sit up and then recognized the room. The guest room. Then she remembered the dream that was returning now. "I'm fine. Thank you," she gasped.

Chad sat down on the bed, resting his hand on her leg hidden beneath the bedspread. She pulled it free of his touch. She didn't want anyone touching her.

"You sure you are okay?" he asked. "What happened?"

"Nothing."

He studied her. "I don't believe you."

"I don't give a shit what you believe. I'm fine. I don't need a babysitter."

He looked away toward Lori's playroom. "Sierra, you know everything about me. I know some of what happened to you. It's okay to tell me anything. I won't judge. You know that."

"Like I said, thank you for waking me up. But I'm fine now. You can go."

He shook his head. "I'm not leaving."

"Fine. Then I will." She crawled from the sheets, clutched the blanket and a pillow, and started out of the room. "I'll be downstairs. Enjoy the bed."

She no more than settled on the living room couch than Chad and Owen came down the stairs. "It is none of your business. I don't want to talk about it."

"Fine. I'll get us some water."

"Damn it, Chad. Don't you get it. I don't want to remember."

"You know you will the next time you close your eyes." Chad stood there, hand on his hips, defiant in his blinking Rudolph pjs. Owen's tail was beating against Chad's leg as he also watched.

"Maybe that dream won't return if you tell me about it," he said. "Maybe, you'll even sleep better if you do."

"Dammit, Chad. Dammit." Tears blurted from her eyes. She curled into a couch pillow, letting them pour unheeded. Chad's hand stroked her hair as she clung to the pillow.

"It … it was my first time. Colton sold me for half a million dollars. I had to do it. I had to." The story flooded out with her tears. "I didn't want to do it. I begged him. Please."

"That's behind you now, Sierra. That will never happen again." Chad said softly.

Sierra looked up at her patient, the man she had been taking care of ever since the hospital spewed her out like trash. She was his nurse. She was supposed to be taking care of him. That was her job. She collected herself. "Uh. Thank you, Chad. I'm … I'm … I'm fine now. Much better. Thank you."

Chad moved back from her. "I mean that, Sierra. You don't ever have to go back to that life. So, please, don't."

"Oh, really." She waved at the blank screen of the television as if the media were once again displaying her reality to the world.

"My life is ruined. One semester left. I would have graduated this May. But not now," she snarled. "All those loans, how do I pay them unless I work? And … Even if I had graduated, what hospital would have me once they did a background check. It was all over the damn news. What do I have left?" She slumped back into the sofa.

"God will …"

She glared at him. "Don't give this 'God-will-provide' shit. Where was He when my parents sold me to Colton? Where? Where was He that night Colton sold me to those johns? Where, Chad? Where?"

"I don't know, Sierra. I've been asking that question too. I don't know."

"Well, at least God can still love you. He hates everything about me. My parents didn't even want me."

Chad stared at her as if she had suddenly grown a horn. "Is that what this pimp told you?"

"Colton showed me the proof. Paper signed by my parents. She … she … she … didn't come for me. My mother was looking at her phone when he took me. No one came looking for me." Tears jerked from her insides. "Colton let me hold the puppy and said there were more in a van. I wanted to see them. He said that was the plan all along. My mother was to bring me to the playground and let him show me the puppies."

"Sierra, Colton lured you away." Chad went to the picture window and stared out at the falling snow. "They lied to you, Sierra. You were kidnapped."

"No. Everyone else's parents sold them. I wasn't the only one."

He turned. "You all were kidnapped, Sierra. They lied to every damn one of you." He walked back to the couch to sit down, his face hard and determined. "They told you this shit over and over until you believed it. Every damn one of you." He leaned toward her. "I bet your parents desperately looked for you. I'm sure of it."

She shook her head. "It doesn't matter. After all this time, they have given up. Besides, if they knew what I have done all these years, they would never want me back. God doesn't even want me. Chad, I am a prostitute … literally. God does not care about us. We ruin his perfect plan."

"Daaaddyyyy?" Lori appeared halfway down the staircase.

Chapter 18

Chad had given her the keys to Margery's car to get groceries for dinner. The chilly air and fresh snow felt wonderful. She could finally breathe.

The very idea that her parents could still be looking for her after seventeen years was … was …. No. Once they knew what their daughter had been doing all those years, they would toss her out like the garbage she was. Like Colton said, "If God doesn't want you, why would your parents? But I do, I love you. I love every one of my kids."

With shopping cart and Chad's VISA card ready, Sierra began the mental inventory of what was needed. Veggies. More fruit. Meat, they were low on that. This would be a great chili day.

"Fantasy."

She turned automatically to the sound of that name. No. It wasn't her name. But the strange man smiled victoriously at her. "I knew it was you. I knew …"

Normally, she would befriend him and forget about groceries … see to his needs. But … but …no. She didn't have to do that now. She …

"Excuse me, but do you know where the Nut Crackers are?"

Sierra looked at the Muslim lady wearing her head scarf who intruded. "Uh, what?"

"Go ask a store clerk," the john growled. "We are talking here."

The woman, who had opened this trap door for Sierra, glared at the piece of filth as Chad's words, *You don't have to do this* reverberated in Sierra's brain.

"Get out of my sight or I'm calling security." Sierra snarled and turned back to the woman. "Yes. Let me show you."

The woman smiled victoriously. "Thank you."

Sierra headed anywhere that could take her out of the produce section. "I really don't know where they are," Sierra confessed. "I'm sorry."

The woman grinned. "You are too pretty to put up with shit like him. Besides, I really don't know where they are. So, I thought maybe I could help you, and you could help me. Have you tried the cheddar ones? They are …"

The woman's chatter was overrun by Sierra's thoughts. In a grocery store! Her past had haunted her down in a grocery store. She was never going to get away from it. Never. That was proof enough.

"In aisle 22."

Sierra realized the woman had stopped to ask a store clerk for help. The happy lilt in her voice drew Sierra back. "My husband just loves the cheddar, but I love the country ranch. Have you ever tried them? I bet if you do, you and your husband would really like them, too."

"Yes." Sierra stammered, "I mean, no, we haven't … I mean I haven't tried them."

"Oh, there they are. You should try them. They are delicious." Waving the boxes in her hands, the woman gleamed as she proceeded toward check-out. "May Allah bless you for helping me."

"Yes. God bless you for helping me."

The woman smiled brilliantly as she turned the corner. Sierra watched her go.

What had made her say, 'God bless you'? Maybe Chad's parents were rubbing off on her. She plucked two boxes from the shelf, cheddar and country ranch, then headed toward the check out. She would get the rest of the groceries from another store, praying the john wouldn't follow her.

"Daddy, here." Lori shoved a letter from her teacher. "Can you do it. Pleeeeease! Everybody else's daddy came to class. Can you? Pleeeeease?"

Stopping at a light, Chad took the letter from his daughter's hand then saw his name—*Mr. Michaels.*

Mr. Michaels, we are introducing our class to the student's parents and are inviting all parents to come speak to the class. Would you be willing to come tell us about who you are, where you were born, what you do as a profession, or anything you would like to share with our class? If so, would you be willing to visit us Wednesday, February 28th.

Thank you for making our class better,

Ms. Hart

"Please, daddy. Can you do it? Can you?"

The light changed. As he continued into the cemetery, he could already see their shock the moment he walked into the classroom.

Monster. He saw it every time he went anywhere, even at his doctor's office. He was a freak now.

"Lori, this is next week. I …"

"Daddy, please. I'm the only one whose daddy hasn't come. Or mommy." He heard tears in her plea.

"Let me think about it," Chad said as he pulled up to the area where Margery was. He started from his truck. "You sure you don't want to tell mommy you love her?"

"Oh. I tell her every night. She knows. It's too cold."

As Chad opened the door, Owen hopped out to race after a rabbit. "I'm locking the doors. Don't touch a thing. You understand?"

"Okay."

He slammed the door shut, hearing the assurance of the short beep of the door locks. Lori's cavalier attitude of 'she knows' irritated him. Or was it confidence? He wasn't sure but whatever it took, he wanted Margery a part of their lives even if her place was now a large empty hole in their lives. She was here. They had that much.

He came to her headstone. Margery Ann Michaels. June 28, 1987 ~ October 25, 2022. The angel carved above her name was announcing her entrance into heaven. The garlands of roses carved along either side were beautiful. But still, he just stared at the stone.

"Hi. I'm back. I guess you have been talking to Lori. She says you talk every night. I miss you every night." A tear froze on his face as he hunkered down to keep an element of warmth. It was cold.

"I love you, sweetheart. I want you back." The words cut like frozen icicles stabbing his heart, drawing even more tears. He swiped at them with his shoulders while he kept his gloved hands shoved into his coat pocket. "Lori wants me to visit her class. I just don't know if I can. Everyone thinks …"

Owen stopped his traipsing about the plots, froze, and then bolted toward the truck. Chad turned to see a black Navigator stop alongside his truck. A man was getting out. Lori! Sierra! Kidnappers! *No. Not my daughter.*

He bolted on Owen's heels as fast as his legs allowed. But that was not fast enough. He stumbled rather than ran. His strides too short. His muscles not stable. The burn scars crippled each stride.

Chad collapsed against the hood of his truck and confronted the short guy in a full cashmere coat. He would tear him limb from limb before he let …

"Excuse me. Do you have any idea where Howard Parks may be buried? I was told it was down here somewhere," the Hispanic man asked. He looked executive with dark black hair and black eyes, as he waved across all the plots. "I don't see any new burials. Do you?"

One glance proved Lori was watching safely from the windshield. Owen was beside him. Chad scanned Margery's area. "I don't see any. You might want to ask the office by the gate."

A long, frustrated sigh escaped the man. "Yes. I will. But I have a meeting downtown and I'm already late. Thank you." He started back to the Navigator.

His driver got out to close the rear door for the man. He, too, had a similar Hispanic look with his black-brown hair, but his eyes were hazel. He nodded to Chad as he hurried back to the steering wheel.

Dismissing the moment, Chad unlocked the truck, let Owen in, and followed into the warmth of the cab. "You were right, Lori. It is cold out there."

"Told ya, daddy. Who was that man?" Lori asked as she snapped herself in her car seat.

"Couldn't find who he was looking for. Lost." Chad started the engine.

"Lori," Ms. Hart announced softly, "Would you like to introduce your father and his …"

"Nurse," Lori stated proudly. His daughter cleared her throat and stood very tall. "Everybody, this is my daddy. Sierra is his nurse. He got burned bad."

"That why you are wearing a mask?" A boy blurted from the back. "It's not Halloween."

"Johnny, that was not nice. Sit down," Ms. Hart ordered.

Chad appreciated the question. The elephant was out of the room. "Doctor says I have to wear it. Have any of you been told to not play with fire?"

Heads nodded.

"Well, I wasn't playing with fire. But let's say, a blast of fire played with me. This is why your parents tell you, not to." Suddenly, curiosity replaced the fear in their faces. Those words had to come from God because he hadn't devised them.

"Was that back right before Halloween? When that asshole blew himself up?" Again, from Johnny.

"Johnny! That was inappropriate."

Chad was starting to really like this kid. "Actually, yes. It was. The blast hit me in the front and did this. Well, not this." He pointed to the beginnings of his first ballooning on his shoulder.

"What's that," another kid who apparently took his cue from Johnny.

Chad couldn't explain it. He just knew what it was … some kind of new hell.

"Mr. Michaels is growing new skin for grafts so that the doctors can use that skin to fix the burn scarring." All attention shifted to Sierra. "How many of you have ever been sunburned?"

Hands raised.

"Well, then you were burned, like Lori's daddy. But not as badly. His burns left scars. Lori's daddy has a lot of them from the fire."

"I don't see any scaring." Johnny again. Chad could see the class agreed. No part of him wanted to do this, but if it kept one kid from playing with fire … Chad slowly removed the compression mask. The room gasped in fear.

Sierra instantly took over. "Scarred skin is different, isn't it?" Heads barely nodded as gazes tore away to listen to her. "It's very uncomfortable as well as hard to live with." She looked at Chad. "Isn't it?"

"Very hard to live with. Very itchy."

"Looks like shit." Johnny again.

After another reprimand, it was obvious they were beginning to understand.

"But Mr. Michaels is not … scary," Sierra continued. "Right Lori?"

Chad welcomed Lori into his lap like a savior. "I love my daddy. He's perfect."

He appreciated the smiles as well as the excitement traipsing impishly about the room now. "Nothing will ever stop my love for you, sweetheart," he whispered. Lori hugged him in front of her class.

"This is Mr. Michaels' nurse, Ms. Smith," Ms. Hart stated. "Maybe she can explain to everyone about burns and scars. Will you?"

Sierra placed her hand on Chad's shoulder, grounding him as

she took command of the class. Chad listened as she drew diagrams of first, second, and third degree burns on the board. Answering questions about their own scars. About how the bulbous part of his arm was going be used for a graft which she drew on the board. About the compression mask, once again back in place, and why he had to wear it.

"Your skin is an especially important organ of your body. It keeps everything inside, keeping you warm. But his skin was burned off from most of his body." She pointed to the mask.

"Can you see?" a little girl asked.

"Obviously, he can, dummy," Johnny answered.

The little girl burst into tears. Lori raced to her friend to comfort her while the teacher scowled to the back of the classroom. "Johnny, say you are sorry."

"Sorry."

Chad felt he had to save the moment. "When the blast occurred, I covered my face like this, so the back of my arms got burned. You try it."

Arms covered eyes; head nodded.

"Is *everything* burned?" another, smaller boy asked genuinely concerned.

Chad felt a blush start up his neck. "No. I turned slightly. Like this." He stood, turned slightly to the right as he had that day. Then the blast hit again. He felt its force heaving him backward into the chair.

Before he panicked, Sierra's hand rested on his shoulder, again grounding him. "Lori's dad's back side is perfectly fine, no burns. But he was burned over a lot of his body on the front."

He fed into her touch, letting it wash through him like cooling water. He listened to the sound of Sierra's voice as she talked. Calm. Collected. Certain. It soothed. Distracted. Chad worked on breathing as Ms. Hart asked the class, "Great. Now. Are there any more questions?"

"Are you a porn star?"

"Johnny! Go to the principal's office. Now."

"Well, my dad watches someone who looks like her ... a lot." Johnny said as he stood up to leave.

Lori's friend burst into tears again, drawing the entire room back to the front. "He's always doing that, calling people names. I am not a dummy!"

Ms. Hart shifted her attention to the little girl. "No, Susie, you are not a dummy, that was not nice. Johnny, again, say ..."

Chad saw something change in Sierra. He had expected her to crumble as his insides had done earlier. Instead, Sierra met the youngster's gaze. "I am a nurse."

"Yes. Well, I think we have learned a lot today," Ms. Hart announced grandly. "Thank you, Ms. Smith and Mr. Michaels, for sharing so much about not playing with fire. Lori, you are an incredibly lucky girl. Thank you for asking them to come today."

The principal appeared at the classroom door. "Johnny, we will be talking with your parents." He turned to Sierra. "Sorry about that," he muttered.

"I'm used to it," she said softly.

Chad knew she was lying. "After today, my appreciation of first grade teachers just skyrocketed," he stated as they left.

The principal rose proudly. "I have to say, we have the best of the best. Ms. Hart is the best."

Things got quiet in Chad's truck. Christian music played on the radio while he drove home. "You managed everything really well," Sierra said to the windshield.

"You did too." He smiled as he turned into their street. "It all started coming back on me. You stopped it. Thanks. Maybe we should have brought Owen after all.

"Definitely. Kids would have forgotten us entirely."

Chad smirked. "You really handled Johnny back there, too," he said as he drove. "A first grader who knows about porn. Says something about his parents, doesn't it?"

It said that my past is going to haunt me forever, Sierra thought. First, the patient at the hospital, the hospital letting me go. The media. Chad's parents. Not to mention the john at the grocery store. Now, a first grader. Why fight it?

Sierra shook her head with disbelief. "I can't believe I said I was a nurse."

He glanced at her. "You are a nurse."

She dropped her gaze to her lap. "Not really. A glorified caregiver maybe. But not a nurse."

Chad pulled to the curb.

"What are you doing?"

Shifting into park, he turned to her. "I can't drive and say this to you, Sierra. What you said to Johnny was right. You are a nurse, maybe not a licensed nurse yet, but you will be one day. You have to keep moving forward." He took her hand in his. "Follow your dream, Sierra. You deserve it."

Normally she withdrew from all unnecessary touching. But she couldn't, not this time. Chad's strength, sincerity, and kindness flowed into her like a transfusion. But it wasn't right. He deserved better.

She eased her hand free. "I'll try."

Chapter 19

The remains of spaghetti decorated the now empty plates along with the leftovers of the bag salad Lori had made … with help, of course. Bottles of Green Goddess and Ranch dressings stood stalwartly on either side of the bowl along with a both open boxes of Nut Crackers.

Chad sat back in contentment. "That was good. I think I like the cheddar flavor."

Owen was begging for another chip, which Lori gave him the moment Sierra got up to begin collecting the dirty dishes. "How'd your doctor appointment go?" she asked.

"First, I got to drive myself for once, which was great," Chad answered. "The appointment was, I guess, okay."

"Does that mean you can take me to Chuckie Cheese?" Lori asked, pleading, hope blazing in her face.

"We might be able to manage that, but not now or tomorrow. I'll have to think about it more."

That was enough hope to charge the child out of her chair toward the living room with Owen on her heels. "Lori, Sierra needs help with the dishes first. Then you can play."

"Yes, Daddy." Lori straggled back into view and started carrying dishes to the sink.

Sierra watched Lori clearing the table. Doing that for Colton and Mario flashed in her mind. She, Onyx, and Levi had the task of taking care of the dishes each evening while Colton and Mario discussed business. Customers. How the other girls were doing. Income. Expenses. The next trip to Europe for whatever playoffs were about to occur or some big event. Who they needed to contact.

As Sierra rinsed the dishes, handing them to Lori, she wondered why these thoughts had begun to return like hot pokers. Normally, she could turn them off simply by studying or taking someone's shift.

"Dr. Kendrick said he wants to start harvesting more skin for the grafts," Chad said as he placed the four-leafed clover candle and green mats to the table. "I am hating the thought of dealing with that again."

Sierra realized Chad was still talking about the appointment. She handed Lori the salad bowl. "Since it's your skin, your body accepts it better. It's cheaper than other processes."

"Well, I've made it this far," he grumbled. "Do I really look that bad?" he asked.

"No! Daddy. You are handsome."

"I think you are very handsome," Sierra stated with a grin.

"Liar," he mouthed at her.

Smiling sheepishly, Sierra dropped her gaze to the dishwater, looking up through her eyelashes. "Well, a nip and tuck here and there might help a bit, especially the end of your nose."

"My nose?" Chad instantly lifted his fingers to the marred area.

"An earlobe maybe … if you want to wear an earring," she continued with a grin.

"Yeah, Daddy, an earring. I want earrings. We could match." Lori closed the dishwasher. "Sierra, are we done?"

"I think so. Go play."

Lori darted out of the kitchen with Owen once again at her heels. They watched them disappear.

"Dr. Kendrick is talking about grafting the back of my hands and neck for flexibility," Chad said seriously as they both walked to their chairs. "Then he wants to graft across my shoulders here, then the backs of my arms. The front of my thighs is optional. What do you think?"

Sierra shrugged as she settled in the chair. "Listen to the doctors."

"I'm getting a beer," he asked. "You want one."

"Not with your meds, you're not. But I'll take one."

Once they returned from putting Lori to bed, Chad put another log in the fireplace. "I knew she wasn't going to make it through to the end of that movie," he said as he stirred the coals.

"You want to watch a game or something?" Sierra asked from her chair.

"Not really. Fire's enough." He was enjoying the silence. Chad sat on the couch next to Sierra's chair with Owen curled up beside him.

"It's quiet without the guys." Sierra said to the flames.

"They got away to go sand-dunning in Oklahoma. Wanted me to join them."

"Seriously?" she asked. "Dr. Kendrick would nix that idea in a heartbeat."

He drank his coke. "It would have been nice though. I'm getting tired of just sitting around here or going to the doctors."

"That's better than being in the hospital." Sierra thought a minute. "You'd be just getting out about now."

Silence consumed the shadows as he studied the growing flames. "That makes hanging out here easier. But I look forward to getting this graft removed. It itches worse than all the others."

"They are renowned for that." Sierra stated. "You want me to get some ointment?"

"No. It's fine. I can manage."

Silence returned. Owen readjusted on his cushions. "How did you and the guys meet up?" she asked

Chad dropped his head back on the couch to look at the ceiling where it all came to life like a movie screen. "We were assigned to the same unit in Afghanistan. Went over and came back together both times. But, instead of six, it was the five of us that came back the last time.

"You lost someone over there?"

He nodded. "We lost a lot of men in our unit. We were a week from coming home and were caught on a crossfire. This scar on the side of my head was a bullet. Hunter took one in the leg. It almost killed him. Ryan got hit in the shoulder. Charlie and Axel got us all out of there. It was hell."

Images of that day started flashing in his mind. Owen settled again. Chad welcomed the dog's restless comfort. He reached for the cold water on the coffee table.

"I'm sorry I asked."

Chad shook his head. "We came back from Germany to Joint Base Anacostia for rehab, went through PTSD therapy together. That's what brought them back to Missouri with me. You could say that mom and dad have adopted them. They all loved Marg …"

Choking on her name, Chad shook his head to clear it. It refused to go until he inhaled deeply. Owen sat up to look directly into his gaze. He draped an arm over the dog to press it down beside him. The pain retreated.

"What're their stories?"

"Well, Axel's dad has Alzheimer's, doesn't even recognize him. He still goes back to Louisiana coupla times a year. He's the sharpshooter of the outfit. He can shoot a flea off a dog and never leave a scratch. You probably guessed that Hunter is from Texas. His parents were killed in a car accident the year before he signed up. Just a grunt like me. Charlie's parents live in Vegas and are divorced, snarling at each other still, after ten years. Both have gambling and alcohol issues. He's our lead man. Ryan, well you know his mom and sisters. What you don't know is his father is in Leavenworth for another ten years for manslaughter. Bar fight. I went with Ryan once to visit his dad. Great guy. He just got drunk and screwed up. Ryan's our MP; he keeps us straight."

Sierra poked at the fire, placing another log on it. "I see why you all are so close. I can also see your mom and dad adopting them. I've never seen greater friends." Everyone she knew were friendly but cut-throat—except the staff at the hospital maybe.

Chad stared at the fire while Sierra sat down. "The military isn't the only reason we are close. We were all addicted to porn."

"What?"

Closing his eyes, Chad nodded. "Yeah. Porn." His attention

opened to the flames. "We all watched it before we went in, but being deployed only added to it. When I came home after the first tour, I was pretty addicted to it. Margery wouldn't stand for it. Almost ruined our marriage. She said sex is either fucking or making love. Fucking is selfish and self-centered. Making love is selfless and centered on the other person. It is, according to her, what God wants between married people to love each other only. Something special and only theirs."

Sierra just stared at him.

So, he continued as if he were hearing Margery explaining it all over again. "I didn't want to lose her. So, I tried to straighten up my act. We went to group therapy and well, she was right. Things got amazing. All the guys noticed. After a lecture from Margery, they also straightened up. We all now have locks on our phones. Not for Lori, but for us. It wasn't an easy addiction to get rid of, but it was worth it."

No expression shifted on Sierra's face as to whether she believed him, agreed with him, or thought he was plain stupid. Chad started running his hand over Owen's fur.

"It is selfish," she said to the fire. "Porn is all about what the johns want as well as the money you get for providing it. You are nothing more than the bed they lay on."

Chad looked at her. 'Were all the johns like that?"

She looked down at her knees and then took a drink from the can of beer. "No. Some just want company. Some just want to talk, well at first, then it's about what they paid for. Some are sweet, lonely. Then others …"

Owen jerked his head up, staring at Sierra. Chad, too, went on alert. "Don't go there, Sierra. I'm sorry."

She shook her head. "I wish I had known Margery. I know I would have liked her." She chuckled softly. "But that also explains why not one of the guys have made even one advance. I wondered if I really looked that bad or smelled like a hospital."

"You don't look that bad. In fact, you compliment those scrubs or sweats. We've all noticed. For the record, you haven't come on to any of them and their egos have suffered, I assure you." As for himself, he had noticed, but kept matters hidden even from his own thoughts. "But, who would come on to me anyway?"

Sierra smirked, letting the fire reclaim her attention. "Any woman who has half a brain cell. They would easily see you outshine them all."

"Well, it would be a waste of their time. I'm not interested in getting married again. I had the best. Now she's gone." A tear trickled down his cheek. He let it run. "Well, I think it's whirlpool time."

Chapter 20

"Chad, I don't think that is a good idea," his mother stated emphatically from her passenger seat as they left the cemetery. "Yes, Sierra has done a lot for you. You have paid her, housed her, and fed her. You do not need to give her Margery's car."

Chad grimaced from the back seat. "What am I going to do with it?"

"Sell it."

"Sierra needs a car, Mom. How is she supposed to make it without a car?"

"He has a point, Mary," his father said as he drove. "There's no point in keeping it. Why not let Sierra have it?"

There were moments that Sierra and his mother were like his mom and Margery, but now this. "I thought you liked Sierra?" Chad asked.

His mother fretted like a puffer fish. "I do like … her. But she's taken enough control over … over the house. Even you." She glared back at him. "And that is Margery's car." She looked ahead. "I'm just afraid she's trying to replace Margery," she finished in a whisper.

"No one will ever replace her, Mom. No one."

"Chad," his father stated. "No one will ever replace Margery. But don't close your heart from what God may have for you in the future. That's all I ask." His dad turned off the interstate.

The car went silent as his dad drove. Thoughts blazed in Chad's brain now. What woman in her right mind would even think of being seen with him now? He was no arm candy. However, he didn't want any woman wanting him. He wanted Margery. So, he was left with no one. Oddly, he had become accustomed to her ghost accompanying him everywhere. He, at least, had that much.

"Dad, right now, all I care about is Lori, making sure she has a home. The government is not going to keep paying for all this. Eventually Southwest will give away my job."

"I just praise God that the paperwork for your DD214 still hasn't arrived," his mother said as they pulled in the driveway.

The garage door rose, relaying the message that Margery's car was gone. He checked his phone. Sierra's phone tracker was at the school; she was picking up Lori.

They pulled in the drive as Margery's car glided alongside them. He felt his parents' reaction to seeing Sierra driving it reverberate through the car like a crushed stink bug. Just seeing it had hit him as well ... as if Margery had finally come home. His mother was right. It was Margery's car.

When his dad parked behind his truck, Chad got out of the car as his dad's window slid down. "Best be getting home," he said. "Looks like it could get bad tonight."

They pulled out before Lori bolted from Margery's car. "Daddy! Daddy!" Chad shifted his attention to Lori racing toward him with her backpack dragging on the ground.

"I have something to show you. I drawed a picture of us. See."

Lori heaved a piece of paper drawn with three stick figures and a brown dog that looked like a hot dog bun. One stick figure was short with brown hair and blue dots for eyes that was holding hands with the other two: a taller stick figure wrapped like a mummy with a strange bump on his shoulder and the figure wearing green scrubs and black shoes had yellow hair and green eyes. Behind them rose a porcupine sun blazing over their heads. "You like it?"

"Yes. I … love it." But his mother had better not see this, Chad thought. "I think I will put it up in my room. Okay?"

"Sure, Daddy."

"Can we help with anything?" Chad asked as he walked with Lori toward Margery's car. The rear of the CRV's hatchback lazily opened.

Sierra appeared from the driver's seat. "Groceries. I picked up the prescripts that Dr. Kendrick ordered. How was the appointment?"

Like it had always been like this, Chad reached for the bags of groceries, handing the prescription bag to Lori. It felt good to finally be of some use. In a small parade through the garage, they all trudged toward the kitchen as the garage door slowly lowered on both his truck and Margery's car. Maybe he should talk to his dad about the car. "Hey Lori, want to go out to play with me and Owen."

Sierra claimed the pharmacy bag of medical supplies for Chad's grafts, another huge jar of Silvadene for the burn scars as well as a few other items she needed and headed for Chad's bedroom.

Never had she considered walking into their closet. Doing so, seemed like an invasion of privacy. She already knew Margery was a creative homebody. Happy to be Chad's wife. But who was she really? Her clothes would hold that answer.

When Sierra gazed at Margery's line of dresses, Kohl's was her first though: long, mid-calf, V-necked in most cases. Her pastel sweaters said the same in polyester. Jeans were stretchy, some decorated with sequins and fake rhinestones. Her shoes consisted of a pair of cowboy boots, flats, loafers, a few sets of two-inch heels.

Sierra grinned. Margery was an average American girl with some spice. Chad was an all-American guy by the line of jeans that stretched beneath polyester polo shirts, sport T-shirts, a few sweaters that Sierra presumed were past Christmas gifts that he had never worn. They were the perfect American couple.

She walked to her room with the child's shampoo, conditioner, and a bottle of body soap, bubble gum scented. What was she now? In the guest closet hung her sets of scrubs—green, blue, and Christmas-themed. Her only two sweats waited for her in the dryer. Her only other pair of black Crocs and tennis shoes sat below them. She was nothing more than a caregiver in scrubs or sweats who wore tennis shoes or Crocs. With no future except porn. Not even a nurse.

Sitting on the bed corner, images of her past self rose in her mind. Silk gowns, cashmere sweaters, expensive stilettos, diamond necklaces that followed the plunging necklines down to her naval. She thought of the rented ruby necklaces that dangled down between her shoulder blades in the open-backed silk red gown she wore to the Super Bowl gala with that Italian suit.

She remembered the warm Mediterranean seas with the yachts where she once basked in the sun in swimsuits half as big as the French-cut lingerie. As elegant as that sounded now, it came at an equally high cost. Her soul.

Colton had seen that all his girls wore the best. He had daily fashion shows with what he brought home as *gifts*. Once upon a time she had been excited to model them for him. Colton had the connections in the right places with the right names. It had been their job to see his name remained on the top of their lists and first in their minds.

You didn't just walk back into that world without connections. The only place where she possibly could get a start would be in Vegas, but that came with mean pimps as well as filthy johns who worked the cut-throat world of drugs and survival.

Colton had threatened them all with their lives if they got into drugs or drunk. "You're dead either way. So, don't let me ever find out you tried doing it. Learn to fake it."

He and Mario made sure they saw the cost of defying that order when they had Delight beaten beyond recognition and was never to be seen again. Rumors said they buried her in the rainforest somewhere.

So, they all learned to pretend to be high or drunk and shared tricks on how to fake shooting up. Anyhow, it only took once to prove how stupid it made you no matter how much it cost you in the end. Usually a beating by Mario.

She was not even going to consider the porn industry where the real money flowed through agents that the girls had to "take care of" regularly as well as their friends. She'd done enough of that.

She could strip. There were a lot of girls working their way through school by doing that. At least, she wouldn't be on her back to earn money. The money was adequate at best.

Still, the thought of men watching her gyrate over a pole or allowing them to put money in the thong as she flashed her butt at them made her sick. There were clubs that wouldn't let the customer touch you. Fondle you. But in a private room, you could come out very rich.

She missed the clean, sterile halls of the hospital, the routines that helped people. Nurses were respected. They were people who could walk anywhere and be proud to say, "I'm a nurse." Now, that world was closed to her. That as well as every other respectable job out there.

Coming home with Chad from another check up with Dr. Kendrick, Sierra saw his house appear in the distance. A new, dark-blue Lexus was parked in the driveway behind his mother's scarlet Lexus. His parents saw them and began climbing out of each car as Chad drove his truck into the driveway. The garage door rose to reveal Margery's car absent.

"Where's Margery's car?" Sierra asked. Something was up. She could feel it.

Grinning, Chad looked at her. "Maybe you should ask Mom."

His mom? Why? Sierra thought as Chad slid past them into the garage. Chad instantly went to hug his parents, but Sierra tentatively followed, silent.

"I like it," Chad said as he strolled around the blue car. "Not bad."

"I think your mom likes it," his dad said. "After all, it has all the bells and whistles. She picked it out."

"Oh, I do like it," his mother said as she came over to stand beside Sierra. "What do you think?"

"Beautiful. I had no idea you were looking for a new car. Where's Margery's?"

"We traded it in on this one," his dad stated with a grin. "Got a hell of a good deal on it, too. What do you think of that one?" He pointed to his wife's scarlet Lexus.

"N-Nice." The sparkle in their eyes set off a new set of bells and whistles in Sierra's brain. "Why a new car? What's wrong with this one?"

"Nothing. But, we started thinking," Chad began. "The only thing wrong with mom's car is … it doesn't have someone to take care of it now. So, Sierra, would you like to have it?"

Sierra staggered back against the back of Chad's truck. They were serious? "You are giving it to me?"

"Yes," his mother said, grinning proudly. "We want you to have it, if you want it."

Of course, she wanted it. It was scarlet, her favorite color. A Lexus of all things. Even used, didn't matter. Sierra's world spun in a million different directions. She studied each face smiling at her as if they were Santa's elves. "You're … just giving it to me? Just giving it away?"

"But only if you want it," his mother stated.

Sierra looked at the car. It was beyond perfect. Barely breathing, she walked around the car, dragging her fingertips over the scarlet side panel. The interior was tan leather. It was too perfect. She looked at the grinning faces. "You can't be serious."

"And after all you've done for our son, you deserve it," his mother stated.

Chad nodded. "We are serious, Sierra. We talked about this. Mom wanted a new car." He held the keys toward Sierra.

She faced Chad. He had not removed one thing of Margery's. Not one. "You just let Margery's car go? Just like that. Now, you want me to have your mom's car?"

Shrugging, Chad nodded. "I couldn't keep her car. Every time I see you drive in, I think Margery is coming home. It was tearing me up. So, Dad came up with the idea of just giving this to you as a … gift. This way, you don't owe anyone a dime. This way, everyone wins."

No one had ever just given her anything. It always came with a price. Not even horse-riding lessons. But she would eventually need something to drive. "I'll buy it from you. I mean I'll get a loan or something. If you can just give me time, I promise I will pay you back."

All three heads shook no.

"I'll take care of the car insurance until you can manage that on your own," his dad assured. "Tomorrow, we can get it signed over to you. Will that work?"

Sierra just stood there, staring at the car. For no sane reason, they just wanted to give her a car.

There ain't no free lunch, Fantasy. No free lunch—Colton.

"I can't. I really can't accept this. I mean it is nice. But how am I going to take care of it, gas, upkeep?"

Chad nodded. "We thought of that too. We should have been paying you all along. You've earned this." He walked toward her. "But, Sierra, please don't think that we want you to leave. We don't. I don't. I still need your help."

"Are you sure?" she asked Chad as he again dangled the car keys before her.

"Sierra, you won't be pinned down anymore." His mother smiled. "You could go back to school, go shopping or do something whenever you want now. After all, all this time you had to be here to take care of Chad, the house, Lori, and Owen. Sweetheart, it's just a gift from us to you. Nothing more."

Chad lay there, feeling every inch of the compression suit covering him … totally now. All day with one hour of freedom. Like packaged goods, he wondered when his expiration date ended. *Never.*

When Chad swung up to the side of the mattress, Owen, who dominated the corner of the bed now, woke, studied him seriously. Unconcerned, the dog went back to sleep.

Chad dropped his face into the fabric of the compression, fingerless gloves. He had expected Sierra to be ecstatic over getting his mother's car.

He remembered Margery's reaction when they handed her the keys to the CRV. She went wild with glee, breaking into tears, dancing, hugging everyone. He remembered her hands shaking with excitement on the wheel when she drove it for the first time. Her smile stuck on her beautiful face for days.

Now, like Margery, the car was gone. And he had just let it go.

A cold, steel rod seemed to slice down his back the moment he realized what he had done. His attention shifted to their closet at her clothes. He felt nothing but anger. If he got rid of her car. It was time to get rid of her clothes. He headed to the garage.

He opened the kitchen door expecting to see the CRV, but he saw Sierra's Lexus sleeping where Margery's car should have been. But it wasn't. Again, that was his fault. He was responsible for this. He saw the box of trash bags and grabbed it.

Marching back to Margery's closet, his closet, their closet, Chad began ripping blouses, dresses, her jeans off the rails, hangers, stuffing them into black trash bags he had snatched in the garage. Something ripped. He didn't care. If he got rid of her car, he would get rid of her clothes.

Owen shied away when Chad threw a pair of Margery's shoes at him. Disappearing, the dog went into the playroom and started barking. "Damn dog."

He plucked Margery's house coat off its hook, the one she always wore, every Christmas morning. Chad saw her standing at the stove, frying bacon, cooking breakfast in it. He plunged his face into the soft cotton fabric filled with her memories and fragrance. Tears poured out as he dropped to the floor.

"Chad? Chad? What's going on?"

When Sierra touched his shoulder, he jerked away. "Getting rid of this shit. Once and for all. Like her car. I'm getting rid of her … things."

Sierra squatted down beside him as Owen observed in the doorway. "Chad, are you sure you are ready to do this?"

NO. NO. He wasn't sure. He wasn't sure of anything. *God, why? Why?* The persistent question reverberated in his brain. Still no answer.

"Just leave me alone."

"You want me to get a sedative so you can sleep?"

"JUST LEAVE ME THE FUCK ALONE! JUST GET OUT!"

Chapter 21

Fantasy, you wanted riding lessons, didn't you? Well, I want you to meet Carl. He's a riding instructor.

Hi, Fantasy. Colton told me you wanted to learn to ride horses. You want to pick which horse you want to ride first?

The image of the stable rose with the scents of horse, wood, straw, and leather. It was the leather that was most pungent. It filled the tack room, where, after a few lessons, she learned the price of those lessons weren't free. They weren't "just a gift from us to you. Nothing more."

Sierra bolted upright in the bed, gasping, dripping with sweat. The room spun slowly. Finally, she realized she where she was. But Colton's words echoed in her brain. *Nothing is free in this world, Fantasy. Nothing. It all comes at a price. You just have to be smart enough to make it work for you.*

Who in their right mind would just give away a car like that? No. She couldn't just accept it. When she had Margery's car, she … she could t drive to the store. Pick up Lori. Take Chad to the doctors. It was part of Chad's belongings that she used to make things work better for everyone.

The Lexus was none of that. No. She could not let anyone own her again. Eventually, something would go wrong.

Chad's parents would want the car back because she wasn't doing something right. They wouldn't like where she was driving. They … they would take it from her or … require that she do something for it. It wasn't just free. Everything comes at a price.

But how could she function without a car? Eventually, she would need transportation. Maybe she could buy it or, get a junker. A junker driving a junker.

Everyone knew who and what she was. She heard them, circling around her, pointing at her. *Fantasy! Come here. Fantasy, you're a porn star. A whore. A filthy prostitute.*

Colton was there, chanting the Bible for all to hear, "For a prostitute is a deep pit; an adulteress is a narrow well. She lies in wait like a robber and increases the traitors among mankind."

She was trapped. She had nowhere to go, to get away from their frothing glares. She saw the teenage girls in the church restroom, giggling at her. They were part of a huge crowd in the parking lot, mocking her, pointing fingers at her like the witches during the Salem Witch trials.

Charging through them, Sierra only found herself in the hospital, seeing the nurses clustered at the main desk, the hospital president, the mayor, Dr. Kendrick. They greeted her with, "I'm sorry, Sierra. But you must leave."

The john in the grocery store appeared with his luring gaze. "Hey, Fantasy."

Those visions were going to follow her to Dallas, to New York

City, to Miami, to Paris, to Rome. They all knew her, knew her past. Even God knew.

There was only one way to get away from them. Getting up, Sierra retrieved Chad's bottle of Ativan, staring at the pills resting in her palm. It was her only escape from this hell.

A small voice whispered from somewhere deep in her brain, *Don't do this. Sierra. Don't. Don't …*

"It's my only escape left. I'm sorry. I just can't take it anymore."

"No, Sierra. No, it isn't."

Curling into the covers, Sierra retreated to her safe place, the one place she would flee to when necessary. The sweet clear waters of the Rio Dulce floated once again into her mind, taking her back into the rainforest full of lush green plants so thick that you could easily hide in the underbrush. She heard the water falling over the cave entrance, hollow and pure. She felt the luscious cool air sweep around her. She smelled the thick scent of dampened soil. It all came to her as faithfully as it always had, either for real or in her mind, offering her only peace.

She heard Levi behind her as she hopped over the rocks.

You can't catch me.

Yes, I can. I have to," Levi called out.

But I know this place better than you ever will.

Sierra, where are you? Levi's voice was worried. *I can't find you. Please, Sierra, don't run away again.*

Suddenly, her world darkened like a storm. She saw the cave covered by roots. The falling water.

He won't find me here. He won't find me …

There you are, you little bitch.

It was Mario. She saw his black gaze, the mass of black hair falling over his face as he climbed into the cave after her.

I'll see you never run away again if I have to break your damn legs to prove it.

She felt him jerk her back into the shadows of night, full of restless birds insulted by this intrusion.

When I'm through with you, you can look forward to a long stay in the closet, Fantasy.

"No. No. Please, I won't do it again. Please. I won' t…" Jerking for her freedom, he dragged her back … back to Colton. *Fantasy, why did you run away?*

She saw it—the closet door, opening, the small dark shadows lurking there. It was full of tears and smelled of urine.

"Daddy, I won't do it again. Please. Not the closet. Please, I won't do it again."

Mario was jerking her closer to the looming hole.

"Please, Daddy, I won't run away again. I won't. Please, Daddy, please."

"Sierra. Sierra! Wake up. Sierra."

"Please, Daddy. Don't do this. Please. I …"

She heard Colton's stern voice, *Mario, let her go.* He turned to her; his eyes glaring. *Fantasy, you promise never…*

"I promise. I promise. I promise I won't run away again. Daddy, please believe me."

"Sierra. Sierra."

The rainforest began to dissolve. Mario's grip left her. She could breathe.

"She's coming around. Sierra."

Slowly, the fuzzy image cleared to a worried face with desperate eyes pleading down on her. "Sierra. Stay with us. Stay with us." She closed her eyes and floated back into the darkness.

"Owen, I'm fine," Chad grumbled. He pushed the annoying dog's nose out of his face. "I'm fine." Suddenly, the dog was standing on his chest.

Shoving the dog off him, he realized that the dog's concern wasn't him this time. Bolting upright, he listened as Owen bolted out of his bedroom to start barking in the play area. The moon beaming through the window lit Chad's way to Lori's room. She wasn't there. Wait. She was having a sleepover at Missy's next door.

Owen had disappeared into Sierra's bedroom. Chad raced to Sierra's bed where Owen was now pouncing on Sierra's stomach. Then, he saw the pills sprawled around his bottle of Ativan. *No. No. She wouldn't* ...

"No. No. Please, I won't do it again. Please. I won't…"

"Sierra? Sierra?" He shook her. No response. Panic flooded his senses.

"Daddy, I won't do it again. Please. Not the closet. Please, I won't do it again."

He jerked her up upright, but she responded like a wet noodle. Her head bobbed on her shoulders. Her eyes closed.

"Please, Daddy, I won't run away again. I won't. Please, Daddy, please."

"Sierra! Sierra! No. Shit. No." He grabbed her phone, stabbing 911. A voice answered.

"Ambulance. Attempted suicide."

"What's your address?"

He gave it. "She's barely conscious. Get here quick."

Absently, Chad tried to answer the barrage of questions pouring from dispatch:

Sierra's age? He didn't know.

How much did she take? I don't know.

How long ago? I don't know.

"She's coming around," Chad spat to Charlie the instant he appeared in the room. "Sierra!"

"We have to get her up," Charlie ordered. "We have to keep her moving until they get here."

Chad didn't care what brought Charlie upstairs, but he was there. With his help, they dragged Sierra' limp body to her feet, carrying her out to the play area. "Walk, Sierra. Please, walk."

Hunter followed the rushing EMTs up the staircase. "What the hell?" he blurted.

"Please, Daddy. Don't do this. Please. I …" Sierra started fighting them like a wet noodle. "Please, Daddy. Don't do this. Please."

"Come on Sierra. Stay with us. Stay with us."

The barrage of questions from the paramedics began:

"How long? "I don't know."

On what? "Ativan, There, by the bed."

What's her name? "Sierra Smith."

You related? "No. She's, my nurse."

Where does she live? "Here …"

They all watched as Sierra's body started to spasm, something was shoved down her throat. She vomited into a provided bag. Chad felt the paramedics breathe but remain intense. An oxygen mask was clamped over her face. One medic began pumping air through it.

"Clear the stairway."

Charlie and Hunter stepped back with Chad as the gurney carrying Sierra was hoisted upward and disappeared down the stairs. Chad turned to his friends, "I have to go to the hospital. Charlie, stay here in case the neighbor's call. Lori is staying the night with them."

"I'm taking you. You aren't driving," Hunter ordered. "Let me get dressed. Meet you in my truck."

Chapter 22

Six hours passed. The sun was chasing the night away as Chad paced the waiting area. Ryan, Axel, and Hunter slouched in the chairs in various poses, reading magazines or blindly watching whatever channel was on the televisions.

"Mr. Smith?" a nurse called out.

Chad hurried toward her. "I'm Chad Michaels. Is Sierra … fine?"

"Are you related to Sierra Smith?"

"She's my nurse … caregiver. Is she okay?"

The nurse sternly studied him. "I'm sorry. I can't share any information to anyone but those related to Ms. Smith."

"Please," he stepped in front of the nurse to stop her going back through those doors. "She doesn't have anyone else but me." That reality hit him.

The nurse melted slowly. "All I can tell you is she is in ICU, in critical condition."

Hunter gripped Chad's shoulder from behind. "That means she's alive."

"Yeah. Alive." *How long?* Sierra needed him. No one was with her. He needed to be there with her. Couldn't they see she needed him? He saw the security guards milling around, so he couldn't just barge down that hall. They would haul him off to jail and he wouldn't be there if ...

Chad scanned everyone around him. Once again, they all had returned to flipping the mind-numbing magazine pages and television channels. Just then Jason strolled into the waiting room. Chad bolted to him like a lifeline.

"Hey? What happened to our girl?"

"I don't know," Chad answered. "I just found her like that. I don't know why she took those pills." The guys gathered around him like vultures. "Is she going to make it? Can you tell us anything?"

"She's very weak," Jason said. "Still touch and go. But she's a fighter. We all know that."

"Can I see her?" Chad begged. No, he wasn't being unfaithful to Margery. He wasn't. It's just ... Sierra didn't have anyone else. He had to be there for her like she had been for him. "Look she was there for me. I ... I need to be there for her."

"I will see what I can arrange," Jason said with a grimace.

A few minutes later, the same nurse reappeared. "Mr. Michaels, you ... only you ... can go in with Ms. Smith. Follow me."

Sierra was fully sedated when Chad walked into her hospital room. Her heart monitor showed a weak heartbeat. Saline bags hung from the IV stand. An oxygen mask covered her face that, at least, was no longer blue. "What the hell were you thinking, Sierra?" He pulled a chair close and clasped her hand. Her fingers tightened around his.

He remembered that feeling when life touched his hand. Only it wasn't Margery's. Still, it gave him strength enough to struggle on. "You gotta pull though this. You have to, Sierra. We need you. Don't you give up."

Chad grinned. The church and the guys were filling Sierra's room with every possible plant that the gift shop had. It had been a long three days in ICU, but now Sierra was out of intensive care and in the psyche ward as law demanded. Those three days had been an eternity, but praise the Lord, she was alive.

"I'm fine," Sierra groused at Chad. "I do not need to be in the psych ward. Just take me home. Please."

"I don't think you have any say in this than I did, Sierra," Chad said, squeezing her hand.

Apparently, Jason had contacted Dr. Kendrick who approved Chad staying with her. So, he was certain that, like Sierra, he had spent his time watching the heartrate monitor or television, the Saint Patrick's Day parade, reading about anything he could find in the room, and appreciating every nurse that said hello.

Sierra slept mostly, but when she was awake, Chad fought every breath to not ask the million questions that burned in his brain. Instead, he just saw that she ate everything they brought her and assured her that he was there for her. It felt good but strange to be the one taking care of someone and not be that someone.

His mother had brought her Bible, but he ended up being the one reading it, praying. Since he was in the psyche ward, he simply prayed aloud to God. After all, the nurses were used to crazy, right? In fact, on one of his excursions into the hall, he had even come face to face with someone declaring he was God himself.

"Why didn't you stop her? Why didn't you wake me sooner? Why? Then he realized Owen had. Maybe it was God... "Did you wake Owen?" Then he remembered Owen charging into the house the first time. "Was that damn dog actually a gift from you?"

How else could a well-trained service dog just show up as Santa's gift to Lori. But nothing else made sense—then or even now. But it had miraculously happened.

"So, tell me, why Margery?" Still, no answers came, but a fragment of peace settled over him as if it were obvious. But it wasn't.

"Okay. Fine. But, you have to keep Sierra alive. She has to graduate. It's her dream. Don't let her die. I need ..."

"Who ... are you ... talking to," Sierra mumbled, awake.

Caught, Chad sheepishly looked at his patient. "I guess you could say, God. How are you feeling?"

"Like ... shit."

"At least you can feel ... like shit." Chad drew her hand to his compression-covered cheek. "You really had us scared."

She just blinked at him.

It all just came out, gushing. "Listen, Sierra, you have to pull though this. You have to. I ... We all need you. The guys and everyone are worried sick about you. If it's graduating. Whatever. We'll help to see you make it." Chad nodded to confirm what he said.

Sierra's lips tweaked a weak smile. "Then tell your God to just take me home," muttered from her lips.

"I remember saying that once," he said as the food trays arrived. "But He ignored me, too."

Chad's mother appeared in Sierra's doorway, carrying another vase of flowers into the room, leading the crew behind her. Lori raced to the bed to climb up on Chad's lap to present her newest art creation to Sierra—a field of shamrocks with three stick figures in the middle of it. Two big, one little, two wearing triangles. the other wearing rectangles on both legs.

"I'm sorry you're sick, Sierra. When you comin' home? I miss you," Lori blurted.

Attempting to smile, Sierra released Chad's hand to touch his daughter on the arm. "I miss ... you too, Sweetie."

Ryan followed with roses. "Hey, beautiful. Want ya to know every petal is for you. You had us worried," he said with his grand smile.

"We've all been praying for you. The church. Everyone has," his mother said, resting a hand on Sierra's shoulder.

"Really? The church? Why?" Sierra asked, stunned.

"Sweetheart, because we want you better," his mother assured. "God has a plan for you. We don't want you to miss it."

Sierra closed her eyes and let the sedative take her away again. Chad's mother motioned for him to follow her out into the hall with everyone else. "Has she said anything about why? Was it the car? What?"

"No. I'm not asking."

"Chad," his dad fretted. "The doctors' offices are calling because you missed your appointments. Look, I can stay here with Sierra while you go."

"You're doing so well, sweetheart," his mother fretted. "You can't let this stop you from getting better."

Sierra felt a strange hand claim hers. It woke her. When the blurry vision cleared, Chad's father smiled at her. She had seen that same look on Chad's face a few times. Like father, like son. She also noticed they shared the same blue gaze and black hair … once upon a time.

"I'm fine," she said attempting to remove her hand from the strange grasp.

"Sierra, you're not fine," he whispered, not releasing it.

Tear brimmed her eyes. "Maybe so, but … I will make it."

"Will you? Or are you thinking of going back to … what you left behind?"

The burning facts started simmering, clearing her mind from the fog. Didn't he understand? She had no choice but to go back to … to servicing men to survive. The tears burned. "Do I have a choice?"

"Yes."

She glared at his innocent stupidity. "You're right. I can choose to go back to doing men, or I can choose to become homeless and die on the street. Sure. I have a choice." Her hand fisted in his as she twisted it free.

Mr. Michaels shook his head, grinning. "You will never be homeless, Sierra. Not if I have anything to do about it." He sighed. A true smile appeared. "I don't know what God is up to, Sierra, but he is up to something. Mary and I have talked about this, prayed about it, and we are certain, it was no accident God brought you into our lives."

"Me? Brought into your lives? By God?" Sierra studied him as if he belonged in one of the hospital beds instead of her.

"Yes. Even if it meant losing our daughter-in-law whom we genuinely loved," Mr. Michaels stated. "Like we have come to love you too, Sierra."

She wanted to laugh but couldn't. Yet, it was true. She had never felt such love anywhere like she had in Chad's family. There were many times she was jealous of even Lori. But her? "You love me?"

"Yes, we do, Sierra. God loves you too. You are his child. So yes, we love you."

"But Chad?" Defiant, Sierra stared at his father. "He didn't deserve this."

Nodding, Mr. Michaels continued, "You're right. He didn't. Chad, like all the others, did not deserve to have their lives destroyed by a selfish man with a death wish." He shrugged. "But it happened. Now God is trying to put things back together ... take a shit pile to turn it into a rose garden, like he always does."

"If he's God, why is he *trying* to?"

"I don't know why or how God does what he does. But, I do know we have to cooperate with him. There in may lie the problem. But Mary and I are absolutely certain that God has used you to help Chad."

Oh, that was too much. Her? A prostitute? A whore? God used her? Sierra sank back in her pillow in disgust. "Me? You mean me? Oh, sure."

"Yes, Sierra. You." Chad's father's gaze rose as soft as a morning sunrise. "Mary always says go shopping with God. He is good at getting what she calls a 'two-fer' or two for the price of one. You and Chad."

"I understand Chad," Sierra stated, defiance rising, Colton's recitations mounting like the cavalry. "But why me? You know my past."

"God knows it too, Sierra. He's been through every moment with you."

"Then why didn't he stop it!?" she yelled. How many millions of times had she wanted it all to stop? How many times had she pleaded for it to stop? How many times did she have to flee behind her waterfall to escape what was happening? "Why … Didn't … He … Stop it?"

Mr. Michaels stood there, studying her. Then he calmly stated, "He did. You're here."

"No. That is not good enough," she spewed. "God hates me. He hates all prostitutes, whores, you name it." She jerked from his touch. "It's truly clear in that Bible that you … you Christians are always spouting from, that God hates prostitutes. He hates us. Read it. Just read it. Google "prostitute in the Bible" to see how many times He makes that point clear."

Her tirade didn't faze him. Mr. Michaels' gaze even lit with a spark of humor. "Sierra, God hates murder; not murders. God hates theft, not robbers. God hates prostitution; not prostitutes. God does not hate you, Sierra. In fact, he loves you enough to die for you."

He picked up her Bible from the table and started flipping through it. He stopped and pointed at a place on the page then he looked up at her. "Read this Sierra. It's a story of a prostitute the priests of the Sanhedrin wanted stoned to death. Jesus stopped them by saying, 'He who has not sinned, cast the first stone.' They didn't like that truth and left because everyone has sinned and come short of the glory of God."

A long sigh escaped, but his gaze remained on Sierra. "Then Jesus said to the prostitute, 'Go. And sin no more.'" A small smile appeared. "I think He's saying that to you too, Sierra. He doesn't want you to go back to that life either."

Tears consumed her. God … didn't want her to go back to … that. Maybe that's what everyone was trying to tell her. She didn't have to go back to serving men. Tears poured out like a poison from her soul.

Arms enfolded her like a warm, soothing blanket, holding her together, arms she had so often wanted to feel and never had. Arms holding her, as if saying, "It's okay. It's okay."

"Shhhhh, Sierra. It's okay. It's okay. You are safe now." His whispers sank into her ears like soft rain on dry dirt. Was it Chad's father saying that or some stranger? She didn't know, but it was not like any other man who had ever held her. Laying her head on his shoulder, she let the tears drain from her soul.

Gasping, she pulled back. "B … but, how?" she gasped.

Mr. Michaels settled back in Chad's chair. "That, Sierra I don't have an answer for. But I'm sure God has a plan. I know we must wait on God to pull it off." Then he looked bravely at her. "But remember, Sierra, God has eternity on his side, so it may take a while."

Chapter 23

"You remind me of two drunks leaving a bar at closing time, but neither of you can find your way home. And you need a taxi," the woman said after she appeared in Sierra's room unexpectedly.

Medium build, kinda frumpy, Chad stared at the woman with salt and peppered hair.

"Hi. I'm Dr. Larson. Dr. Kendrick told me about both of you. That's why I am here. I'm your taxi driver."

"I thought there was something about HIPPA," Chad said, smelling the odor of counselling.

Dr. Larson laughed as she walked to the foot of Sierra's bed. Her brown gaze sparkled. "You signed papers saying it was okay to professionally share your information. Right? Dr. Kendrick is worried about both of you."

He didn't need any therapy. He wasn't the one who tried to kill himself. But if it helped Sierra. Fine. Chad reached for the one remaining chair, pulling it closer for the doctor to sit down.

"Thank you, but I'll stand for now," Dr. Larson studied Sierra.

Chad saw a glare rise in Sierra's gaze as she endured the interest.

"I'm glad to see you are doing very well, Sierra. You truly do look better."

"I am."

Dr. Larson nodded. "I'm glad to hear you say that. Would you agree that you've been over some of life's nasty roads lately?"

Sierra hesitated. "You could say that."

"I'm going to be honest, Dr. Larson," Chad said to clear the air. "If I'm included in your chats with Dr Kendrick, for the record, I don't need therapy."

Dr. Larson studied him. "You haven't had any outbursts, flashbacks, night sweats, popped off at family members?"

How the hell did she know about that? "I've had moments, but I'm managing them."

The doctor glanced at Sierra who was staring at him as if he were a liar. "Oh, really?" Dr Larson smirked.

Enduring the scrutiny, Chad continued, "Look. I've been through therapy for PTSD when I got back to the States. I'm good."

"That is good news, Chad. But this most recent episode regarding the bombing, scarring, is that resolved?"

No, but he was managing to get through it. "I think so."

"Well, I would like to help you when it does get difficult. And it will." Dr. Larson looked to Sierra, "Dr. Kendrick is also concerned for you regarding what the media has said about your past. You've been involved with the porn industry and human trafficking under the name of Fantasy. Is that right?"

"It is." Sierra bit the bottom of her lip. "Does this have anything to do with me getting out of here?"

"It most certainly does, Sierra. But it also has to do with helping you out of this trap that life has put you in. I've helped a lot of girls deal with this complex trauma. I know I can help you." She looked at Chad. "Even your PTSD, Chad."

A long sigh escaped the woman. Chad had seen his mother take on that same stature before she began a lecture. So, the doctor was about to expound on something.

"What most people don't understand is that many sufferers of PTSD and complex trauma don't think they have a problem, that they can manage it. But both situations are extremely difficult to heal from."

"What's the difference," Sierra asked. "Trauma is trauma."

Dr. Larson shook her head. "It's not the same at all, Sierra. Chad's trauma is episodic: a rape, or bomb blast, IED, a beating. In his case it's his tours overseas as well as the destruction of what the fool did in the Market that day. It's like being in the Twin Towers on 9-11 mid-building when the plane hit. You run down the stairwell as the floors above are collapsing overhead. You no more than get out the side door than the building collapses behind you. The concussion blasts you into the ambulance. It whisks you to the ER where they save *you*—but not your friends."

"However, Sierra, what you've dealt with is far more complex. It's what abused children are raised in, or a wife experiences over years of an abusive marriage. It's a long line of episodes. It's like driving down into an underground garage where the first floors are typical issues: parents take away your cell phone, ground you. That's Level A. Level B, your boyfriend dumps you for your best friend, your best friends stab you in the back. Level C, your husband cheats on you, your boss sexually assaults you. With each level, the abuse gets worse in a downward spiral. Chaining to beds, starvation, locked in closets, repeated rape, beating. With each level one light bulb goes out until Level Z. That floor has only one lightbulb. The cars are parked helter-skelter. Water is rising. Panic sets in. You want to escape."

Chad felt Sierra's hand grip his.

"The thing about complex trauma is that to escape, it requires you to go out the way you came in, each spiraling ramp by spiraling ramp, while trying to find the exit. Unfortunately, when you do escape, you are plunged out onto Normal Street where everyday traffic blissfully zooms by, unaware of the hell you just went through. But, Sierra, I do know what you've been through. I do realize the hell you have survived."

Tears defiantly brimmed in Sierra's hard gaze.

"It is a difficult recovery, for both of you," the doctor pleaded. "Let me help you so you can stop what has happened to both of you." Sympathy lay soft in Dr. Larson's gaze as she waited.

Chad scratched the cheek of his compression mask. "I can't afford this."

"Nor can I," Sierra said coldly. "I can't even graduate or get a job now."

Dr. Larson took in a deep, brave breath. "Don't worry about that. My office can help. But keep in mind, things will change *for the better* if you let me help you." She drew a business card from her pocket. "This is a big decision to reach out for help." She put the card on the bed. "But I can help you through this. Let me drive you home."

Chapter 24

After leaving the hospital, Charlie and Ryan had a feast waiting for them when she and Chad walked into the house. The fragrance of Gates BBQ and smoking brisket floated over Sierra like a delicious cloud.

"We'll get the rest from the car," Axel barked at Chad's parents following on Sierra's heels. He and Hunter headed to the car for the plants, flowers, and her backpack.

Owen was jumping for joy while Lori hugged her, instantly chattering about what her class had made for Sierra. "It's on the fridge. Come. I'll show you."

"I can't wait to see it," Sierra muttered. It felt so wonderful.

She remembered another time when everyone greeted her when she had come home from the hospital after one of Mario's beatings. She blocked the association. She wanted all that behind her now, forgotten.

Once inside, Sierra stepped before the fireplace. "I want to talk to everyone," she commanded. Obediently, with Owen sitting like a good dog beside her, everyone surrounded her. "I'm sorry for what

I did. I shouldn't have put you through all this." She lifted her chin. "I promise this won't happen again."

Everyone went into assurances that they were glad she was better, glad she wouldn't do it again. Said they would be there for her anytime. Sierra knew they would be.

"You better not," Lori warned. "That was not fun."

"Lori, can you help me and Gampa with setting the table?" Chad's mom asked, proffering a hand toward her granddaughter.

"Fine." Off Lori went, bounding away with Owen.

Sierra melted into the closest leather chair as Chad sat down in his. "Are you going to be okay in that bedroom?" he asked. "Lori can sleep with me. You can have her bed."

Flashes of nights when Colton wanted Sierra to sleep with him fired in her brain. "The guest room is fine." Even though it wasn't. She knew everything still lurked in that room: the memories, the waterfall, the cave.

Chad's touch on her wrist jolted like a hot poker. "Sierra. I mean it. You don't have to sleep there. Remember, we need you. All of us."

Looking out at dusk setting itself in his yard, she said what had to be said. "You aren't always going to need me, Chad. You will want to get on with your life. I need to do the same."

"But Sierra, not now. Not tonight. Let God manage that."

She laughed sadly. "You think God knows how to handle this?"

"He usually does," Chad answered with a smirk.

"Dinner is served," Ryan announced. "Come and get it before Axel gets started."

Prayer was said and then everyone chowed down. Biscuits, smoked ribs bathing in Gates rub and BBQ sauce, Cole slaw, and Ryan's very own mash potatoes with gravy, along with apple slices smothered in butter, brown sugar, and cinnamon, a gift from his mother. Again, it was too much.

Nibbling on each item before her, Sierra watched everyone feast. Flashes of past birthday parties, celebrations, and holidays flickered before her. One in particular, when Colton drew everyone together. *Hey, everyone, come meet the newest member of our family. Fantasy.*

She had wanted to go home to her mommy and daddy, but the strangers seemed welcoming. They appeared to want her to be a part of them. Later, she learned they all had been sold to Colton by their parents too. They seemed happy. In time, she thought she was, too.

Her insides were knotting. Owen found her and sat beside her. She put a hand on the soft chocolate head, letting the warmth soothe through her.

Dr. Larson had talked privately about this happening before she left the hospital. "Honey, you are going to remember so many things over time. Some good. Some bad. But remember, it is your past. Let me help you make those moments better so you can move forward into a better future. I can help you, Sierra. It definitely takes time, tears, talking. And I am good at listening."

Sierra had agreed to her initial appointment, which was set for tomorrow. First, she had to get through the night. Until then, she continued to pick at the biscuit on her plate.

To put some normality back into what was overwhelming her, Sierra insisted on helping with the dishes. Just letting the faucet's warm water flood over her hands helped calm her nerves. Even handing dishes to Lori helped. Chad's mother got busy putting food away. Talk and chatter abounded. Sounds of scraping chairs and the television blasting a basketball game amid groans and cheers managed to intrude with a strange peace. The routine allowed her to breathe again.

Threats of tomorrow loomed, which seemed to hide in the corners of her heart with the other shadows. Chad's father's voice whispered in her mind. *Sierra. Let God handle this.*

She couldn't. It wasn't right to keep everyone involved in her misery, not after what they had done to help her. She could pretend to be happy about moving on with her life. Maybe even keep the gifted Lexus. She didn't know. So, maybe she would let this God of theirs handle things. At least for now.

As everyone left for the basement or home, she walked toward the looming stink of depression waiting in the guest bedroom. Chad followed her closer than Owen. "I mean it. Lori can sleep with me. You can have her room."

"No." She didn't want to be the reason Lori slept with her daddy. "I'm fine. Really, Chad. But maybe Owen can stay with me tonight."

Giggles and "gotcha" greeted Sierra when she reappeared from the shower. Chad, Lori, and Owen were playing tickle on the bed. The instant they saw her, the play halted as if caught. She smiled at the guilty gazes. "Go to bed. I'm fine," she ordered with a laugh that almost felt real.

As she pulled the sheets over her, the memories returned. Once again she pulled the blankets up to her chin. The luring sounds of falling water, the cool chill of the cave returned. *You little bitch …*

She attempted to block the memory by turning over. And over again. It was eleven o'clock by the alarm clock on the side table. Not 2:30 in the morning. Something pounced on the bed, circled around, then plopped protectively on the foot of the bed. Owen. The warmth of that damn dog floated over her. Sleep came.

"Sierra?"

Dragging her eyelids open, Sierra saw a little pathetic urchin beside her bed.

"Can I sleep with you?"

Without a thought, Sierra opened the blankets, scooting toward Owen to make room for her guest, and a sweet eternity returned.

Chapter 25

Sierra stopped by the patio door, which was partially open. The old routines easily returned. As she picked up the family area, hearing the drier beep that it was finished, Chad and Lori had joined the guys outside.

The guys were busy smoking a turkey on the grill or cleaning the winter crap from the yard. Like the others, Chad was now standing in the studious group staring at the pile of pavers while leaning on shovels, deliberating over some new fire pit.

She could see Chad was getting stronger. The compression suit was his biggest bone of contention. As everyone does, he hated it. "I can't breathe in this damn thing."

"Sorry," had been her only answer. "You have to wear it."

His most recent skin-graft on his neck was healing much better. The ballooning on his side was nearly ready to harvest for the next surgery. The first few days after those surgeries were usually rough. Flashbacks came with the painkillers. Otherwise, he seemed better on that score. A smile trickled over her lips as she listened.

"Then we can put in benches around here." Hunter waved an arm about the area.

The doorbell rang. Owen barged past her, nearly knocking her over. She followed his tail wagging joyously to the front door. She opened it to a strange couple in jeans and sweatshirts imprinted with *K9s for Vets*. Once Sierra stepped onto the porch, Owen jumped up on the guy's chest.

"Choco, we found you," the guy said as Owen sat obediently before him.

"May I help you?" Sierra asked.

Lori came, searching for Owen and stood like a shield before Sierra.

"Well, yes, you can," the girl answered. "We've been looking for Choco for some time." She smiled. "We can see he's been very well taken care of. We …"

"Can we help you?" Chad asked as he came out on the porch and stood behind Sierra. The guys followed, peeling out through the door one at a time. Owen moved to Chad and sat beside his leg. It was noted by the couple.

"I'm Steve and this is Elyna. We run a *K9 Service for Veterans*. We specialize in training service dogs," this Steve stated bravely. "Choco is one of our dogs."

"NO. He isn't!" Lori screamed, "Santa and God gave him to me as a Christmas present, and his name is Owen!"

The couple studied at each other. "Well, Choco disappeared from our location around December," Elyna stated to Steve. He nodded.

"I said his name is Owen."

"How did you happen to find Choco … I mean, Owen?" Steve asked Chad as Lori strangled the dog with her arms.

"Apparently, Santa," Chad began, "brought Owen to my parent's house in Odessa just before Christmas. Praise God he did. He's been a lifesaver for us."

"Us?" Elyna asked. "Service dogs normally bond with one person."

The tension mounted on the porch like rumbles of thunder.

"What brought you here?" Sierra asked.

Steve motioned to Owen. "The paramedics who were recently here, told us about Choco."

"Owen," Lori corrected. "He's my dog. Santa gave him to me."

"Owen. Yes. Well, he was already purchased by someone before he disappeared from our facility," Steve continued.

"He ran away to Santa, and Santa gave him to me. I love him!" Lori burst into tears. Chad knelt beside her, hugging her.

Funny, no one was correcting Lori for being rude, Sierra thought. Maybe because she was saying exactly what was on everyone's heart. Owen was one of them now.

Elyna sighed. "I'm sorry. But our dogs go to war vets. It's our policy. No exceptions. We have no choice but to take … Owen."

Chad and all the guys raised their hands, all but saying the pledge of allegiance, and announced, "I am a vet and I have PTSD."

That stunned the two dog trainers. "Well, uh," this Elyna said hesitantly. "Well, thank you for your service. But, we will need a DD214 as well as references from your doctors before we can consider releasing Owen to you."

"Wait here," Chad said, heading back in the house. He was gone for less than five minutes and reappeared with the needed paper. "And I will have the medical references tomorrow. Even though Santa brought Owen to my daughter for Christmas, he's been there for me through every flashback. He is an amazing dog, so we all will do whatever it takes to keep him."

"Until then, we will have to take him back with us until we have all the necessary paperwork completed," Elyna chirped.

"NO! Daddy, don't let them take Owen!"

Dropping down to his daughter, Chad hugged her. "Lori, Lori, it will only be for a few days," he assured.

"Can't you make an exception?" Sierra pleaded as a cold glare from the guys encircled her. Chad needed the dog. She did. Lori did. They all needed Owen.

She continued, "You see, I'm Chad's nurse. I can tell you that his flashbacks are unpredictable. Dr. Larson, his therapist, will confirm what I say, as well as Dr. Kendrick, his burn specialist. Owen has become more valuable than you know. Chad needs him ... here."

Just then, Owen started licking Chad's face. The couple watched as sweat beaded around the eyeholes of the compression mask. Touching the dog's head, Chad closed his eyes in relief.

"*We* ... need the dog ... *here*," Hunter stated bluntly. The other guys braced like a wall, almost daring the trainers to touch Owen.

"Apparently you must be a burn victim by your compression mask?" Steve asked. "Maybe the one at the Farmer's Market incident?"

"Yes. That's him," Ryan informed sharply. "Chad's been through enough hell since then. Owen has saved his life more than once. As well as Sierra's." He grimaced at Sierra. "Sorry. But the dog did."

"He's right." Sierra nodded to the couple. "I wouldn't be here if it wasn't for Owen."

Elyna sighed dubiously. "I get it, but we still must verify everything with your doctor as well as the VA first. It's best Choco goes with us until then." The woman pulled a leash from her belt.

The air instantly became electric. Axel stepped forward, sliding his hand to the small of his back where he always kept his revolver. Ryan was exploding into a black goliath. Hunter's blue eyes turned laser. Charlie's snarl set off fire sparks from his gaze. Chad draped an arm over Owen while Lori clung to the dog's neck.

"Uh, Elyna, wait," Steve said hesitantly. "Maybe we can make an exception here. 'He added a pleading gaze toward his partner. "This one time?"

Stalwart, Elyna appraised the situation and melted. "We do not normally do this. But, if the expectations are not met by the end of the week, we will return for our service dog. Is that clear?"

"How much proof do you want?" Ryan snarled.

"His," Elyna pointed to Chad. "will be enough."

Chapter 26

She had no choice but to see Dr. Larson for follow-up visits in order to leave the hospital. The first few visits had helped take the edge off sleeping in the same bedroom. Now, Dr. Larson wanted to help her face one of her reoccurring nightmares. The riding stable.

Fantasy, you wanted riding lessons, didn't you? Well, I want you to meet Carl. He's a riding instructor.

No part of Sierra ever wanted to walk into another barn after Carl. But, Dr. Larson wanted to take her to visit her own small stable. And there she was, facing the doctor's private horse barn.

Even as Sierra opened the door of Dr. Larson's Cadillac, she felt knots twist in her stomach. Her gaze hardened at the view of the little six-stall barn with solar panels stretching across the roofing. Sliding barn doors were pushed back on either side of the front entry. A rear entry created a breezeway to a working arena behind it, where a student trotted past.

Very good Fantasy. Up. Down. Up. Down. The memory of that voice drew Sierra to a halt in front of the car.

"It's coming back on you, isn't it?" she asked.

Sierra nodded, nothing more.

"Good. It's a beginning." Resting against the warm engine hood, Dr. Larson continued, "Do you want to destroy this? Whatever is happening to you right now?"

"I don't know … if I can."

"Oh, you can, Sierra. Think of it like facing a dog that has bit you. Look into its eyes and make it cower before you. You can do this."

Swallowing, Sierra glared at the stable as a shadow of someone led a horse from a stall to crosstie it in the hallway. There it was. The dream of every girl. A horse waiting for her to ride. A horse she got to brush. A horse ready to carry her away. Oh, she had loved that part. Imaginary places she wanted to flee to on Valjean, that bay gelding who was so kind, caring, willing. But then, …

"What's happening?"

"He's in there."

"No. He's not in there, Sierra. I promise you. He is not." Dr. Larson motioned to the man brushing the horse. "That's Simeon. He's a groom. Not an instructor. Just a hired hand. He works for me. He's very kind. You will like him."

"Colton said that."

"Sierra, I'm not Colton. This is different place; a different memory."

Making herself breathe, Sierra glared into the brutal memory of that stable, all white, painted and perfect. Clutching her fists, she forced her feet forward into the mouth of the beast. A new memory. A new memory. A good new memory. Could it be?

Then it hit her. The smells of horse and straw. The sounds of rustling hay, stamping feet, nickering. She froze in the doorway.

"It's all here now, isn't it? All of it. Face it, Sierra. Nothing is going to happen here that *you do not* want to happen. This is your barn."

Her barn? Her barn? She stood there. Everything was saturating her like the waterfall cascading over her, drenching her to the skin.

"What are you feeling?"

"W … water. I'm … I'm dr … drowning."

"Could it be simply cool water? Soft water. Washing away the fear? If so, let it."

It could be, Sierra thought. Moments passed. She had loved playing in the cascades of the waterfall. She remembered dancing in it. The trembling stopped.

"Would you like to meet some of the horses?" Dr. Larson walked to the first stall where a gray horse with a star on its forehead greeted her. "This is Silver. Hey, boy."

Sierra watched the horse nuzzle Dr. Larson for a treat, remembering a gray mare doing that. Easing toward them, the horse turned to her. She stepped back. So, Silver returned to Dr. Larson for more attention.

An element of assurance taunted Sierra to draw closer, to stroke the gray neck. Oh, the memory of that satin caressing her palm. Something nuzzled her other hand.

Dr. Larson handed her a carrot. "Here. He loves carrots."

Feeling the nibbling in her palm, it tickled with innocence. "Hi … Silver," struggled from her lips.

Slowly, Dr. Larson introduced her to the other horses stirring in their stalls, each one was given a treat. By the time they got to the last horse, Sierra was breathing again. That was until a bay gelding poked its head out, the black forelock falling over the star on its forehead. The black mane. Brown fur. *Valjean.*

Sierra froze in front of the stall door.

"This is McGregor. Mac meet …," Dr. Larson looked back at Sierra. "What is it?"

"No. No I can't." The horse seemed to beckon to her, come closer. "I want to leave."

Dr. Larson grinned at her. "Oh, so the dog is growling now, and you are going to let it chase you away?" She waited. "If you want to leave, we can, Sierra. This is your day. But do you really want to do that?"

Staring at the horse but seeing the black-haired man with locks of hair falling over his face again, an anger began to simmer deep in Sierra's guts. This wasn't that man. It was a horse. A horse called Mac. "I don't know. Maybe he'll like a treat."

"Oh, Mac would love a treat, Sierra. In fact, he's a bit of a glutton."

Treat given, Sierra began to breathe again, enough to even gaze down the line of stalls as if she knew every horse there. In fact, it was beginning to feel nice.

"Let's go out to the ring. It's right out here," Dr. Larson offered jovially to the rear door. "Do you want to see it?"

No. Not really. But the sky was a brilliant blue. April breezes slight. Sun was shining outside the barn.

Walking in stride with the doctor, Sierra remembered her exercise arena, the sounds of "Good. Good. Pull left. Use your leg to push. Yes, that's it. Shorten your reins. Good. Very good."

Sierra stood at the rail, watching the female instructor work with her student, a young girl not too much older than she had been. She saw the same joy in the rider's gaze as she passed by them.

"What's she doing," Dr. Larson asked, curiously.

Answering was like spitting nails from her mouth. "Trotting. She's learning to post."

"Looks hard."

"It isn't. You … you move with the outside shoulder. It … it goes forward … you go up."

"Why?"

Sierra looked at the doctor, her hair pulled back behind her neck. Her middle-aged face was plain, no makeup. "It's easier … on the horse's back."

Dr. Larson smiled. "I bet you were very good at this."

Sierra quickly shook her head. "No. I quit. I quit."

"Oh, that is unfortunate, Sierra. I think you enjoyed, at least, this part of being with horses. Didn't you?"

"I did."

"Oh, I understand, Sierra. It's the rest of the story that ruined this part. Are you ready to destroy that part?"

Lightning struck Sierra's insides. Her heart climbed into her throat as she shook her head.

Shrugging, Dr. Larson said, "We don't have to today. Not today. But eventually, you must face that memory, Sierra. Let's destroy it now."

"You mean the tack room?"

"Yes." A clever smile emerged on the doctor's face. "Look at what you have already accomplished, Sierra. You have walked through the stable. You have watched a girl ride as you once did. This was a hard walk. But you made it. Agreed?"

Feeling the air around her, the sky above her, the clouds floating innocently by, even the air had a warmth to it. Glancing at the rider, Sierra saw that she had made it this far. Farther than she ever wanted. It was as if she had walked past that growling dog, snarling at her. Just doing that had given her strength enough to move forward.

Until the heavy smells of fresh, clean leather assaulted her the instant she stepped into the small tack room. The saddles were lined up on their supports, horse blankets covering them. Bridles hung like lace against one wall. It was the middle of the room that captured Sierra's full attention.

The worktable. The table where tack was cleaned. It was where she did Carl for payment for the lessons. She would have fled except Dr. Larson was behind her.

"It happened here, didn't it," she asked.

Whirling about, Sierra snapped, "What do you think?"

"But, Sierra, it's not going to happen today. This is nothing more than just another tack room with *all* the same stuff." Walking deeper into the room, Dr. Larson wandered around the worktable, adjusting blankets, running a hand along the table edge.

"None of this had anything to do with what happened to you, Sierra. Nothing. Give all this a second chance to prove that to you. None of this is going to harm you."

Gazing about the room, Sierra realized the doctor was right. This was just a room. But the memory was as thick and smothering as if it was the same tack room.

Dr. Larson remained stalwart with a brave look in her eyes. Waiting. Waiting for what? Sierra studied her, hearing the imaginary dog behind her, growling.

Fantasy, let me show you the tack room before you go home. She could feel his hot breath on her back, on her neck. She felt his hands slide over her breasts.

Sierra raced to the other side of the table, just as she had then. She glared back at him—only Carl wasn't there. It was just an open door. Saddles. Bridles. Blankets. Didn't move. Nothing moved.

Nothing. Not even the table. Sweat poured down her face as she realized it wasn't sweat but tears.

Pretending to be busy, Dr. Larson took a saddle from one of the supports. "Have you ever cleaned a saddle before?"

No answer. It was clogged in her throat.

"I say, let's make use of this table for a better reason, Dr Larson sat a saddle on the island. "Let's destroy what is going through your mind right now. Will you help me, Sierra?"

The soap lathered over her hands as Sierra dragged the sponge over the side panel of the saddle. Before long it was as if she were removing a stain from the saddle's seat. Under the saddle. Along the stirrup leathers.

Drying the leather with a new cloth, Dr. Larson handed her the saddle oil, and again, Sierra went over every inch of leather, smelling the familiar aroma again. This was different. It was cleaner, fresher. Memories were fading.

Sliding the stirrup up its leather strap, tucking it away like all the other English saddles, Sierra felt a sense of pride filter through her. The memory was almost gone, removed like a …

"Hey, thanks," Simeon said as he sauntered into the tack room. Sierra's peace shattered as a busy, happy Mexican stepped in the room.

"Oh, Simeon, would you mind going back out in the hallway for a bit." Dr. Larson sweetly asked.

"Sure, Ms. Larson."

The short Mexican left. Dr. Larson faced Sierra. 'Sierra? Sierra? Was that him?"

Frantically nodding, Sierra fisted her wet hands, pressing them to her thighs.

"No. Sierra, that was Simeon. Not Carl, who is not in every

tack room, Sierra. He is not everywhere. Destroy him. Destroy the memory, Sierra. Do not let him take any more life from you than he already has. Take it back. Demand it back."

Sierra glared at Dr. Larson, not seeing her. But seeing the image of her riding instructor, who was fading ever so slightly. She hadn't wanted anything to do with Carl. But she did to survive, like all the others. She did because that was what everyone had to do to live with Colton. To live.

Since she had escaped, gone to nursing school, the life she wanted was obvious. It was wonderful. It was clean. Clean like that saddle. Like Carol had said on her truck, "Whatever happened to you, Sierra, has to die before you could get on down the road."

And she wanted it dead.

Nodding, Sierra inhaled deeply. "I want my life back."

"Good." Dr. Larson's eyes gleamed. "I will help you get it, Sierra. You can do this."

Chapter 27

Chad grinned. He couldn't wait to tell Lori that Owen was officially his service dog. The papers had just come in the mail. He didn't think the couple wanted to bring it by because of the guys.

He gazed over what they had accomplished this last month. As much as he didn't want to admit it, the guys had done all the work of cleaning winter out of the yard, mowing, building the new outdoor kitchen and fire pit. At least, he had been able to help while enduring Sierra's constant fretting about him tearing loose the latest graft.

He had thought itching was bad before he had to wear the damn compression suit. Ha. He could not be more wrong. It was worse than any mosquito invasion. Fortunately, his personal torture chamber was covered up by jeans, an oversized polo shirt.

After that frigid day at the cemetery, stumbling back to the truck to protect Lori, he realized he had to get back into shape. Again, the guys helped, and resistance bands had been installed in the basement. Charlie, the perfect platoon instructor without a heart, had him out every morning … running down the block. Little more every day. His physical therapists loved Charlie now.

Chad flipped the hamburgers on the new grill. Tonight, everyone was there for the lighting of the first fire in the newly completed firepit.

Charlie handed him a beer. "Hey, how's the chow?"

"Getting there," Chad answered, as his friend pulled a folded piece of paper from his jean pocket and handed it to Chad. "See any resemblance?"

Unfolding it, Chad stared down at the poster of a missing, six-year-old girl who was the younger version with the same green eyes and blonde hair as Sierra. *Our daughter is missing. Please, if you see her, contact Mike and Stella Ogden. Seattle Oregon ....*

"Oh shit, that's Sierra's parents," Chad said in shock. "Where'd you find this?"

"Internet." Charlie nodded toward Hunter, Axel, and Ryan taunting Owen with his ball by a blooming redbud tree. "We got to thinking that maybe we could find her parents and found this."

Chad seriously stared at his friend, remembering the panic in Sierra's face when he had mentioned searching for them. "Sierra believes they didn't want her. Sold her, to that bastard Colton or whatever that prick's name is. She also thinks her parents would never want her back after all she's done."

"That's a lie and you know it," Charlie sneered. "They've fed her this crap all her life."

The other guys closed in around him. "Even so," Hunter assured. "Don't you think her parents should know? They've been through hell, too."

"I don't know, man." Ryan ran a hand over his face. "You go tellin' them and they just show up here, Sierra will likely go crazy, maybe even run. This ain't no surprise birthday party for her."

Chad stared at the innocence on the poster, picturing if that was Lori. "I'd never stop searching until I found her. I wouldn't care what she did or how old she was. I would want her back."

Ryan nodded. "But you gotta think of Sierra."

Chad couldn't imagine of that kind of hell Sierra's parents had gone through. Worry flooded over him because Lori was with his parents for the weekend. What if his mother didn't watch out for her? Thoughts of going to get Lori raced through him. What if …. No. He had to trust God. And his parents.

"Hey guys. What's up?"

Chad swiftly folded the poster, shoving it into his pocket as Cheyenne and Allyssa walked through the patio door with a bounty of food. Charlie sheepishly glanced about the group before he strode toward the cute redhead, who greeted him with a possessive kiss that he accepted eagerly.

Hunter claimed Cheyenne, a cowgirl in black leather vest and long-legged jeans that trailed down to black leather boots. Her long brown hair danced the two-step over her shoulders as she claimed Hunter's arm and handed him a beer. He kissed her in gratitude.

"That's the new firepit?" Cheyenne asked, waving her bottle toward a firepit. The front was like any other firepit, but the back rose into a protective shell of grey pavers. A pyramid of firewood was ready for its virgin flame. Next to it was Margery's bench swing and a few random folding chairs.

"Yep, we got it done," Ryan stated proudly. "After they decided to listen to me finally."

"You are so full of shit," Charlie blurted. "It was my idea."

"No. I found it on Pinterest and showed it to you," Allyssa corrected.

"Yeah, well, she did," Charlie admitted with a grin.

Sierra appeared, as usual, wearing the same green hospital scrubs, Crocs, no makeup, hair braided into a gold rope dangling down her back. She was carrying a bowl of chips with three bottles of salsa all of which seemed to threaten her control.

Before the jars dropped, Chad hurried to help her. "Here."

"Thank you," Sierra said with an appreciative smile. "Where do you want them?"

"Here," he said, waving to the grill. Normally, the guilty memory of Margery would flash like a warning. He was glad it had skipped that moment.

"No way, man, we can't let you do this," Axel announced to the world. He waved at Charlie. "No offense Allyssa, but we can't let this happen."

"Too late, Axel. We're getting married," Allyssa dangled her left hand, wiggling fingers for everyone to notice her engagement ring.

Charlie tried his best to look as if he were trapped. But it was obvious to Chad that he was happy about the announcement. Flashes of himself telling the guys about his engagement with Margery intruded. Pete had been with them then. The loss of his best friend in Afghanistan and now Margery ached deep in Chad's gut.

"Hey, a toast to you both," he stated, raising his beer to Charlie and Allyssa. "Much happiness."

"When is this going to happen?" Ryan asked.

Charlie looked to Allyssa who gleamed up at him. "We haven't set the date yet," she answered.

"This fall possibly," Charlie said.

While the rest of the guys proceeded to insult Charlie by tackling him out in the yard, Cheyenne examined the diamond solitaire. "Oh, that has to be at least a half carat."

"Three quarter carat," Allyssa corrected, as she admired the engagement ring as if for the first time. "It's so perfect."

Sierra joined them. "It's lovely, Allyssa. It fits you. Much happiness to you both."

Back to flipping burgers, Chad noticed something in Sierra's gaze differed from Cheyenne's excitement. Something lost, something hoped for but impossible to have. The days around each other apparently had made him more sensitive to Sierra than he should be. But still. Something was off.

"Where's the honeymoon going to be," Sierra asked as she tore open a bag of Doritos.

"We're dreaming of Capri," Allyssa said, sliding her hand into her jean pocket.

"Capri is beautiful in the fall," Sierra remarked as she dug a chip into the salsa.

"You've been there?"

"A few times."

A few too many times, Sierra thought as Allyssa continued, "Capri is my dream, but Charlie wants to save for a down payment on a house. I don't really care. I just want to spend my life with that crazy man."

"You couldn't get a better one," Cheyenne offered, "Next to my cowboy, that is. As your maid of honor, we need to go shopping for your wedding dress."

"Oh, maid of honor, is it?" Allyssa argued with a grin. "Okay.

Maybe." Her attention shifted to Sierra. "If you thought you could ever get out of those scrubs, maybe you could be my bridesmaid." She giggled. "Just kidding about the scrubs, Sierra. But we really need to teach you how to dress."

Biting at the insult, Sierra smirked as if it were just a joke. Simmering, she walked back into the house with thoughts of all that she had left behind. The silks. Jewelry. Designer clothes. Designer perfume and designer makeup. Limos. More than either of those country bumpkins would ever see.

Maybe it was time to show these them how to really dress for a man. If she could destroy a stable memory that easily, she could destroy Fantasy as well. Yes. She would face what she had been to prove that person no longer mattered.

As Sierra trotted upstairs, she remembered Onyx's last Christmas gift—a black silk, Versace tracksuit still hidden in the bottom of her backpack. Memories of Onyx's beautiful face, her brilliant eyes that laughed with joy when she watched Sierra open her outrageously expensive present. It outclassed anything Sierra had ever given Onyx.

The richness of the track suit floated over Sierra's body like a cloud. She drew the zipper up only halfway, showing more lace bra and cleavage than she should. Rummaging in Margery's makeup drawer, she found the colors she needed. So, Chad would not recognize Margery's' fragrances, she dotted two of different perfumes on her wrists, rubbing them together. Sierra remembered that trick from a perfumer. Sniffing proved it was perfect.

The old familiar routines fell into play. Finding a can of hairspray under the sink, she flung her loose hair over her head and started spraying. The only thing left was earrings.

Feeling in the upper pocket of the suit jacket, she found Juliano's

Tiffany's chain earrings—vine leaves dotted with diamond chips and with marquis diamonds dangling from both rear and front chains.

She saw Juliano again, handing her the robin-egg-blue box giftwrapped by Tiffany. His large brown Italian eyes gleamed as if he were giving her the world. The desire to brush her hand along his chiseled jawline that bore a constant 5 o'clock shadow ran through her.

Oh, the hours they had spent together in Rome, on the Amalfi Coast, racing across the waters in his speed boat to feast on each other on the beaches of Capris. It was there Juliano had presented the jewels to her.

He was the only man she had ever thought she could love. But, like so many others, he had married money and could not leave his toys behind. She was one of those toys. The earrings were his farewell gift to the wonderful memories. Angelina had found out about her.

One last check in the mirror, said it was show time. The appraisal was fair. She had done much better in the past. But this would do.

Move over, country bumpkins, here comes the real deal.

Chapter 28

On her way out to the yard, Sierra claimed two bottles of red wine and two plastic wine glasses. She knew the ground was going to be cold, but she was not about to wear Crocs or tennis shoes with a Versace. So, as barefoot as Eve, she appeared on the wooden deck.

Mouths dropped open as she strode across the lawn. Onyx's gift made her feel luscious. Setting the wine on the patio table, Sierra snatched Hunter's cowboy hat off his chair and snuggled into it gleefully to sashay toward him. "How does this look, cowboy?"

She shook her head, swishing her hair over her back. "No. It's better on you. Here." She set the hat askew on his black hair, tapping the crown with her fingertips. "Yes. It does look much better on you, Handsome."

She played in Hunter's gaze for a breath then turned to Axel whose foot slipped off the firepit's stones the moment she settled her focus on him. Putting on her best pleading gaze, she begged, "Are there any hamburgers left, Axel? I'm starving."

"I'll ... yeah, I'll get ya one."

"You are a life saver, as always," she whispered in her best cooing voice.

Ryan was next. Tripping innocently as she started toward him, he caught her on cue. "Uh. You all right?" he asked.

Looking directly into his warm chocolate gaze, Sierra answered with a coy grin. "I am now." She claimed his arm as if she needed support. "Oh, Charlie, Allyssa, I am so happy for you two. But the world will miss you, Charlie."

Daggers shot from Allyssa' gaze.

Leaving that battle front, she turned to Axel who appeared with a brimming plate of food. "Thank you, Axel, you are the best."

"Uh, sure. A... Anything else?"

"Oh no. This is perfect," Sierra assured with one of her best smiles ever forged on her lips.

The intent observation from Chad dampened her efforts slightly. But hey, she had dealt with men who failed to melt to her well-honed charms. However, the girls had not. Cheyenne now clung to Hunter as if to say, don't you dare come near him again. Allyssa was turning greener than the grass at her feet. Eyes could not burn any hotter. Like the many other times, Sierra knew, in that instant, she had won the day.

Chad watched the gold *Versace* logo emblazoned like a gang emblem on the black silk jacket parade into the yard. That same gold name *Versace* stretched along each arm and down the outside of each long leg. Whoever *she* was, had hair flowing over her shoulders like a golden waterfall that swayed with her every step.

The guys were as stunned as he was. Ryan stood there frozen with Sierra draped on his arm. Axel scurried toward her with a plate of food like an obedient servant. Like a deer caught in the headlights, Charlie was speechless. Hunter, still wearing his cock-eyed cowboy hat, stood there immoveable.

Even Cheyenne and Allyssa, at first, were equally as stunned. But that changed quickly enough. Cheyenne now blazed a murderous glare at Sierra. Allyssa's gaze was seething with fury.

"Uh," Hunter jerked everyone's attention to the fire pit. "Let's get this firepit lit up. Okay?" Lighting a fire stick, he tossed it into the firepit.

Plooooomb!

The firepit exploded into flames. Chad froze, seeing the man in the trench coat again. He saw the hand disappear inside the lapels. The blaze...

"GET DOWN! GET DOWN!" No one moved! They were going to die, die like Margery. Noooo! "GET DOWN!"

Sierra dropped Axel's plate when she saw Chad plunge into a flashback of the bombing in the Market. Arms up over his eyes, slightly to the right, left leg covering his crotch, yelling for everyone to get down.

But everyone had frozen in place, except for Owen who barged toward Chad as he fell to his knees, pleading, "Get down! Please. Get down! Everybody! Get down."

Sierra raced to him. "Chad. I'm here. I'm here. It's okay. I'm here."

"Why won't they get down? They're going to die. Die like Margery."

She waved everyone to get down. Slowly, like broken sticks, everyone lowered to the ground. Except Axel, who had flung the cooler full of ice and beer into the firepit. It now dangled from his outstretched arm. Bottles began popping like bullets as the flame died.

Flinching with each pop, Chad lay face down, hands over the back of his head, one hand began grappling to pull her down with him.

Slumping down beside him, Sierra felt Chad's body trembling against hers. "It's okay," she whispered. "Look. It's over. You saved us, Chad. We are fine. See, we are all fine."

Still trembling, Chad peered upward. Everyone was fully reclined, waiting for their cue to get up. Only Axel remained frozen, holding the cooler in his grip. Owen started nosing Chad to move. Chad's grip on Sierra's arm loosened.

Pulling up, Sierra drew Chad first to his knees, then helped him regain his feet. Then, everyone followed suit, rising from the grass, brushing it off from their jeans, glancing nervously at each other. Ryan eased toward them. "Is he okay?"

"I'm fine, asshole. Fine."

"Yeah, sure, bro. Just ... fine." Ryan growled back.

Charlie and Allyssa closed in slowly. "Uh, we're leaving. We'll take everything inside, clean up tomorrow. Okay?" The remnants of fury still lingered like burning coals in Allyssa's gaze.

"Yeah, we're leaving too. Axel, Ryan, you staying?" Hunter asked as Cheyenne clung to his arm.

"Uh, yeah, sure," Axel answered as he swept the glass debris back into the firepit with his foot. "We'll stay."

Ryan leaned in close to Sierra, "We'll be in the basement if you need us."

"Good," Sierra answered, casting a weak smile to the worried face.

Slowly, things settled as the night creatures claimed the growing darkness with their chirping. Sierra managed to get Chad to the patio swing, moving it with her frozen toes.

Chad just rode along, sitting tight beside her, staring blindly at the black firepit. The air was turning crisp enough for blankets. But she couldn't leave him to get one.

He looked at her. "What made you do that?" He flipped his hand toward her attire. "This?"

Feeling the sting of Allyssa remark again, Sierra wilted as if Axel had dumped the cooler over her. "I don't know. Allyssa said something about teaching me how to buy clothes. It just hit me wrong."

She smirked to the black pit before her. "I've worn gowns worth more than all the clothes Allyssa has in her closet." She shrugged. "I simply wanted to prove something."

"You did more than prove something, Sierra."

She looked at Chad. The panic in his eyes was gone, but his gaze was colder than the night's chill. "Did I?"

"Oh, yes. Who we saw tonight wasn't the Sierra we know."

Shit. He was right! She had become Fantasy. She had not destroyed her. In a blink of an eye, she had turned into exactly what she had been, what she was good at, what she never wanted to be again. The black filthy firepit loomed. The swing swung.

"I thought ... I thought ... I just wanted to prove I knew how to look normal, like everyone else," she muttered to the pit. She shrugged against Chad's arm brushing against her. "I'm tired of just wearing nothing but scrubs and sweats. I just needed to feel ... normal."

She turned to Chad sitting there, listening. The evening shadows had claimed the delicate blue in them. "But you're right. I guess you can say, you all just met Fantasy."

He lifted his can of beer in a toast. "She's something. I'll say that. But you know, the guys aren't going to be able to see you the same now. Sierra has been replaced."

Oh God! Sierra slumped back onto the swing. Claiming her wine glass, she raised a toast to Chad. "To me. Once again, I've screwed up my life. Just like I ruined it everywhere I've ever gone." She looked at the stars, tears drizzling from the corners over her eyes into her hair.

Chad brought the swing to a halt. "I wouldn't go that far, Sierra."

She rolled her head toward him to give him a sick smile. "What do you mean? Why not?"

She lifted her head to let Chad stretch his arm across the back of the swing as he started moving it again. She felt his warmth against her shoulders, smelled a taunting scent of his aftershave.

"Okay, they now realize the beauty you really were ... I mean ... are, Sierra. Why shouldn't we ... I mean ... they see that? Sierra, you are ...." It took him seconds to evaluate her. "Attractive doesn't even come close." He looked at the pit. "God truly made you noticeable."

"God?"

He nodded." Yep. 'Beautifully and wonderfully made' as Lori would say."

Ruined like Rome, laying in broken debris. Sierra submitted to the gentle sway. "You aren't mad at God anymore?"

"Yeah, I'm still pissed. I don't like what happened to me any more than your past that keeps biting at your ass constantly. But it's useless to fight it. It is what it is." He shrugged. "Maybe Dad's right. God is up to something. I don't know."

Chad studied her, his gaze warm, soothing. A spark lit in it. "Sierra, stop wearing that hospital crap. Be you. We'll get used to it. Maybe it's time for you to be who God made you to be."

"And who is that?"

Chad chuckled but it wasn't happy. "How would I know. I don't even know who I am now, Sierra."

Back and forth, back and forth, the swing swayed as they both studied the black pit before them. Sierra wondered if it was symbolic of both of their lives. "Chad, at least you are the same person you were before all this shit happened."

"No. I'm not that same man." He told the firepit. "Who the hell wants to be seen with a one-eared Freddy Krueger? You better than anyone know what I look like now. I'm nothing but a freak."

"I know exactly what you look like, Chad Michaels," Sierra snarled, "Every inch of you. You are simply damaged on the outside. But you are the same man inside. At least your scars will heal, fade with time.

Chad smirked as if she had lost her mind.

"Me?" Sierra continued. "You saw the real me tonight. My talents are seducing men and doing them. That's who I am. I'm ruined inside regardless of how anyone sees me." She toasted her glass of wine at him. "People will love you no matter what. But me ... once they know, they will never accept me for who I am."

Turning, Chad drew close enough for her to smell the beer on his breath, the sweat under his suit, him. His gaze warmed through her, even to her toes. She could no more draw away than she could run. Nor did she want to. She wanted, no needed, to feel him that close.

His gaze sank into her soul. "I'll tell you who you are, Sierra. You're still a virgin."

She spit wine in his face. "Me? A virgin? I don't think so."

Unblinking, Chad smirked. "Yes. A virgin because you have never known the love of a good man. One who treats you like you should be treated. Not like a thing or an object, but the beautiful person that you truly are." His heart was in his gaze.

Never, not once, had she ever felt drawn to anyone like this. Not even Juliano. But she needed to feel his mouth on hers. Chad's gaze brushed over her face, over her lips that drew toward hers. She lifted her lips to accept them, wanting them.

Suddenly, as if yanking her heart from her chest, Chad bolted to his feet. "I ... I ... can't. No. I ..." He bolted from the swing and stepped away from her as if caught in some illicit act.

Stabbed, Sierra glared at him, at the true man before her. She rose slowly to her feet. "Oh, you can talk sweet words, Chad. Kind words that are nothing but filthy lies. You can't even touch m..."

Before she could finish the word, Chad wheeled about. His lips fell on hers, consuming her senses, melting her insides. His arms claimed her, holding her safe. Holding her exactly where she wanted to be, had never been, and never wanted to leave.

The wineglass fell from her grip as her hands glided up Chad's back, feeling every inch of the compression suit, knowing full well what lay beneath it. For first time in her life, she wanted to feel that flesh on hers as raw as she knew it was.

Chad pulled away, taking her heart with him. His gaze as hot as she felt. It lingered. She lingered, wanting his lips back, wanting him holding her. But she could see that wasn't going to happen. It was a stolen moment. Nothing more.

"I, uh, I am going up ... to the whirlpool. I ... I won't need ... your help."

"Yeah. I need to clean up ... the kitchen."

Chapter 29

The kitchen was immaculate when Sierra found her way inside. Still, she began wiping down the counters. What the hell had she done besides ruin the last good thing in her life? Her plan had been to prove she did know a thing or two about looking attractive. After all, her entire life had been seeing that she did. It was her paycheck.

What she hadn't expected was to fall back into her past, back to who she didn't want to be any more. *Fantasy*. Admittedly, the thrill of it had rushed over her.

Yes. It was fun to tease, taunt, play for attention. Glean men's interest away from their girls. But usually, it was other girls just like her, not couples who were in love. She and Onyx had assured themselves that, if they could pull a man away from their girl that easily, that they were doing that girl a favor.

But, what she had done tonight was over the line. Allyssa and Charlie didn't deserve what she did. Nor Hunter and Cheyenne. Not after all they had done for her and Chad. Allyssa even mentioned wanting her in the wedding. Leaning on the kitchen counter, Sierra saw the fury in Allyssa's eyes.

This time, she was responsible for destroying her life. Not someone else. Not some john. Not some newspaper article. No. She had done this. She had no choice now but to start making plans to leave. Start again. Somewhere. Somehow. No part of her wanted to, but it was coming, just like a storm.

At least, she had time and a car. Chad still needed her to watch over his skin grafts, making sure everything was kept as sterile as possible. She didn't want to think of seeing him naked ... as a patient. Not after feeling alive in his arms. She had ruined that, too.

"Oh, God, what have I done? Why did you let me do this to Chad? To his friends. To Lori?" As odd as it felt talking to Him, something felt good to at least clear her heart to someone. She only hoped, if there really was a God out there, that he was listening.

Slowly, Sierra climbed the stairs, hearing the whirlpool going. But she also heard Chad in his bedroom, talking. She hesitated outside his door.

"I'm sorry, Margery. I'm so sorry. I didn't mean that to happen." Sobs poured from Chad's soul as he sat on the side of the bed. He had felt every ounce of that kiss with Sierra. And he had wanted every ounce of that kiss. In fact, he wanted more.

Visions of seeing Sierra walking into that backyard, swaying her blonde hair over her shoulders as she glided out there had stunned everyone, him included. Watching her gush over Hunter, wearing his cowboy hat, tapping it on his head, Chad had felt every tap. When

Axel turned into a puppy, he wanted to turn into that puppy. Seeing her clutching Ryan's arms when he caught her had sent a spasm of jealousy through him he had forgotten could exist.

But when she taunted Charlie over no longer being single, that stung. Allyssa and Charlie didn't deserve that from her. Then the firepit blew up. Ending it all. All but the kiss.

After everything calmed down. He was sitting there beside her, watching her sipping wine, hearing her admit to what she had done, realizing her mistake, at least that melted some of his annoyance. Regret had coated her. Then, he realized Sierra had tripped back into this Fantasy. Shit. How many times had he had flipped "soldier" on Margery? Too many.

Just watching Sierra crumble before him, made him realize she really was a virgin. She had been used by every john out there who had made her their object. They never cared about her. They loved her as much as their car that took them speeding down some blind highway. If any car could do that, any hooker could do that too. Sierra deserved better.

He had to admit, it was easy to see that Sierra was good at what she did. No doubt about that. That was no excuse for him to cheat. But was he ... cheating?

Time had proven Margery wasn't coming home. She was gone. Buried. Visions of Margery's tombstone rose in his brain, knocking him back onto the mattress. More memories continued to display on the ceiling. Her funeral. The flowers. The 'I'm so sorry for your loss.' Her body in that casket.

"I don't have anyone, except Lori," he whispered to the bedroom walls.

His brain farted, *"You have Sierra."*

Why would an exquisite woman like Sierra ever want to be seen with a Freddy Krueger? In time, Sierra would move on. Why wouldn't she when he had nothing to offer her. He could easily envision Sierra on the arm of some high-powered doctor, charming everyone at the grand opening of some hospital, cocktail party, or political gala. "God, why would she ever want to be with me?"

I don't have anyone, except Lori. Tears brimming, Sierra left the side of the wall by Chad's to her room, dragging her heart on her heels. Chad was sorry he had kissed her, even touched her. It was plain now; she was nothing more than his caregiver. So, if his God has some magical plan, fine. She'd play along. What other choice did she have?

She heard Chad calling her a virgin. *Yes. A virgin because you have never known the love of a good man.*

"What good man would ever want me?"

Chapter 30

Sierra watched from the deck as Lori raced about the backyard in search of Easter eggs before Axel got to them. Her yellow Easter dress flounced about the backyard as gleefully as Owen pouncing along on her heels. Ryan was with his nieces and nephews, so he was missing out on the mayhem she was watching.

"Hey, not fair. You guys are pointing the eggs out to Lori before I get 'em," Axel barked.

"Nope. We're just milling about the yard. Hunter and I can't help it if we stop by an Easter egg," Charlie stated so innocently.

Lori had caught on immediately, watching like a hawk where Hunter and Charlie ventured next. Then miraculously, Lori managed to get to the egg just seconds before Axel, who proceeded to grumble, trying pathetically to get to the next egg before she did.

Absently watching the frolic, Sierra replayed the recent past. She finally got to apologize to Allyssa who seemed content with the basic explanation that she wanted to show that she did know a little bit about looking decent.

Dr. Larson had burst into laughter when Sierra had told her what happened. "Lesson learned, I bet." She then proceeded to dissect what, why, how she had done it, and why it all went wrong.

Sierra had refused to tell about the kiss. She didn't want anyone knowing about it. She wanted to forget it as well. But couldn't. She blushed with the memory every time she so much as looked at Chad.

Chad had slowly returned to his cordial self. Yet, he insisted on his own whirlpools now and was dealing with the Silvadene. Occasionally, he would ask for her help if he couldn't reach a spot ... like his back. They both got noticeably quiet in that awkward silence as she rubbed ointment on the new scar created by the graft.

Along with his back, his shoulders and legs were growing into a patchwork of minor scars from harvested skin. One graft had come from his scalp, which he now refused to be used for more. "I look enough like a monster. I don't need that making it worse."

Sierra found herself simply running the house as a "Margery." Laundry, housecleaning, cooking, grocery shopping, playing with Lori and Owen. Or, if Chad couldn't pick up Lori from school, she did it.

Chad had checked to see if the job with Southwest was still his. Apparently, it was. The world had lifted off his shoulders with that news came home. Everyone celebrated by going out for pizza, which included stares from customers.

So, as Chad was getting his life back, she wasn't. Graduation at the nursing school was coming up in less than a month. Her student loans were coming due again. She also had a car to somehow care for. Chad's folks were paying her a stipend, but not enough. It was never enough. Sierra recalled Rosie's chatter in her head. "Darlin,' leave that to God. He has a plan."

"Well, Rosie," Sierra thought, "God had better be letting me in on this little plan of his soon, because things here are coming to an end."

"You look nice," Chad stated as he joined Sierra on the deck.

She scanned him, new trousers, new polo shirt covering his new compression suit. "Thanks. You do, too." She pointed to a Trump cap that covered the top of his mask. "You are actually going to wear that to church?"

"Yep. Republicans smile when they see this cap because I'm a vote. Dems frown because I'm not. Somehow, they both forget to see *me*, and I win." A true smile emerged from behind the compression mask.

She wanted to linger on that smile but forced her attention back out to the ongoing Easter egg hunt. Things were good now. So, don't blow it, she warned herself.

Chad's mother had been relentless about Sierra going to Easter service, refusing to allow her to remain home as was the norm on Sunday. Submitting, Sierra found a dress on Amazon covered with spring lilac designs with a wide purple belt, as well as a pair of purple flats to go with it. The dress felt good for a change. It made her feel like a woman instead of … a caregiver. She even dared to let her hair trail loose down her back. That, too, felt good.

"I won!" Lori announced.

"By one egg," Axel grumbled as he once again counted the contents of their baskets. Sierra saw him sneak yet another egg into Lori's basket. "Owww, man. By two. That's not fair."

Chad checked his watch. "Time to leave for church. Everyone ready?"

"Where in tarnation have you been, girl?" Rosie called out as she hurried across the church lobby toward Sierra, arms wide open. Regality flowed with her.

Images surfaced of Onyx in her black habit rushing toward Sierra. If she ever had a sister, it would have been Onyx. They had shared everything. Enjoyed everything until the night Sierra had fled to the Santa Rosa Convent, naked as a newborn babe while escaping on Levi's Yamaha. The nuns had protected her that night from Mario's search party.

The instant Rosie's arms wrapped around her, Sierra burst into tears. "Mercy me, Darlin.' We gotta talk." Rosie pulled her away to the pastor's small office, kicking the door closed, as they both sat down on the blue loveseat. "Now, tell me, girl, what's going on."

Sierra look up at that beautiful chocolate face. "I don't know what I'm going to do, Rosie. Everything is coming to an end. I don't know how I'm going to survive ... without going back ... I ..."

"Oh, Sugar, Sugar, I know one thing, you ain't going back to that life again. You hear me. Like I told you, God's got a plan." Rosie said, patting her face, then arms, then gripped Sierra's hands in hers. "Honey, you keep forgetting that you are a child of the most high God. He loves you. I love you. We don't want nothin' ever harmin' you ever again. Tell me, what's goin' on?"

Swiping at the river that had flooded her face, Sierra slumped back in the loveseat. "I know you keep telling me to trust God. But I can't. I can't take any more."

"Baby, is anyone hurtin' you?" Rosie asked dubiously.

"Oh, no! I just don't deserve their kindness," Sierra assured. "Chad, his parents, the guys are so wonderful." The tears were welling up to spill again.

"Baby girl. You deserve all the kindness you can get from this world." Rosie face turned stern. "But I get where you are coming from. I didn't think I deserved anything good either. In fact, I was repeatedly told I was nothing and didn't deserve shit. You see, my daddy was a beater, then I married a beater. They beat me down to nothin.' Made me believe I deserved that shit. No, honey, that's a demon lie for sure."

"You couldn't be more worse off than I am," Sierra assured.

"Oh, honey, I was. Then I met Jesus." A smile eased across her radiant face that filled her eyes. "Now, that man knows how to treat a woman with real love."

A riled nerve climbed up Sierra's back. "Not this 'go and sin no more' shit. Please."

Rosie scowled at her. "Baby, God is love. That's all he wants to do. It don't matter what you've done. He loves you." Rosie's brown eyes darkened to anger. "Sugar, they lied to me. And they lied to you … to make you into what they wanted.

"You see, Jesus hates porn, not prostitutes. It destroys people: johns, girls, pimps, everything porn touches." She sat back. "Look what it's done to you. How long did you work the streets?"

Sierra shrugged. "Since I was six, I guess, but not the streets. High end."

"Fucking is fucking whether in a back alley or a penthouse. Look at me. Baby, either way you ain't nothing but a *fuckinal* to your johns. Men urinate in a urinal; they fuck in a *fuckinal*. That's why God hates prostitution. It's selfish. It's all about money, greed, and lust.

"But now, Jesus loves you with a real love that is unselfish, self-sacrificing. You are somebody to him, not a some *thing*. Jesus loved us so much he died for us. For you. You know any man who would do that?"

Sierra shook her head. What man would die for her? It was almost funny. She didn't laugh.

"Well, Baby, let me tell you. Don't you give yourself to anyone else until you know the love of Jesus. He knows how to treat a woman. Then, you wait for a man who will love you like that. Don't you ever settle for less."

There was a soft knock on the office door. Chad poked his head in. "Is everything okay? Uh, the service is starting."

"We'll be right out." Rosie glanced at Sierra. "Another thing. Like I keep telling you, God has a plan for you. Don't give up on Him, ya hear."

Drying her eyes, Sierra smirked up at Rosie. "If God has a plan, he'd better be letting me in on it."

"Darlin,' you ain't got nothing to do with the plannin' except to go along with it."

Ryan was waiting by the double doorway into the sanctuary booming with praise music, concert-style. Sierra felt the intense sound vibrations as she crossed the main area with Rosie.

Ryan's gaze swept over Rosie and intrigue followed. Swiftly, the image of those two together appeared in Sierra's brain. That brought the distraction she needed.

Ryan directed them to the third row in the back where the stage was only seen though the forest of hands waving to the ceiling. Sierra stood beside Chad as Rosie settled in the only available chair which happened to be the one by Ryan.

Everything quieted as people sat, eagerly waiting for Pastor

Pete to appear on stage after his long absence. The short, Hispanic man with coal black hair and beard strolled to center stage. "In the name of Jesus, Welcome! Today, let's all give God praise!" His face beamed with happiness.

Sierra froze. Couldn't move. Couldn't breathe. *He found her.* Mario. *He knows where I am.*

Panic cut knives through her as she trampled over everyone to escape. She had to get away like she had that horrid night Mario decided to punish her for refusing his orders.

Yes you will, Fantasy. You don't have Colton to protect you now. Now you will pay.

I won't do it.

She remembered Mario dragging her by her hair out before the cheering crowd where a donkey waited to climb onto her. She fought each step until a sudden burst of smoke exploded in the stands—her signal from Levi to break away and flee to his motorbike waiting outside. The frigid air sliced at her bare skin as the bike roared toward the convent. She knew Mario would never give up trying to find her. Now he had.

Chad's hand gripped her arm, wheeling her about. "What the hell, Sierra. What happened in there?"

Claws out, she raked at his face, missed, finally realizing who it was. "That's him. Chad, that's Mario. He found me. I have to get away. I can't stay here." She'd seen Mario play lots of roles. If he wanted to, he could play God. After all, he thought he was God.

Hunter's truck pulled up and the passenger door swung open for her. She bolted into the cab as Chad, Ryan, and Charlie piled in the back. "I have to go home."

"Sierra, that wasn't that pimp guy. It's Pastor Pete," Chad assured from the rear of the cab.

"I think I know what he looks like," snarled from Sierra's lips.

"Wait," Charlie commanded. "Could this Mario guy look like Pastor Pete?"

If she knew anything, she knew Mario better than her own hand. "That was him."

"Sierra, I don't think you've met Pastor Pete," Charlie said. "He's been on a trip to Africa and while there got some bug and was laid up in the hospital. This was his first sermon after getting back."

"I don't care what they told you but that was him."

As Hunter drove up the interstate entrance ramp, Chad suddenly blurted, "We have to go back. Lori is in Sunday School still."

"Call your folks. They are still there," Charlie ordered. "Sierra has no business going back there right now."

Chapter 31

"Twenty-one. Two. Three ...," the therapist counted as Chad went through the automatic movements of the exercises that therapist wanted, making him feel like a circus monkey. Meantime, Chad watched Sierra talking to Rosie outside on the patio.

Watching her laugh from one of Rosie's comments trickled pleasantly over him. He recalled Sierra a couple of days ago, under the table with him, laughing uncontrollably. A lawn mower had backfired, and a flashback had plunged over him. He started ordering everyone to get down; so, she did. Then Lori found them, causing even more laughter.

He couldn't stop thinking about how absolutely beautiful she was. He could easily see why she had become a successful high-end call girl. After that Versace night, the trusted nurse, who had seen it all, was gone, replaced by a very hot female.

He had no choice but to stop relying on Sierra because ... at least, he had discovered he was very much alive, which was a relief. However, what woman would ever want to be with a strawberry-swirl Freddy?

One night after a whirlpool, he had studied himself again in the full mirror. Thanks to the compression suit, the swelling was down over his entire body. He saw an improved male body starting to show. Still, the image was repulsive.

From the lack of an ear—likely no future of a fake one—to the rough batches of hair above his forehead, his left cheek, misaligned mouth, damaged nose tip, was proof enough he was still a mess. And the reality continued to his ruined jawline, neck, chest, to the front of his arms, his belly, to the front of his thighs. There was nothing but red, shiny, mottled flesh streaked with white. So much so, he could only think of it all as swirls of strawberry ice cream.

Turning to view his back proved it was nearly as bad, since it had been harvested for skin grafts. "It will fade in time, Chad." A wonderful way to say, he would look like shit for the rest of his life.

However, patterns had shifted. Since everyone had seen Sierra at her worst as well as her best, she was now family—someone that Margery would have liked. She seemed more comfortable with herself as well. Especially after a visit from Pastor Pete, which, at first, had been like Lori seeing him in the hospital without bandages. But Pastor Pete won the day.

There was no real explanation for this change other than Sierra wasn't pretending to be a nurse, caregiver, or something else anymore. Even a call girl. She had no pretense to do so now. She was just being herself, which he hoped stayed that way because she was a natural nurse.

But there were moments when Sierra was alone that he noticed her lost in some abyss that he couldn't touch. During one of his appointments, he had talked to Dr. Kendrick about Sierra's situation with the school and hospital. "I'm working on it," was all the doctor could report.

Something had better happen soon, or Chad wasn't sure what Sierra would do, he thought as he finished the count for the therapist.

"That's great, Chad," the guy announced. "I don't think we need to continue coming. I'll talk to the office about taking you off the schedule. Okay?"

"Uh, sure. Yeah. That is good news."

After escorting the therapist to the front door, Chad walked into the kitchen as Ryan headed to the deck like a servant, bearing two glasses of iced tea.

Sucker, Chad thought with a grin. "Uh, hey, how about me. I'll take an iced tea," he ordered as he joined everyone.

"It's in the fridge. Get it yourself, bro." Reclining in a deck chair, Ryan had planted himself next to Rosie and avidly listened to the girls' chitchat. Seems Rosie had no problem at all including Ryan in their conversation. The gleam in Sierra's gaze said she was reading the same message as he was.

He returned to the kitchen and opened the fridge for the pitcher of tea. By the time he filled his glass, Sierra appeared in his shadow. "Hey. Is there enough for a refill?" she asked, holding out her glass

"You want to go back outside," he asked, nodding toward the couple flirting out at the firepit now.

"Sure."

A mower started in the neighborhood. One glance sent another shared memory through them which brought smiles to both faces.

Chad forced himself to look out at the fence, the redbud tree, anything but not Sierra's lips. The urge to kiss her seared through him. Instead, he drank the iced tea as a substitution for a cold shower.

Still, he could feel her standing there beside him, smell her fresh scent. Oh, it would be so easy just to put his glass down, turn to her, lift her chin, kiss her. Damn, he really wanted to.

"I think Rosie and Ryan have hit it off," he stated.

"Oh, I know so," Sierra said, sitting her glass on the railing. "They fit."

He nodded. He wanted to fit. Being alone was suffocating. He had no idea how much of his life Margery had claimed. Now she was gone, leaving him alone … with Lori.

For now, he just wanted what he had right there. Right now. Just a comfortable silence on a sunny spring day with Sierra, enjoying a glass of tea. He didn't mean as a couple. But as friends.

Setting his glass beside hers, Chad faced Sierra. "Sierra, you don't have to leave. I… I mean we really want you to stay … if you want to. Lori will miss you if you go. It would be like losing her mom all over again."

Sierra kept staring out at the fire pit. "She's a sweet girl. I'll miss her, too. But I'm not sure Kansas City has anything for me now. Not after all this."

"Stay here until you know for sure. Okay?"

"Sure."

Their gazes held for an intense breath. Her smile turned brave. "Uh, do you want me to go with you to the doctor's appointment in about an hour?" she asked.

Reality swept back in like stink. "Oh, uh, no. I'll drive. And I'll pick up Lori."

"Then, I'll go get groceries for the weekend."

Chapter 32

The guys were all going to be there that weekend, with the girls. Possibly Rosie. So, Chad would need groceries for that and for the next week. So, here she was, doing her "Margery" thing. As Sierra claimed the grocery bags from the rear of her car, she remembered what Chad had said.

Sierra, you don't have to leave. I... I mean we really want you to stay ... if you want to. Lori will miss you. It would be like losing her mom all over again..

Simply hearing Chad say that meant everything. But, she knew she'd just keep doing the "Margery" things and become a pet like Owen.

Chad would go ballistic if he knew that she was considering moving to some small town that had strip joints that would pay her bills and she could pay off the loan and then save enough for nursing school somewhere. She just hadn't found that place yet. But it was time she started making plans to move on to whatever God had planned ... if he did, anyway.

"So, whatever You have planned, God, best be making it clear," Sierra whispered as she started toward the store.

Checking the avocados, Sierra played with ideas of fixing Mexican that weekend. Ideas of sour cream, extra lettuce, more salsa managed to add themselves to the grocery list as she tied the plastic bag closed.

A cart bumped into hers. She looked up into her past.

Levi stood there all so perfect, calm, smiling. A vagrant lock of blackish brown hair dangled over his chiseled face. But it was his hazel eyes that took her breath. As usual, they were dancing.

"Levi?"

"Hey, beautiful. I didn't expect to see you here. You're looking great, Fantasy."

Her throat closed. Mario? One glance around the produce area proved Levi was alone. "What are you doing … here?"

The delight in Levi's face melted like morning dew on a scorching day. "I have to talk to you, Fantasy." He nodded toward the Starbucks area. "Can we talk over there?"

Every step toward the small tables weighed like concrete. "I'm … I'm not Fantasy anymore. Sierra. Sierra Smith."

Oh, Okay. Sierra," he said dubiously. Levi waved toward the corner table.

As he bought two cups of coffee, Sierra watched the smooth, confident movements of the boy who grew up with her, watched over her, held her when she was coming apart at the seams.

As he started toward the table, memories returned of another time when they had planned her escape—Levi sitting across from her at another small coffee shop in Guatemala.

He sat and pushed one cup toward her., "You remember what

Mario said he would do if he caught Onyx beyond those convent walls?"

Clutching her paper cup, it burst like a volcano. Hot coffee flooded the table. It went ignored. "He. Didn't." Her body shook. She couldn't breathe as she watched every inch of Levi's face.

As the employee cleaned up the mess, Levi looked out of the window where people were going on about their normal lives. Meanwhile Sierra's was crumbling into a pit of lava.

Tears drizzled down his cheeks as his lips quivered. "Fantasy, I had no choice. But I did it for her." His hazel gaze turned toward her, pleading. "For Onyx. That's the reason I started searching for you. You had to know."

People were pretending to not watch or listen to the conversation. Something very cold solidified inside her. "What … happened?"

Levi looked down at his coffee. "Mario," his chin quivered. "Beat her. Fantasy, he beat her. I tried to stop him. I tried. But they made me watch." He cleared his throat. "He … he said unless I kill her, he would continue until she was dead." He broke into sobs.

Every ounce of her knew Mario would do this. How many horrors they all had been forced to watch. Sierra rested a hand on his wrist. His tears dripped onto the back of her hand. "I'm sorry, Levi." Sobs of her own mounted past her frozen heart. "I hate him. I hate that bastard."

Gasping for air, Levi stiffened upright. Using the harsh napkins to wipe his face, he looked directly into her eyes. "You're next. I had to warn you, Fantasy. He's looking for you."

Sierra slumped back in the bench seat and clutched the table edge. Her attention froze on Levi's face. "You. Found. Me. That means, Mario will too."

"Yes. So, Fantasy, I mean Sierra, we have to get you away from here. Go with me. We can go to Seattle. Denver. Nashville. Or just keep moving until he gives up."

That would work. Her and Levi. But she couldn't go back to that life. She couldn't do that now. "Levi, I'm not going back to ... that. I'm not.

"No. No. You don't have to. I'll get a job and pay for everything, so you can finish your nursing degree ... online. Whatever."

"How did you find me?

"I read about that suicide bomber in the paper. I saw your picture. *Patient and Porn Star* or something like that." Levi straightened his shoulders. "Sierra, Mario knows I helped you escape that night. So, I can't go back either. We can start a new life. You know. Be normal. We don't have to do that anymore. Either of us.

"But Sierra you can't stay here. You don't want that bastard to know about that guy's little girl." His gaze said to read his mind. "Because you know Mario will come for her."

Sierra slumped back in the chair, strangling a napkin with her hand as if it were Mario's throat. A whine crawled from her heart. "Lori. No. Not Lori."

Chad heard a motorcycle putter into the drive as the garage door rose to let Sierra's car pull in. None of the guys had a Harley. They had dirt bikes, usually keeping them out at Mike's Bike Shop in BFE, Kansas, so they could go dirt bike riding out there.

He went to the garage door to help Sierra with the groceries and to find out who came home with her. The Harley Fat Boy halted behind his truck and a guy dismounted. Chad found his way to the raised hatch of the car as Sierra gathered the sacks.

"Uh, Chad, this is Martin, an old friend from nursing school. He's on his way to Nashville. He, uh … we ran into each other at the grocery store."

"Really?" Chad asked.

This Martin strolled into the garage, with his leather jacket and a helmet tucked under one arm. "You must be Chad," he said with an outstretched hand. His hazel gaze danced with a strange familiarity as if they had met before.

Chad accepted the handshake. "I am."

Shifting his attention to the groceries as if discovering a new need, Martin quipped, "Here. Sierra, go on inside. We got this."

Chad stepped aside as Sierra obediently disappeared into the house. "Hope you don't mind, but Sierra asked me to stay for dinner," Martin said with a pleading gaze."

"Sure. I guess."

Martin loaded his arms with the plastic bags, leaving a few for Chad. "I really appreciate it, man. Been on the road, so a home cooked meal is a blessing from heaven. Trust me."

"Glad you can join us." Chad motioned toward the Harley. "Nice bike."

"Yeah, just rented it at a shop out in the boonies of Kansas recently. It's a sweet ride. I'm thinkin' of keeping it."

"Wouldn't be Mike's, would it?"

Martin brightened up. "Yeah. Sounds familiar. You know the place?"

Something stopped him from saying he did. "Not really. I don't ride myself. Heard it about it though."

Loaded with bags, he and Martin managed to go inside. "So. You met up with Sierra at nursing school?"

"Crazy, huh? I couldn't cut nursing school, so I'm headed to Nashville. Heard the music is great there."

"Yeah, I've heard that too," Chad said as he led the way into the house. Something itched about this guy.

Once inside, the bags went on the island; Sierra begin putting things away. "Do either of you want a beer?" she asked.

"Love one ... Sierra," Martin stated, taking the proffered can.

Chad filled a glass with water instead. He didn't like the vibe around this guy at all. What was strange was that Sierra hadn't texted him about asking this guy joining them for dinner. That wasn't like her.

"Excuse me," Chad went into the small bathroom to text his mother. Something wasn't right? Pick up Lori from school. Keep her for the night Will explain later.

She wrote back immediately that she would see to it.

Owen scratched at the patio door. Sierra opened it and the dog eyed Martin seated on the love seat then came to sit beside Chad. Oddly, not greeting Martin as the dog normally did with everybody.

"So, you didn't make it through nursing school?" Chad asked, brushing a rewarding hand over the dog's head.

Swallowing a mouthful of beer, Martin glanced at Chad. "That vocabulary was just too big for me. Put it in normal English so we all can understand. Say, do you mind if I crash here tonight?"

"That's up to Sierra."

"Sure. If the guys don't mind." The smell of frying onions filled the kitchen as Sierra started dinner.

"You going to stay in Nashville or keep moving?" Chad asked after a short draw on the beer.

"I don't know," Martin shrugged. "I'll get a job there, stay a while. See if it fits."

Hunter, Ryan, and Charlie bustled through the front door, laughing, taunting each other. The instant they saw Sierra's guest, curiosity spawned. Owen escorted them to the fireplace.

Ryan took a chair as Hunter lounged by the fireplace, arm on the mantle. Charlie evacuated to the kitchen to help Sierra, or in truth, to take control of cooking, which she abdicated instantly.

Intros were made, hands shook. Axel was reportedly out, "Doing his thing," Hunter assured. "Pity the coyotes tonight. You know Sniper. He's never gotten Afghanistan out of his blood."

Talk around the dinner meal shifted like the weather: Royals, favorite places, sports. Chad watched Sierra who ate little, sipped more wine than usual, made contrite responses to any comments that came her way. Something was off; he didn't like it.

"Hey, we got this," Chad ordered as everyone pushed away from their plates. He wanted to talk to Sierra. "Why don't you guys see if Martin is any good at pool."

The usual banter down the stairs exploded as the process of cleaning up after a dinner began. "Where's Lori?" Sierra asked as she started rinsing dishes, handing them to Chad to put in the dishwasher.

"Spending the night with mom and dad." Chad leaned back on the kitchen island as Sierra left the fridge to rinse an empty out jar of salsa "Did you really run into him in Hi-Vee?" he asked.

She looked out the kitchen window. "Uh, yes. Funny coincidence, huh?" She cast a weak smirk at him.

"And, he flunked out of nursing school to travel the world?"

"I guess."

"You going with him?" The question just popped out of his mouth.

Her face paled. "No. Why would you think I would just take off and not let you know? Seriously, Chad?"

"Because you didn't ask me about your friend joining us tonight."

Chapter 33

"Chad, I've never seen grafts do this well." Dr. Kendrick stated as he wrote in a chart.

"I have to say it's all Sierra."

The doctor chuckled. "It was a good day she came into your life, Chad. However crazy that was."

As Chad was zipping up his compression suit, he asked, "Any luck with the school?"

Frowning, Dr. Kendrick studied him. "Still working on it, but it's showing some promise. We have a new president." Putting the chart down he smiled. "See you next week. How's that?"

"Great."

Pulling his truck over to the side of the road at the cemetery, Chad stared at the head stones and found Margery's. A restless sunlight drifted across the flat area and seemed to settle on it.

Months ago, he wanted to be there with her. But, time had changed that. Even though he was a freak, a monster, he was alive. The people he cared about didn't care what he looked like. So, it was getting easier to deal with gawkers. But what bothered the most was, it was getting easier to live without Margery.

There was no doubt in his heart that he would always love her. Nothing was ever going to change that. But it wasn't the same now. She was here. He was there. They weren't together.

Sometimes, Lori brought Margery up, things they did, things she liked, memories. "Remember when she …" Oh, he could remember. Those times were getting easier to talk about. He could even smile at a few of the funny moments. But Lori would also talk about Sierra the same way, the fun things they did. "We cooked you some cookies, Daddy. See."

But Sierra was restless, thinking too much lately, not telling him anything. She would just come up with some bullshit story, or "just thinking. It's nothing."

He had to find some way to get it through to Sierra, he didn't want her to go. He didn't want his daughter to go through all this loss again. Hell, he didn't want to go through this again.

He got out of the truck and walked to Margery. "Babe, I miss you. Everyday. I want you back. I want me back. I want what we had back. I hate what happened to us. I wish we had never gone to that damn market."

Tears brimmed but didn't fall as they normally did when he came there to talk.

"Lori whispers every night she wants you back, too." He smiled. "Like it's some secret between us." The smile faded. "But you aren't coming back, are you?"

His knees buckled. He gripped the edges of the headstone to remain standing. "I know you are in a good place. I'm glad for that, but I'm not happy without you. Margery, I hate this hell. I hate it!"

He slapped the stone with his palm. Again. Again. Nothing cracked. Nothing released. Nothing. "I'm not even the same man you married. I'm not, Babe. I'm a freak. A monster."

The birds chirped. A butterfly futtered over the stone as if all that didn't matter. Maybe it didn't matter.

"Sierra. You'd like her. She's, my nurse. Well, you know all that. But seriously, she's just my nurse, Margery. Nothing more." That was a lie. Sierra was more than just a nurse n ow. She had become a friend, a true friend. Maybe even a special friend.

"Margery, she's become a friend, too, I guess, really. Like the other day, Axel was mowing when the damn mower backfired. I flashbacked and yelled 'Get down! Incoming!'" He wanted to laugh but it caught in his throat. "I dove under the damn table. Sierra dove with me, stayed under there on all fours until it passed. We laughed."

He sat down in the wet grass. "Margery, I haven't laughed like that since I lost you." His smile melted as he continued. "Lori found us there and asked us what we were doing under the table. For the life of me, I could not explain it.

"I can't explain any of this. I can't, Margery. I want a reason for all of this, dammit. I want to know why God took you from me!"

He sat there, listening for an answer. All he heard were the spring winds traipsing about the field. In the distance, he heard the sound of a blower clearing burial sites. A few birds chirped in the trees. The sun was warm.

He let Margery's stone support him. "Why?" muttered from his lips. "Why? I just want to know why." Still, everything stayed the same. Nothing changed. No answer.

"I don't want to go on without you, Margery. But I'm different now. Something is pushing me. I don't know where, Babe. I just know I have to go there. I need you. I need someone. I'm lost."

Two blue birds landed on the nearby red bud tree, a blue male, and a grayish female. They hopped about teasing each other like he once had with Margery in the back yard. They had been playing chase and he'd finally caught her.

The birds stopped to study him as if they were witnessing his memory. The male bird glanced at the female. For a breath, she looked at him, then bolted up into the air. She was gone.

The lone bird, alone like he was, flew off in a different direction, to another tree. It was as if something was telling him it was time to move on, let Margery go.

"Go. She needs you."

Stunned to hear a voice, Chad looked around to find where it came from. No one. Nothing. Yet, the words played again.

"She needs you. Now."

Chad stared at the front of his truck remembering the day the black Navigator pulled up in front of his truck. The businessman asking about a recent burial did look like Pastor Pete. And the driver with hazel eyes—*the same eyes* of the guy Sierra called Martin.

"Nashville. My ass."

Chad bolted for his truck, only this time he could run. He punched Hunter's cellphone number in as he started the truck. No answer. He left a voice mail as he U-turned in the road. "Get the guys. Meet me at home. It's Sierra."

Chapter 34

Sierra took off Ryan's cross, placing it on the top of her Bible laying on the foot of the bed. She remembered her first night there, 'No way in hell I'm staying here.' Now, looking around the room, she realized it had become a home to her, a special place.

But that part of her life was over, ending unexpectantly. She had to move ahead anyway, make her own life without Chad. Without everyone. She couldn't get past what Levi told her about Onyx. It was exactly what that bastard Mario would do. Now the bastard was hunting her. And maybe Lori.

"Shit," Levi snapped. He looked up from his phone. "We gotta go. NOW! Fantasy. Now."

Fear struck. "Why?"

Jabbing the cell into his pocket, Levi stared at her. "It's Mario. I put a tracker on his phone. He's flying in from St. Louis. If we leave now, he'll to try to follow us. Otherwise … I don't know what will happen."

Her insides shattered into small ice particles. Mario was coming for her. She had to protect Lori. She had to go now, or they all would be dead. Dead as Margery. Dead as Onyx. She couldn't let that happen. Lori, Chad, the guys didn't deserve that.

Swinging her backpack onto her shoulder, Sierra followed Levi through the living room. Flashbacks of Christmas, flashbacks of sleeping on that couch, flashbacks of Chad's hospital bed assaulted her as she raced through the dining area, the dinners, the firepit outside, the guys fussing in the kitchen, Charlie frying bacon. Avoiding any more, Sierra raced past her car to Levi revving his bike. He handed her a helmet and moved so she could climb on behind him.

Chad wheeled into his driveway as the garage door rose to reveal Sierra's Lexus. But the bike was gone. That meant that asshole was gone. Maybe Sierra didn't go with him.

Hope lodged in Chad's throat as he slammed the truck into park and raced through the garage. The house was too silent. Too empty. "Sierra!" No answer.

Hunter's truck pulled in the drive. Truck doors slammed. As Chad raced up the stairs to her bedroom, Hunter, Charlie, and Ryan burst through the front door. "Chad, You here? Where are you?"

Footsteps followed like a herd on the steps as Chad stared at the Bible and the necklace. Then everyone filled the doorway, "Any sign of her?" Charlie asked.

Not turning, Chad answered, "She left with that asshole."

"That Martin guy?" Ryan asked as he, too, saw his necklace on the Bible.

"That isn't his name. It's that Levi guy from her past. He came for her. I knew something wasn't right about that fool last night." Cold memories at the cemetery flashed in Chad's brain, colder than that day ever was.

"I remembered him now. That limo pulling up at the cemetery. That suit who, now that I think about it, did look like Pastor Pete. His driver was that asshole who Sierra just left with. They've been watching the place all this time.

"Where's Lori?" Charlie demanded.

Chad stared at his friend. "With my folks."

Hunter wheeled to Ryan. "Get your cop friends out to Chad's parents' house, in case these assholes go there."

Chad didn't know which way to turn. What if the creep made her go? Kidnapped her again? But what if she wasn't? What if she went to keep them away from there? Maybe, she chose to go with that prick. A million questions pierced his brain.

"Didn't this Martin guy say he was headed to Nashville?" Charlie asked, moving into the room.

Chad looked at his friend. "He did."

Hunter shrugged. "If it were me, I'd tell you Nashville and head to Denver."

"Wait. I put a tracker on Sierra's phone." Hope sprang inside Chad, as he started poking at his phone screen. He found Sierra's little dot, heading toward the Benton curve. "She's moving ... west I-70. Denver." He scanned the worried faces around him. "Something tells me, he's headed to Mikes. He said he rented the Harley out there. Probably has a car out there."

Hunter nodded. "Yeah. I remember seeing that bike out there last week, for rent."

Chad looked at Hunter. "Where's Axel?"

"Roaming the hills out by Mikes. Can't reach him. I just tried."

Ryan rejoined them. "Parent's covered." He closed his phone. "So, which way we headed—Nashville or Denver?"

"Mike's. My truck. Now," Hunter ordered. They all bailed toward the stairs.

As Chad jumped into the passenger seat, he demanded, "What is everyone carrying?"

"Luger 9 mm in the console," Hunter answered. "Two AR-15s under the seat."

Ryan. "9 mm. Shit. I forgot my AR."

"No time to get it." Chad announced.

"Something tells me this could get ugly," Charlie stated. "Everyone got ammo?"

"Nope." Was the general answer.

"I can fix that. Problem solved," Hunter informed as he tore out of the driveway.

Levi swerved around a car speeding along on the interstate and then fell back into the right lane. The wind blew through Sierra as if a hole that had opened in her soul.

The instant Levi had pulled away from Chad's house, it was like being torn in half. But there was no other choice. She had to get on with her life anyway. And she had to protect Chad and Lori.

She couldn't allow this hell onto anyone she loved. Did she love them? Yes. After all, they had given her more than she had ever known.

"I thought you said we were going to Nashville?" Sierra asked through the mic in the helmet.

"It doesn't matter. We just gotta get out of town to throw Mario off track. I know a few backroads in Kansas that will throw keep him lost till we get to Denver or San Antonio." Levi swayed dangerously around a line of cars, darting in before a semi. It honked at him.

"Slow down or the highway patrol will pull you over," Sierra ordered.

As commanded, Levi slowed into normal flow of traffic. The reality that Chad would be furious with her ate at her. He had given her the first sense of a real home. A real family. Knowing Lori had just lost her mom, and now her; the fact cut deep. But that was nothing like being kidnapped. Protecting Lori was far more important.

Besides, Chad didn't need to deal with this threat as well has the hell he was going through. He had suffered enough with losing Margery. Chad would give his life to keep anything from happening to his daughter. She couldn't risk putting him in that situation. Not if she could prevent it.

Each mile that whizzed past, somehow, snapped a ribbon that connected her to them. Each snap hurt. Tears drizzled from her eyes, unhindered.

The morning replayed. Everyone had left for work. Chad had gone to his doctor's appointment. She was standing at the patio doors remembering the days that Axel hunted for Easter eggs with Lori. Or, Charlie fretting over the smoker while Ryan and Hunter argued over which paver should go where. Right after they all left for work or the doctor's appointment, Levi appeared from the basement.

"I smell coffee."

"Yeah, I'll get you a cup," Sierra started toward the kitchen.

"I'll get it."

She watched Levi make himself at home. "I'm not going back into the business."

He had claimed his steaming coffee mug and walked toward her with that grin of his. "I don't blame you. But," he took a sip, "what are you going to do?"

"You said you would get a job so I could finish school."

"Oh, yes. Of course," Levi shrugged. "I doubt I can make enough for both of us, though. I don't have what you have, Fanta ... Sierra. Brains and a body."

"I mean it, Levi. I'm not going back to doing men."

He stared out at the backyard and sighed. "First, let's live long enough to figure that out." He put the cup on the table to look at her. "Let's get this show on the road."

There they were, speeding up an exit ramp wearing a road sign of State Highway 73. "Where are you going?" she asked.

"Trust me." Levi stopped and then gunned the bike to the right. "Like I said, we have to take the back roads."

Minutes later, Levi turned left onto a deserted dirt road that soon became rural scenery of old farms with wide pastures of grazing cows. Even that evaporated into just rolling hills. No houses. No farms. Few livestock. Dust blew up behind them like a wake.

It was as if Levi knew exactly where he was going. What choice did she have other than to see where this ended? Maybe where she didn't want to be.

Chapter 35

"Sniper, where are you?" Charlie asked from the back seat. Chad listened as Charlie talked to Axel on dash speaker.

"Out here looking for coyotes."

"You near Mike's?"

"Close enough."

"Good. Targets are headed your way.

"What targets?"

"The asshole we told you about last night is. He's with Sierra."

"Where are they now?"

Charlie looked to Chad.

"The tracker on Sierra's phone says they just left the interstate, moving to 73." Chad informed. "Mike's Bike Shop is out that way, isn't it?"

"Yeah. Only one near 73. How will I know it's him?" Axel asked. Wind blew through the phone.

"They're on a green Harley Fat Boy." Chad stated.

"Goin' there now." There was rustling of grass and wind. The connection was lost in the hills.

Silence filled Hunter's cab as he drove through the usual traffic at the infamous Benton curve.

"You know where Mike's is?" Chad asked.

"Like a homing pigeon. Axel's favorite hunting grounds. I've been with him many times. Once we get through this shit, we're golden. Move over, granny!" Hunter barked at the old lady driving ahead of him who was clogging traffic. When he made the infamous curve, everything opened to the skyline of the city.

"Uh, everyone, before we get to State Line, figure out what you need at the gun shop."

"Affirmative," resounded in the cab.

The clicking of guns being checked sounded behind Chad as he endured the mass of buildings, exit ramps, overpasses. All he could think about was seeing that asshole closing the Navigator's rear door, seeing those same hazel eyes.

Why would Sierra leave with him so easily? Obviously, the prick hadn't forced her since she left Ryan's cross on her Bible. Why, Sierra? What were you thinking?

He knew things were changing. They both did. He'd be starting with Southwest the first of the month. He was managing his own finances again, taking Lori to school, etc. What he couldn't manage, his father or mother could. The guys were there if he needed them. But Sierra was one of them now. He had pictured her graduating, becoming a nurse. Things were going perfect.

How was he going to explain this to Lori? He could hear her little voice now. *Where's Sierra? Why did she leave? Doesn't she want to be with us anymore? Daddy, I don't want to lose her, toooooo!'*

As the neighborhoods of Kansas City whizzed by, he saw Sierra's past in the rundown districts, potential future—strip clubs. His heart sank. She was so much better than that.

God, don't let her go back to that.

Chad cleared his throat of emotion as Hunter pulled into a small parking lot of a Kansas gun shop near a small strip mall. They all climbed out, did recon, while Hunter checked the chamber of an AR-15 that he handed to Ryan.

"Sweet. When did you get that?" Ryan asked

"Last year," Hunter answered as he inspected the other AR-15 from under the passenger seat.

"Holy shit man, where did you get all this firepower?" Charlie demanded as Hunter dug for a plastic container behind the back seat that revealed only two magazines.

"From who else? Sniper," Hunter answered. "Everyone know what they need?"

Orders were stated. Hunter looked at Chad. "We go in. Everyone else stay here."

The door dinged their entry. Glass cases ran down both sides of the narrow shop, which ended with a narrow case where "mom and pop" were. Pop stood up from behind the register the instant the door opened.

"Good morning … or is it afternoon. Whatever it is, what can we do to help you?" Pop asked.

"Five boxes of 9 mm, four magazines of .223 Remington," Hunter stated.

"You boys out for some serious shootin'?" Pop asked as he placed the ammunition boxes on the glass counter.

"Likely." Hunter's wrist phone lit up with a message: he answered. It was Charlie. "Targets arrived. We move. Now."

Boxes claimed, they bolted toward the door, Hunter tossing a credit card on the counter. "Call the cops. Mike's Bike Shop," he barked, as they charged outside.

"Harley has arrived. Sierra's with that prick," Charlie informed as everyone piled back into Hunter's truck. "There's also a Navigator with a Pitbull carrying an AK-47. Second Pit's in the car. Shop's empty."

"Tell him to keep his eyes open for company," Hunter muttered as he fled down the interstate ramp.

Levi pulled up to the only building Sierra had seen for miles. "Mike's Bike Shop" blazed across the open garage door. There had been nothing but rolling hills, scrub brush, blue skies, and bright afternoon sun.

Her guts caved at the sight of one of Mario's bodyguards carrying an assault rifle. One appeared from the building while another got out of a black Navigator parked outside the shop's open door. Levi shut the Harley down and started removing his helmet.

She jerked hers off. "What are they doing here."

Ignoring her, Levi walked to the guard waiting by the car door. "Everything in place?" he asked as Sierra dismounted the Harley.

"Should be here any time," the guy stated.

Sierra didn't need an answer to who. Mario.

Her insides froze as she searched for an escape. Nothing for miles. She bolted toward the thick sage and thorn bushes. Before she made twenty feet, a hard hand clutched her hair and dragged back to the bike, tossing her to Levi's feet.

The instant Levi's grip bit into her arm, lifting her from the dirt, she spat in his face. "You bastard. You filthy bastard," seethed from her lips. "You lied to me."

Releasing a pitiful sigh, Levi leveled a hard cold gaze on her, one she had never seen in him before. "I'm sorry, Fantasy. I had no choice. I either find you or lose Crystal."

She didn't have to ask who this Crystal was—a new girl he thought he loved. She had been traded for her.

With the guard following them while holding an assault rifle against his belly, Levi shoved Sierra into the open double doors to the garage shop. After all the years with Mario's thugs, she knew it was hopeless to resist. She was as dead as Onyx.

As she was dragged into the garage, Sierra scanned everything around a large, well-kept work area. It was lined with toolboxes her: a staircase to balconies displaying supply shelves lining two walls. Around her were workstations with individual tool cabinets, dismantled bikes, a window to a back office. Opposite the wide double front door was a matching door to the rear that revealed a hard packed dirt runway, obviously well used by private aircraft. Nothing provided an escape.

The sound of an approaching plane filled the air. Levi yanked her to the rear doors as a dark speck appeared on the horizon that grew larger with each breath. Sierra immediately recognized the sleek, black, Dassault Falcon 900 from the thousands of trips she'd flown around the world.

The jet landed in a plume of dirt, slowing enough for the dust cloud to consume it. It eased to a stop, engines decelerating to a slow whirr. Not only did the jet stop, so did her insides. He was there.

Sierra jerked helplessly in Levi's grip. She had to do something, anything to get away. But how? Two guards were by the front door. The jet hatch opened, revealing two more guards with assault rifles. Mario appeared, black Armani suit, no tie, black shirt, open collar, black hair whipping in the Kansas wind.

"Hold her. Don't lose her," Levi ordered as he shoved Sierra toward the nearest guard to go out to meet Colton's heir. The man who thought he owned her. No. Not this time. She would die before letting him touch her.

Jerking at the steel grip on her arm, Sierra watched Levi talk with Mario who smiled, nodded. In step, they walked toward her.

Chapter 36

"Slow down. Don't need a dust cloud announcing we are here. Pull over there," Charlie ordered, pointing toward the dirt patch right before the big curve in the road. Hunter stopped. Vacating the truck cab, everyone began assessment of the area and the weapons. Ammo clicked into gun barrels; handguns revealed a full load of bullets ready.

"Sniper, what do you see?" Charlie asked his smart watch. They all huddled like linebackers to listen to Axel's update.

"Pitbull-one is guarding the rear office door. AK-47. Sierra and your target are inside with Pit-two by rear doors. Pimp's inside. Pit-three just appeared at front door. Pit-four is watching the jet."

"Can you take out Pit-one?"

"If I get to blow up the jet?"

Charlie rolled his eyes. "Civilians are inside!"

"If I get them out?"

'Sure. Fine. Whatever. But take out Pit-one first. Wait for my cue."

"Roger."

Laying on their bellies behind a hill, they watched their first target milling around the office door. As the jet engines whirred to stop, Pit-one peered around the front corner.

A soft report popped from the distant rise, and Pit-one's brains exploded over the office door. His body thumped to the dirt. Apparently, Axel had his silencer on, Chad thought as they crouched in a run toward the shop. The instant they arrived at the bloody doorway, Chad retrieved Pit-one's AK.

Charlie's arm blocked anyone as he eased the door open. Forking two fingers at his eyes, he motioned toward the office. "Window. Keep down," mouthed from his lips. Understood. He eased the door open, allowing each man to shuffle inside.

"Well, Fantasy. I see you are just fine." That had to be the pimp Chad thought, as the bastard's laugh was cut short. A slap rang out. "Bitch, you'll pay for that."

"Hold on, Sierra. Hold on," Chad prayed.

"I'm never going back with you, you asshole." Sierra sounded defiant.

"Oh, yes you are, Fantasy. Dead or alive. Preferrable alive. You have an engagement you failed to appear at. The crowds are still waiting."

Whatever it took, there was no way he was letting Sierra on that jet. Chad scanned the familiar office filled with a desk covered with a mass of receipts. Except for the door into the garage, calendars, receipts, pictures of Harley bikes covered the walls. Dust coated every surface.

As if turned to stone, they all watched Charlie crawl toward the desk and eased a drawer out to retrieve a .38 revolver. He checked; it was loaded. Plugging it in the back of his jeans, he peeked through the picture window into the shop area, swiftly read the situation going on in the garage. He dropped down to start texting Axel.

Every nerve in Chad's body blazed as he knelt in the compression suit that felt like it was strangling his entire body. Sweat poured where it could, as his lungs begged for air.

Then, Charlie's gaze met theirs with an order ready to deliver. With his finger, he drew a box in the floor dirt— the garage area. The box had two blanks along two walls which were obviously the garage doors. He stabbed his fingertip at each door...indicating with two fingers—Pit 2 at the rear door and Pit 3—three fingers—at the front door. He drew a cross outside the garage- the jet, and stabbed four fingers there, Pit 4 He read their faces. They nodded. He drew an S and L in the center of the shop—Sierra and Levi, then he added a M for Mario.

Choking down desperation, Chad forced his attention on the plan being drawn before him. All he really wanted to do was barge in, firing, killing those bastards while saving Sierra. It was insanity. He knew it. The training that had been drilled into him in Afghanistan stood fast. Make a plan. Stick to it. He forced himself to wait, pay attention.

After texting something to Axel, Charlie pointed to Hunter and drew a line outside the box, around to the rear door, X-ing P-4 by the jet, then X-ed P2 and studied Hunter who nodded. Looking at Ryan, he X-ed the P-3, motioning to stab the Navigator tires. Ryan pulled his knife from his pocket. Charlie looked at Chad, then pointed to himself, pointed to the interior door. Charlie pointed at L then at himself and Chad.

Charlie looked into the intent gazes, pointed at M, and then drew an X. Meaning—whoever got the best shot ... take it.

There was more—Charlie thumbed toward the jet then placed

both hands palms together as if flattening something. "Jet tires ... go flat ... move," he mouthed. Heads nodded.

Hunter and Ryan softly exited the rear door. Chad and Charlie eased to the office door into the garage area.

Levi's hand clutched Sierra by her left arm as the man she hated more than anyone in the world gloated before her, pacing about like a proud peacock. Every part of her wanted him dead.

She had enjoyed spitting into Mario's arrogant face even if it did cost her being slapped. But everyone had gotten used to that from Mario. She could easily see him beating Onyx like he had all the others, only this time he killed her. She knew she was next.

Levi always had two guns on him. Maybe she could get the one tucked in the back of his pants. It was a death wish, but Mario would be dead.

"You know we've been watching you all this time, ever since you made the national news. *Patient and Porn Star*. Was that how you paid your student loans in the hospital—by servicing patients, Fantasy? Clever," Mario smirked as he continued his parade before her. "We even visited this Chad and his daughter out at the cemetery. Bet your sugar daddy didn't tell you about that, did he?"

Sierra's heart halted. That was the day Chad almost had a full-blown panic attack. "It's nothing. It's nothing," he had told her. But, it was something.

Mario shrugged in his silk suit coat. "Oh, we could have taken his daughter any time we wanted to. But I decided to wait for you, so you could see us train her. Make you perform for her." Mario raised a finger to the tin roof as if to claim a brilliant idea. "Yes. Once we get you back, we will come back for the girl."

"Chad will kill you."

"I doubt that." Mario smirked. "However, we will see that he is planted with his dead wife."

Pop. Pop

The sound of the jet tires fizzing flat burst in the air. Then, the jet windshield exploded. A passenger window burst apart. As the crew fled toward the garage, the guard by the jet suddenly jolted from a bullet and fell, squirming beneath the wing.

"Get them back on board," Mario yelled at the guard by the rear doors. The guard bolted toward the escaping crew, then suddenly spun to drop face down in the dirt. The crew froze like sitting ducks caught between the garage and the jet.

The guard by the front door raced to the other side of the wide doorway as if to locate the shooter. He barely stepped from the doorway before two shots were fired. He also fell into the shop with half a skull.

Mario grabbed her around the neck jabbing a gun muzzle to her temple. "Get me out of here," he bellowed at Levi.

Just then the office door burst open, slamming back against the wall. Bullets sank into Levi, jerking him about then dropping him to Mario's feet.

Mario halted, strangling Sierra with his arm, the gunpoint almost impaling into her skull. "Drop your guns, or she dies before you pull a trigger."

"Chad, don't," Sierra pleaded. "He'll kill you."

"Chad," Charlie calmly said as he placed his gun on the ground. "Do as the asshole says." He motioned to get down.

To prove a point, Mario jabbed the muzzle against her temple. Sierra felt the dangerous glare burning in Chad's gaze as he lowered the AK toward the ground and knelt with Charlie, lifting his hands in as if to surrender.

Mario's gun was still driving itself into her brain. That she could endure. If for a moment it left her skull, she would …

The jet suddenly detonated. Black smoke and golden flames burst toward the sky. The concussion rocked the shop with its heat and shrapnel. The force flung her from Mario's grip. His gun fired. The breeze of the bullet caressed through her hair as she fell to the oily floor.

Chad and Charlie plunged for their guns, but bullets pelted from both side doors. Mario's body ripped apart as Ryan and Hunter unloaded bullets into him.

For a breath, nothing moved. Sierra wasn't sure if she was alive until a hand clutched her arm and she looked up into Chad's blue gaze. "You okay? Sierra. Are you okay?"

Without a thought, she leaped into his arms. His strength flooded into her. He had saved her. "Are you okay?" she demanded as she pulled back to look for blood anywhere on him.

"Never better."

Chad's gaze feasted on the emerald tears in Sierra's eyes. She was alive. She was in his arms. Just then, Axel sauntered into the garage, grinning like he ate the prize.

"Damn that was fun. Everybody okay?"

"Yeah, but I got the pimp first," Hunter announced, beaming

like a true Texan. "Since you gave up your weapons," he smirked at Charlie.

"Oh, no. I did," Ryan retorted.

"Yeah, but I got the jet," Axel announced. "Was that fucking cool or what?""

The guys began bantering over their victory, and giving high-fives. Smiles were shared all around. Sirens sounded in the distance. Reinforcements were coming. He needed to get Sierra away from everything.

"There is a sink out back," Chad said and led Sierra to an outside wash area behind the office, roiling with the smell of kerosine from the burning jet fuel.

Memories tried to assault his brain, but he shoved them back and tore a paper towel from the roller. He had the towel ready as Sierra rinsed her face with the cold water. Color returned to her face.

"Why did you go with him?" he demanded.

She looked desperately up at him. "Chad, they knew about Lori. I believed Levi that, if I left with him, we would draw Mario away from here."

"Sierra, we would have stopped them long before they ever got to Lori … or you."

"I couldn't risk that." Her body started shaking uncontrollably, chin quivering. "Levi lied to me, Chad. I believed him. Like I did the puppies."

Clutching Sierra into his arms, Chad held her, pressing her head to his shoulder, absorbing her tremors.

"Sierra. They're dead. You're safe. With me." He stroked her hair again and again as if pressing that fact into her brain. Just holding her that close assured him that she was alive. Life surged into him; a life he had forgotten existed. He could breathe again.

Chapter 37

Patrol cars plowed down the dirt road gathering like a flock of Canadian geese, creating a parking lot equal to a rock concert. Sierra froze as highway patrol officers strode toward the garage like an army, guns drawn, eyeing every weed. She pressed close to Chad's body, using it like a shield.

An officer appeared from the rear doors and halted, his shadow draping over them as he read their every move. "Are you Mr. Michaels?"

"Yes."

The officer's hard gaze shifted, slicing through her. "Are you Sierra Smith?"

"She is."

The man's gaze cut back to Chad. "Let her answer."

Sierra managed to nod as Colton's voice barked at her. *If you are caught, don't tell them anything. You hear me, Fantasy. Run if you can. Run.*

"Both of you. Follow me."

"Chad. I ... No. I can't," Sierra pleaded in a desperate whisper.

"I can't." She clung to his shirt, begging. The officer waited a few paces away.

"Can we have a moment, please?" Chad asked. He leaned close, holding her by the shoulders, "Just tell them you were kidnapped. Nothing else. Okay?" Chad drew back enough to see if she understood.

She understood. Clearly.

Letting Chad lead her toward the rear garage door, Sierra witnessed more officers questioning Axel and Hunter, taking pictures, starting to draw yellow outlines around Mario. Levi. It all happened again. The bodyguards. Levi still holding her. Mario parading before her. The explosion. Bullets.

The officer opened a small notebook. "Mr. Michaels, can you tell me what happened here?"

The instant Chad's arm dropped from her, Sierra bolted toward the flames bellowing from burning jet fuel, roiling with the black curtain of smoke.

"Sierra!"

Ignoring Chad's call, she pumped her legs through the suffocating smoke, down the dirt runway toward the shrub brush, toward the gully running along the runway. The smell of kerosine followed her, choking her, taking her breath. A ravine was just beyond the dirt strip. She would disappear in there.

"No! Sierra, please stop!"

Glancing back, she saw Chad bolt from the black curtain to collapse.

Run! The word kept replaying in her brain. *Run. Get away.*

Chad tried to get up, stumbled and then fell again. "Please stop! Sierra!"

He was on his knees, reaching out to her. Calling for her. Pleading for her to stop. He pulled himself up from the dirt, but his legs buckled again. "Sierra!" He fell, reaching for her.

She heard the pain in his voice, pleading. Beyond the flaming curtain of smoke, Hunter was blocking the officers from coming after her. *Run! Get away!*

She couldn't just leave Chad there. A spark of hope sprang in her heart. They could escape together. She raced back to clutch his hand. "Chad. Come on." She grabbed him by the waist to help him up. "We can…"

He pulled her to him, to his chest, enfolding her in his arms, tying her to him. "You're safe, Sierra." One hand rested on her head, pressing it, again, to the safety of his shoulder, cradling her. "It's over. You don't have to run any more. It's over," gasped in her ear. "You're safe. With me."

His face pressed against her head, the warmth of his breath, his smell, his arms, the sound of his words, *Safe. It's over*, melted through her.

She pictured Mario's body dead; his head blown off. Levi, laying there, dead. Colton was dead. They were all dead. All of them. She gave into Chad's arms, clinging onto his quivering body. Smoke drifted around them as they clung to each other in the dusty dirt of the runway as the sound of angry crackling flames feasted on its prey.

Gazing up, she drowned in the soft blue gaze pouring like a waterfall into her soul. A quivering smile emerged from beneath the mask. It was so beautiful. His lips rested on her lips. Her heart floated toward them, letting him claim it.

Once again, the flashback in the Farmer's market ripped through Chad with a fresh reality, plunging him back into the burning flames, black smoke, the same roar. Like the shroud that had killed Margery, it had taken Sierra from him. *NO! Not again!* He had to save her.

The inferno swept around him with the scalding flames, the smell of kerosine. The stench of smoke strangled him. But Sierra wasn't there. He kept going. He had to. He had to find her. Finally, he saw her racing down the runway toward the scrub brush.

"Sierra." She was getting away from him. He couldn't keep up. "Stop. Sierra."

Reaching for her though the million miles between them, Sierra was gone. He lost her. She was gone ... gone like Margery.

A hand clutched his arm. "Chad. Come on."

No! She wasn't gone! She was alive. She was pulling him to get up. He clung to that source of life enfolding it to his heart. "It's over, Sierra. You're safe. It's over."

Coughing, Chad gazed down into Sierra's gaze. It drew him. His mouth covered hers, knowing he could never let her leave him again.

Chapter 38

"An international sex trafficking ring was recently uncovered and destroyed …."

"What's a sex ticking ring?" Lori asked. The innocent eyes looked up for the answer.

"Something you don't want to know anything about, princess," Chad said as he flipped the television off.

Charlie plucked Lori up from the loveseat. "And if I have a say in the matter, you will never know," he announced, tossing Lori to Hunter. Her squeal of delight was their reward.

"Not ever," Hunter echoed. She was tossed back to Charlie then onward out to the backyard. Owen tried to catch her with each toss.

Axel leaned on the fireplace mantle. "Just give me another jet. Please."

"Don't get your hopes up, bro." Ryan got up. "Heading outside. You comin?"

"Yeah."

"Don't let Axel near the grill," Chad ordered over his shoulder as the family area suddenly grew quiet. His arm slid off the back of the loveseat onto Sierra's shoulders as if to keep her there. They both looked back to the patio door where Axel was already chasing Owen while Lori chased them both.

Hunter, Ryan, and Charlie had gathered around Chad's dad, advising him on how to finish the flank steak. "Gates, Mr. M, you gotta use Gates."

Chad's dad just smirked at their attempts. "You wait and see. OJ, cumin, salt, and pepper are all you need."

"Naw, man, you need Gates. I'm tellin' you."

Sierra melted back beneath the weight of Chad's arm, resting in its security. It was over. Along with Mike's being permanently closed, the flight crew had revealed years of flight manifests of Colton and Mario's connections with international cartels in every country that she had been taken to. Names, companies were exposed. It was going to be years before this was resolved.

Not only was Mario dead, but his entire stable had been located and the children were returned to their families. A weak happiness fluttered in Sierra's chest.

Escaping the entrapping comfort lingering on the couch, Sierra got up. "I need to start the sides," she stated as she headed toward the kitchen. The aroma of Charlie's very own recipe of black beans and rice cooking in the crock greeted her.

"I'll help," Chad stated as he followed.

"Great." Sierra hunted in the fridge for a head of lettuce. It was Mexican night, so she needed to start the sides. Chad's mother was at a church group with Rosie. They would be coming in with groceries all too soon.

She tossed the head to Chad "Here. Start chopping."

He caught it. A beam of pride flashed in his gaze as he tore the cellophane off to begin rinsing the leaves. Rummaging for the cheese grater, Sierra grumbled. "I know it's in here." She stood, frustrated, as Chad retrieved it from the dishwasher.

"Here."

"Thank … you." Sierra was struck by a delight she never witnessed in his gaze. Contentment, with a dash of joy, gleamed from the compression mask. Those laser blue eyes had gone through so much these the last seven months: terror, pain, anger, worry, fear, yes, all of those, but not joy. Yet, most of it remained hidden behind the mask. Suddenly, she wanted to see what was hidden from view. She reached for his head, for the Velcro straps that kept the compression mask in place.

He jerked from her touch, joy switching to surprise. "What?"

It had been months since she had seen what lay beneath the compression fabric covering Chad's entire body all day—23/7. One hour off. That one hour of freedom had become private. From the start of Chad's hell, she had watched his healing personally. She knew every scar, every burn that was now wrapped from her view.

"I want to see your face."

Chad drew back further, looking for an escape. But he didn't leave. "No. No you don't. No."

"Yes, I do, Chad." She reached again. The sound of tearing Velcro filled the silent kitchen. Once the straps were loose, she used both hands to ease the fabric from his face.

Her heart clogged her throat. Mottled flesh, red brimmed with white, mixed with the colors of normal flesh. Her fingertips feasted over the one eyebrow, the half an eyebrow. Touching each scar wrinkling the edge of each eye filling with tears. Her hands continued, gliding along his cheeks that no longer matched. Each had their own signature burn. Retracing each scar, her hand caressed the streaked flesh that had endured as much as pain she had.

Her gaze ran along his maligned nose, trailing down to the tight corners of his mouth, his warped lips. As her hand cradled his missing ear, Chad's eyes darkened with pain as she examined all before her. "You're beautiful."

As if stung, he jerked from her touch. "You're blind."

"No. I'm not blind, Chad." She shook her head, smirking at his disbelief. She drew closer, close enough to taste the blotched flesh of his cheeks with her lips.

Chad stopped breathing, becoming statuesque. His chin trembled as she pressed another kiss tenderly on it. Drawing back, she then found yet another place—his eyes, brimming with tears. Rising on tiptoes, she placed yet another delicate kiss over each scar, first the left side of his cheek, then the right. It wasn't enough. There was so much more she needed to consume.

Slowly, softly, she rested her lips on his, feeling them come to life. His arms slid around her. She pressed in for more, anything the remainder of the compression suit would allow to seep free.

His hand moved up her back, cradling her head as his mouth consumed her breath. Something inside her stirred for the first time in her life. Something warm, joyous, exciting ... alive. Something totally new. Totally hers. Chad.

The sound of the garage door rising jerked them apart. Chad snatched the mask and raced to the side bathroom before his mother and Rosie entered the kitchen, chattering like birds.

Sierra slumped back against the counter, feeling abandoned, which evaporated to a blush of contentment. Another strange feeling, she had never known.

"Honey, that smells delicious," Rosie cheered as she appeared. She dropped the grocery bags on the island, and then came in for a hug, but abandoned it for the crock pot to inhale the fragrance pulsing from it.

"Oh. That's Charlie's Black Beans and Rice. Don't ask. He won't give you the recipe," Sierra assured. Somehow a smile had implanted itself on her face, refusing to flee.

Chad reappeared with the mask in place. "Hi." It was stated short, crisp, with a tight smile. He glanced at Sierra as if to understand the terrain. "Hey, gorgeous. Guys are in the back," she stated cheerfully.

"Oh, thanks. Hi, Rose."

Rosie hesitated, as Chad escaped to the deck. "Wow. What's he runnin' from? But I say, Darlin, you do look happy."

A long-satisfied sigh accompanied Sierra's nod. "I think I am, Rosie."

"Well, God be praised."

Chad's mother appeared with the next load of groceries. They both rushed to relieve her of the bags. The kitchen came to life with the chatter of putting away groceries, latest news at the church, where to put this or that. The doorbell rang.

"I'll get it," Chad's mom announced and darted into the living room.

Stuffing plastic bags into another bag, Sierra heard a man ask, "Is this the house of Chad Michaels?"

That voice raked through her, freezing every nerve to solid ice.

"Possibly. May I ask why you want to know?"

Helplessly drawn, Sierra walked to the dining room doorway. There standing in the front entry was a man, a woman, and three adult kids. The moment she appeared in the living room, their gazes locked on her.

"Sara? Sara, it's you," the woman gasped. Tears flooded both faces as they looked across the living room. The woman started forward.

"Stella, wait," the man ordered, his hand grasping her arm, halting the woman.

Flashes of a younger woman looking at her cellphone on a park bench flashed as clearly in Sierra's mind as if yesterday. *They sold you to us. They don't want you anymore.*

"You are?" Chad's mom asked, sternly.

"Mike and Stella Ogden," the man stated. He then looked to Sierra as if praying she recognized their names.

Ogden? Ogden. She remembered. Oh God. She remembered! Sierra started backing up until she bumped into Chad's body.

"Sara, please. Please, Sara."

"I'm ... not Sara. I'm ... not ..."

Chad stopped her from fleeing. "Sierra, it's okay. I've got you." Chad's voice steadied her enough to let her feet plant beside him.

"Like we talked, Stella," her father stated softly to the woman who let Colton take her. "It's been a long time. We have to give her time to figure all this out."

"Come. Sit here," Chad's mom insisted as this woman nearly melted to the floor. Glancing at everyone frozen in the doorway, she ordered, "All of you. Come in."

Rosie bumped into Sierra as she passed through the doorway with glasses and a pitcher of iced tea. "Ya' all come on in, sit down. We can talk about this."

It was like watching an invasion as this group of strangers eased carefully into the living room. The boy with tawny hair about high school age remained stalwart beside his father. They remained behind the woman's chair. Their daughter settled in the next chair closest to her mother. Another man, different from the others, stood behind the girl's chair like a sentry.

Sierra couldn't breathe. Her heart was going to burst from her chest as she grappled for Chad's arm to steady her. Stella. That was her mother's name. Her father's—Mike. Ogden. What captured Sierra's gaze was that both mother and daughter had blond hair and green eyes identical to the one she saw every day in her own mirror.

Why were they there? They had sold her. To Colton. They didn't want her. Why were they there? She turned on Chad. "Please. Please. I can't do this. Please."

That same soft blue gaze rested over her. She saw that same smile lurk behind the mask. Encircling her waist, Chad drew her to him. "Sierra. It's okay. It's okay."

"Who told them?" she demanded. "Did you?"

"No. Neither did the guys." He turned to the quiet bunch lurking in the dining room who were now shaking heads vigorously.

"Sara, I mean, Sierra," her father started, "They had nothing to do with this. We saw your picture on the evening news. We couldn't believe it was you." Tears glistened in her father's eyes. "We've been looking for you all this time, Princess," quivered from his lips.

Princess. She remembered hearing 'princess.'

"God answered our prayers," her mother pleaded. "We never stopped praying for you. Never."

"Every night, Sara ... Sierra," the girl glanced at the young boy standing with his father.

The boy nodded. "Every night."

Shaking her head blindly, Sierra looked at Chad. "He … he showed me the money. They sold me. They didn't want me."

Her mother bolted to her feet like a warrior. "That's a lie. Sara! They lied!"

Her father pulled his wife into his arms, "Stella! Sara doesn't know that."

Lori appeared beside Chad, claiming his hand. "Is that Sierra's mommy and daddy?"

He plucked her into his arms. "I think so. Yes."

"I'm Susan, your sister," the girl announced. "This is Mike, we call him Junior. He's your brother. He's a senior this year." She waved at the man beside her. "This is my husband, Larry. We just got married six months ago. We're nurses at Seattle Hospital."

A thick silence filled the living room, allowing Susan to continue, "Sara, all our lives, we have wanted to meet you. Every dinner we prayed for you to return. Every Christmas we bought you gifts. Mom set a plate for you every holiday. We celebrated your birthday each year, May 15th."

Colton had told her that her birthday was the day she came to the ranch, October 9. She never liked that birthday. It felt wrong. It always felt wrong.

"We did, Sara. Every year," sobbed her mother as she started across the room. Her father reached to stop her but failed.

It all came crashing down inside Sierra. The walls. The past. The loneliness. The nights crying for her mommy. There she was, open armed, coming for her.

Then she felt it. Arms surrounding her. Lost arms, arms she had ached to feel, holding her, assuring her everything was going to be all right.

Another set of strong arms encircled her. "Princess, you're alive." Sierra looked up at her father's tear-filled eyes. "We never stopped loving you."

"They said … they told me … you … didn't want … me."

"Princess, they lied to you. It was all lies."

Who would want you if they knew what you have done? But we do, Fantasy. You aren't one of them anymore.

Stepping back, Sierra braced for the next reality to slap her. "You … don't want me now. Not now. Not after what I've done. No. I'm sorry but I…"

Her mother gripped Sierra' arms. "We don't care, Sara. We love you. We never stopped. We don't care what you had to do to survive. We never want to lose you again. Ever."

"Your mother is right, Princess," her father said. "All that is in the past now. We have you back, Sara. We start here. Together."

Slowly, pulling away, Sierra tried to breathe. The guys were still there. Chad's parents stood by the dining room wall. Rosie remained beside Chad, with Lori watching from his hip. Owen was the only one with life; he came to sit beside her leg.

The television was silent. No fire in the fireplace. The stairs to her room held no one. Evening sunset glowed in the picture window. Sierra's attention returned to the people in front of her. They were waiting. Waiting for her to do something. What?

She didn't know. But everyone's gaze said she did. They were just waiting for her to figure it out.

"It was … all a lie?"

They nodded.

"You … didn't sell me … because you didn't want me anymore?"

"Never," her mother pleaded. "I … I don't know how it happened that day. You just disappeared in the park. Believe me, Sara, I looked everywhere. Begged everyone to help find you. The police. They searched everywhere. We put signs up. A child alert went out. We did everything we could think of to find you."

"You ... don't care what I have done all these years?"

"We don't care. Only that you survived, Sara," her father stated. "It's over. You're home, Princess."

Sobs flooded the horrid past from Sierra's soul, buckling her knees. Her father caught her, held her. Again, her mother's arms enfolded her. Her family swept around her, touching, holding brushing back her hair from her face so she could see them. *They wanted her! It was all a lie!*

The aroma of grilled flank steak with black beans and rice soon filled the house as Charlie and Chad's mom and dad worked their magic. Axel finished chopping lettuce while Lori and Rosie grated cheese. Ryan bussed the table as Chad showed Sierra's father around the yard. Sierra listened to her mother and sister talk about nursing. Meanwhile Mike, Jr. tried to fit in with the guys talking football.

So, everyone could eat, the guys moved all the leather furniture back into the living room, making it look like a warehouse again. Owen had planted himself at Sierra's feet, ready to assure her he was there.

"You are so beautiful," her mother said, touching her face. "Don't you think so, Susan."

"Of course. I'm jealous, but sisters are supposed to be jealous."

"You're a nurse?" Sierra asked, forcing the words out from her disbelief. Somehow, some way this was a dream, and she was going to wake up to have it all disappear.

"Yes, I enjoy helping people get well. My favorite floor is obstetrics."

"I ... had one semester ..." Sierra started to announce but couldn't finish. How could she tell them why she didn't graduate?.

"Sierra saved my life in the Burn ICU." Chad said. "She was my nurse. Best nurse out there, in my opinion. She should have graduated this May, but I got in the way." Chad smiled at her. "She's planning to go back to finish nursing school next fall."

He made it sound too innocent. So simple. "Yes. Hopefully." How was she going to explain that she would never become a nurse? No nursing school would have her now? Or hospital.

"I figured you must be a burn patient from your compression suit. How are the grafts doing?" Larry asked.

Chad shrugged. "Itching constantly but well enough."

Larry smirked. "Sounds right. I work in the burn unit in Seattle. They left me with the debridement."

"Oh, then you know more cuss words than most people have vocabularies."

Larry smirked. "You could say that."

Chapter 39

Chad flipped in the bed sheets, trying to evade the memories of being trapped in the ICU and then seeing Sierra for the first time. When he rolled to the other bedroom wall, memories of Margery's funeral greeted him, complete with the looming hole beneath her casket. The one he had wanted to be buried in with her.

That theater production shifted to Lori crying for Sierra. "Daddy, I want her back. Why can't she live here like before?"

Evading the worst episodes of his life, Chad propped himself up on his pillows to swipe his cell phone alive to his photos. The emitting light displayed Margery, Lori, and him, the once happy, perfect family enjoying a once happy, perfect life. Only this wasn't his family nor his life any longer.

He wasn't that man and never would be again. That man was a monster who didn't want anyone to see or remember anything about him. So, no pictures of *it* appeared in the phone's glow.

Soon, it was going to be a year that started his hell. A hell for him and Sierra. Dr. Larson was right—they were like two drunks stumbling down the streets of life, trying to find their way home.

But Sierra had …found her way home. Meanwhile, he remained in his own personal hell with a daughter who, now, had lost another person in her life.

Owen's brown eyes appeared along with a slobbery lick of assurance. "I'm fine." Chad pushed the dog aside and got up to piss.

As he walked into the bathroom, he looked at the empty whirlpool, recalling the early days when he had to endure the crippling pain of the burns, barely remembering Sierra jumping in the water to keep him from drowning.

He remembered her making him walk. "Keep moving, Chad. Yes. Just keep moving." Hovering over him as he struggled with the walker. "Don't lean forward. Keep your weight on your heels."

His gaze fell on Margery's picture laying facedown by the sink. The instant he lifted it, another flashback of the horrific blast exploded. Yet he wasn't sure if it was the suicide bomber or the jet now. Either managed to set off its own episode. He didn't care anymore. Both had devastated him in some way.

He put the picture down to remove his compression mask. What the mirror reflected was still repulsive. However, that day in the kitchen when Sierra told him he was beautiful, he almost believed her.

He wanted to believe her. She made him feel good, normal. Even perfect for those few moments. But the reflection in the mirror reminded him again that this was his pathetic "new normal."

Returning to the bedroom offered him little respite. So, he went to Sierra's bedroom, once again, to witness the medics working to save her life. He made for the stairs. That was when he saw Sierra asleep on the couch, or wished she were.

No. She was with her family in Seattle. Yet, his little, pathetic story continued flashing at him, pictures of Versace, Sierra taking the keys of his mother's car. Fussing over Owen. Fussing over him. The emotional baggage as heavy as concrete. He needed a beer.

He saw the letter still laying on the dining room table where he had tossed it after reading it. The city mayor, a new hospital president, the very assholes who had ruined Sierra's life, wanted him to meet the other survivors of that bastard who had ruined their lives. They wanted to recognize him, to give him the keys to the city for saving so many lives on that momentous day. They all can go to hell with that bastard bomber as far as he was concerned.

He walked toward the fridge, his gaze avoiding the kitchen sink. *You're beautiful.* Gripping the island to keep standing, Chad felt every second of Sierra removing the mask. It had been like she was removing flesh. He felt her hands, her fingers touching his face, her delicate kisses, caressing the hole in the side of his head, whispering, *You're beautiful.*

He had been helpless to stop her. Once again, his insides melted as he felt it all again, stirring his soul alive, a soul that he thought had died with Margery.

Claiming a few beers from the fridge, Chad slumped down in the leather loveseat as more recollections of Sierra taunted him. The first one replayed her telling him of what she had gone through all those years. He replayed her strolling out to the fire pit like a New York model. *Versace!*

Another beer helped him remember Sierra spitting wine over his face when he called her a virgin. The next beer recalled that asshole pointing a gun to her temple. Then Sierra had disappeared into the cloud of black smoke. He didn't want to remember any more. It was as if the black cloud had claimed him.

"Chad! Chad!"

A rough hand shook him awake. Chad managed to look up at Charlie. "What the hell man? Leave me alone." He slapped Charlie's hand away.

"You okay?" Charlie asked.

Chad cleared his head to see the pile of empty beer bottles strewn everywhere. His head throbbed. "Yeah, I guess. Couldn't sleep."

"So, you came down here for some liquid refreshment."

"Something like that." Chad tried to move, sit up. Sucking in his breath, he worked his way to the kitchen bathroom. Reliving last night's reminiscence, Chad listened to Charlie starting breakfast with his usual with bacon.

The aroma ignited another flashback from the pits of hell. What normal flesh left on him that could sweat, did. He couldn't breathe. Chad threw water on his face and looked up at his raw reflection. More cold water barely staunched the looming tears.

A strange familiarity settled over him. He knew Margery was gone, never to return. An acceptance of that had knitted together what remained of his life, enough to continue living. But now another hole had burst open. Sierra. She was gone. She was alive, but gone. Every bit of him wanted to bring her back to what they had.

How could he do that -- take Sierra away from her family now? No. It was wrong to even consider that. "God, I miss Sierra. She's back with her real family. But we miss her," he told the reflection. "If you are listening, God, please show me how to go on without her, too. Please. Help me."

He couldn't believe he was talking to God, but who did he have who would understand what he felt about Sierra.

The small room became suffocating. Chad escaped to the kitchen to lean against the counter as Charlie moved the bacon strips about. "Can you get the eggs?" Charlie asked.

"Sure."

As Chad retrieved the carton, Charlie asked absently, "Heard from Sierra?"

"She texted that, apparently, there's a school in Seattle that will accept all her classes and she'll get graduate."

Charlie studied the popping grease. "I'm happy for her. But ..." He leaned back against the sink. "I wish she were still here."

Chad put the eggs by the stove top. "Me, too."

Charlie returned to shifting the strips of bacon and then waved at the invitation on the table. "Are you going?"

"Not unless they blackmail me." Chad started pouring orange juice into two glasses.

Bacon was draining fat onto the paper towel as Charlie cracked eggs. They both stood there, watching them turn white. "Want me to make enough for Lori?" Charlie asked.

"She always wants Uncle Charlie's eggs. You know that."

Charlie grinned as he poked one to bleed yellow. "Miss Lori doesn't like her eggs runny."

Toast popped up at the perfect time. "How's the wedding planning?" Chad asked while rummaging for silverware.

Charlie smirked up at him. "How would I know? I am only to show up on the right day, at the right time." He filled the plates. Before he sat them down, Charlie locked eyes with Chad. "You going to make it okay without her?" he asked. The plates added the last crescendo as he set them down on the table.

"Do I have a choice?" Chad pushed his plate away. "I want what is best for Sierra. She deserves to be happy."

"Doesn't Southwest fly to Seattle? You could transfer."

Chad studied his friend. "Leave you all here? My folks? Lori would never go for it. Damn hospital," Chad growled. "If they had let her graduate, she'd be here now."

Charlie motioned to the crumpled letter tossed in the trash by the island. "You don't suppose you could bargain with them about that? I mean, if they want you to show up, they have to take Sierra back?"

"What are you saying?" Chad asked.

"Maybe you could, at least, give Sierra some options. Here or Seattle. Let her decide."

"Daddy, when's Sierra coming home today?"

Chad turned to the little sleepy urchin rubbing her eyes. Charlie went to the stove top for her plate.

"She's with her family," Chad answered, drawing his daughter onto his lap.

"Then, she's gonna come back. Right?"

"I don't know, Lori, What I do know is, Uncle Charlie made you your favorite eggs this morning. See." On cue, Charlie presented his masterpiece like a grand chef.

"Thank you, Uncle Charlie." Then tears plummeted. "But I want Sierra's."

Chapter 40

"Don't go. Please, Sierra. Don't go. Owen and I need you. Pleeeeease!!"

"I promise, Lori, I'll come back soon. I promise."

Releasing Lori to Chad at the airport had torn Sierra's heart out. But the little girl's pleas replayed into her brain every night. Months had passed since she returned … *home*. To her childhood bedroom that was exactly as it was the day she and her mother had gone to the park. All pink and sweet.

The room was now livable. It was barely a week before Sierra appeared there with buckets of white paint. Alas, her bedspread was now scarlet. Her bed pillows and sheets were a mix of blues, yellow and scarlets. A large canvas print of a beautiful black woman, exploding with an array of color, filled the wall between the windows curtained with black. The print reminded her of Onyx. They talked every night.

The smell of coffee floated in the air. Soft mutterings drifted in from the distant kitchen. Her *family* was up, fixing breakfast, drinking coffee as usual. She could hear her younger brother talking about football as he was getting ready to leave for school.

Susan and Larry had stayed for the first few days, helping her repaint and shop for furniture. They had gone back to their apartment now. But, as their schedules allowed, they came *home* when they could.

Each night, conversations turned to nursing, about the new procedures. Sierra and Larry talked about the burn unit. He made her think of Jason. It didn't take long to realize, like Chad's parents, the Ogdens were a good family, one that she had been denied.

The first week entailed all the gifts she had missed, most of which went to Goodwill. They all even laughed a few times. They had toured the city of Seattle. Endless car rides to the mountains, the beach, the Space Needle. It was fun, until Larry made the mistake of driving by the park where kids were swinging on swings, flying kites, chasing dogs. A white van was even parked along the street.

A cold sweat broke over Sierra's skin. Breathing choked in her as she gripped Susan's arm. But when Larry started to wheel the car away, she stopped him. Dr. Larson said moments like this would happen. "Try to face them. Make them new. Let someone help you through this, Sierra."

"Stop. I need to get out."

Timidly, they walked to the same place where it all happened. Her mother stood beside her, watching her, seeing it all. The story slowly eased from Sierra's lips.

"You were sitting on the bench over there, looking at your phone." Sierra pointed to the bench. "I was playing over here." She swept her hand toward the kids chasing the kites and kicking soccer balls about.

It took a few breaths before she could turn to the bushes that she once played in. They were gone. Sierra made herself walk to the spot where the puppy came rushing at her. She saw Colton hidden in the bushes, just smiling, trying to call the puppy back. She had scooped it up to take it to him.

Here's your puppy.

Oh, thank you, sweetie. He is an ornery little fella. He's always getting away from the others. You want to see them. They are just over here.

Uh, I can't. My mommy said…

Colton had glanced at her mother. *It won't be but a minute. She'll never miss you.*

Sierra remembered it all, right there. She forced her steps toward the invisible bushes. Each step gained strength. Breathing became easier. "It happened so fast."

To her shock, her mother claimed the rest of the story. "Sara, I searched every inch of this park. Everyone here helped. I was so frantic. I begged them to help me find you." Sobs started taking over her mother. "I will never forgive myself."

"Mom, it's okay. It's over." Sierra couldn't believe she was saying this.

Her mother didn't hear her. "We hung posters with your picture everywhere. We put them on every pole, post, car in the area. We had to wait days before the police would even start a search. I called all your friends. Every parent. Your teachers. The church."

Sierra watched as the panic churned on her mother's face. There was no question that Colton and Mario had lied. Lied to every kid they brought to Guatemala, convincing them that their parents had sold them off because they weren't wanted. Lies.

Knowing all that now tore that cold cloak from her soul, something that needed destroying. Sierra saw her mother in a new light. She went to her and let her cry in her arms. "Mom, it's over. I'm home. I love you."

"Sara, we never … stopped loving you. Never." Her words struggled out through gasps.

Tears flooded unheeded as Sierra attempted a smile. "I know that now."

Stella smiled bravely. "God answered our prayers, Sierra. He did. You're home."

"Finally," Mike Jr blurted. It was enough to break the moment. Everyone laughed and breathed again.

Now, things were moving into a new routine as things always do. Larry and Susan went back to work. Mike Jr's games were starting that Friday. Sierra didn't know if it was normal, but her brother didn't seem all that pleased with his position as linebacker on second string, whatever that was.

Both retired, her parents volunteered every chance they could at the hospital, leaving Sierra with way too much time on her hands. "Spoil yourself, Sara … Sierra. I know. I'm sorry. I just can't seem to get that out of my head," her mother stated as they left.

They were finally accepting that she would never be Sara. She couldn't accept it herself. Sara seemed to disappear in her past with Fantasy. But now, it was legally Sierra Marie Ogden now.

There was a knock on the door to her bedroom, stunning her out of her thoughts. Her dad appeared in the doorway. "Princess, everything okay?"

"Sure, Dad. Fine." It was getting easier to say dad and mom. It was almost as if she were talking to Chad's parents. "I'll be down."

"This came for you." He presented an official letter from the

University Seattle, School of Nursing, with another one from Lori addressed in Chad's handwriting.

"Thank you. I'll ... be down in a sec."

The door closed and she looked at the picture. "Onyx, which one do I open first?" The official envelope from the nursing school drew hope. Larry, Susan, and her mother had said they all talked to the nursing school about her finishing her degree and that it should not be a problem transferring. She had visited the hospital with Larry in the burn unit, which was impressive, but the same as the one in Kansas City. Burn Units were hell everywhere.

Lori's card pulled at her heart strings. Flipping the card back and forth like a fan, she could see Lori and Owen picking it out, *This one. This one, Daddy.*

Finally, tearing it open, Sierra drew a handmade Fourth of July card into view. Amid streaks of what one could call fireworks, Owen was standing with a toothpick of a girl with tears in her eyes, with the entire stick-figure gang standing behind them. Even Hunter wore his cowboy hat. There was an orange fire in the circle that had to be the firepit. It was signed by all the guys as well as Chad.

A piece of paper dropped onto the bed. Unfolding it, Sierra recognized Lori's grandiose writing.

I MIss YOU CoMe Home LORI

Tears blurred the card. She missed them so much. Chad was coming up on his first anniversary of the ruination of his life, and she wanted to be there for him. She knew so much hell was about to return in horrid flashbacks. But should she go? Would she even be able to come back to Seattle? Back Home. But was Seattle home? She wasn't sure.

Dropping the mail on her bed, Sierra stared at Onyx. "I can't go back there. I can't leave my parents alone again. I can't do that to them. Not after what they went through."

Sierra waved the unopened letter from the Seattle Nursing School, knowing there was an acceptance letter waiting in it. Her dreams to be a nurse could easily happen right there in Seattle.

She still had heard absolutely nothing from the school in Kansas City. Chad mentioned Dr. Kendrick was dealing with the politics there. After this long, she didn't believe anything would change. *Patient and Pornstar* would forever haunt her there.

Still, she missed Chad. They had been through so much. He had been there for her every time she really needed someone. In the hospital when they let her go, even though he should have stayed. When she nearly killed herself, never leaving her side.

You're still a virgin. That was absolutely insane, but Chad had no idea what that meant to her. *You've never been loved by a good man.*

Well, he was a good man ... still in love with his dead wife. Even if she could land a "good" man, once that guy found out about her past, she would be history. In truth, she wasn't sure she wanted to be with any man. Being a nurse was all she was reaching for now.

The night she went to a Christian Rally with Larry and Susan flashed in her mind. Everything came together. She understood what Rosie and Chad's parents had been talking about. She'd not only found Christ that night, but met a girl, Michelle, who was trafficked too.

Michelle had fallen in with a guy she thought was her forever boyfriend, who then proceeded to break her down like Mario. She was saved at a truck stop by a trucker trained in TAT–Truckers Against Trafficking.

Michelle was part of a group saving other girls now, helping them get their lives back. She had invited Sierra to come to share her story as well as meet the other girls.

Maybe God was working in her life after all. Maybe God had been all along. Like Chad's father said, "I'm sure God has a plan. I know we must wait on God to pull it off ... but remember, Sierra, God has eternity on his side, so it may take a while."

Chapter 41

The doorbell rang, halting Sierra's thoughts. It was midday. No one was expected. Sierra walked through her parent's ranch style house to the picture window to see a strange Rogue Sport in the drive. License plate – California. The doorbell rang again. This time she heard Lori's voice.

"It couldn't be?"

Sierra raced to the front door to open it to Chad and Lori who were considering whether to leave or stay. Joy exploded at seeing their faces as she joined them on the porch. "What are you two doing up here?"

Lori immediately clutched Sierra's waist. "To take you back home," she said, "You have to."

Chad's smirk remained contained in his compression mask, but it was real. "Lori, we talked about this flying up here."

"Come in, both of you." Sierra stepped back, holding the door. She waved to the couch by the wall. "Want something to drink?"

"Water's fine," Chad said

"You have lemonade?" Lori asked, trailing along toward the

kitchen with Sierra. Chad also followed as far as the dining room table in the breakfast alcove.

"Let me check," Sierra answered, claiming glasses from the cabinet to begin filling them with crushed ice. "How's Owen?"

Lori started off with a tirade of stories of Owen's antics as well as misbehaviors. Sierra laughed as she poured water into glasses. She shrugged, "No lemonade."

"You have anything else?"

A natural bliss floated around Sierra as she went on the hunt for 'something else.' Rummaging in the fridge, she located a bag of fruit juice. "Will this do?'

"Oh, yes, thank you, Sierra." Lori glanced at her dad for approval. He nodded, still standing there watching, his blue eyes dancing.

"Okay, tell me you didn't come all this way for me?" she asked as she handed Chad his glass. They ventured back into the living room.

"Well, everyone misses you. Even Axel," Chad said as he sat down in the chair.

Lori immediately claimed the space on the couch beside Sierra. Instinctively, Sierra wrapped an arm around the girl as she listened to Chad relaying what the guys were doing, his new job. It was music to hear them, see them, but it had a note that felt strangely off key.

Had they wanted her back in Kansas City? Did she want to go? Yes, but … everything here was setting up perfectly. She wasn't sure of anything, even if she did return.

Her family was here in Seattle. She could now finish her final semester, have her nursing degree as well as a future there helping other trafficked victims.

"How is the job?" she asked, to stop the growing feeling of a trap.

"Great," Chad stated. "Really great. I've passed my initiation with Southwest, so we can fly free now. That's how we got up here which is nice if you carry on everything."

"You're able to manage the baggage?"

"Good thing I worked out with the guys like I did," Chad said with a smirk. "The first week was hell. But I like it. Not sure about winter though. That should be interesting."

"You look good," she said. He really did. Chad seemed happy in a content way. She had spent a lot of time praying things were going well for him. He deserved it. Was he having flashbacks? What were the doctors saying about his progress? Had he seen Jason? Dr. Kendrick? Her questions were endless. But she let Chad talk. She wasn't ready for those answers yet.

"Charlie and Allyssa got married last month. They missed you being there."

"Married?" Sierra sank back in the couch. She'd missed it. Allyssa had wanted her in the wedding. The pit of her stomach dropped. No one had said a word.

"It was a small wedding," Chad said. "I guess they decided to put the money in their house instead of a honeymoon."

"So, they didn't go to Capri?"

"Nope. Branson. For the weekend." Chad shrugged. "They got a nice house though, in Lee's Summit."

"Yeah, our house," Lori informed.

"What?" She stared at Chad. "You sold your house?"

"We haven't closed, yet. But, the drive to the airport got really old. So, I am looking for a house up north. We can stay with mom and dad until I find the right place. Or, I can even stay with a few of the guys on the ramp."

Sierra studied the stranger telling her all this. "You really sold your house … to Charlie and Allyssa? After all the work you put into it?"

"Yep. Figured, I've got to move forward." He remembered something. "Oh, I need to get something out of my luggage. I'll be back."

Sierra looked down at Lori whose gaze was on her. "Is it a surprise?"

"Maybe," Lori smirked. "But I really want you back, Sierra. I miss you." Tears wrinkled her delicate gaze.

"I miss you every day, Lori."

Light blossomed in the girl's blue gaze. "Then, you'll come home?"

"Lori, this is my home. This is where my parents live. And, they haven't had me with them for very long. So, I need to stay here for a while."

"They could come, too."

Chad reappeared through the door. "Got it." He walked toward Sierra with envelopes in his hand. "These are for you." He handed her letters from both the school and the hospital, as well as one from Dr. Kendrick's office.

Holding them as if frozen, Sierra studied Chad. She wasn't ready for what she might find inside them. Not now. Not yet.

"Uh, would you guys like to see some of Seattle?" She glanced at Lori. "The Space Needle?"

"Sure! What's a Space Needle?"

"Come on. I'll show you."

The drive into town eased the anxiety. Chad drove while Sierra directed as if she knew where she was going. He could see she was almost as lost as he was. *Thank you, Google Maps.*

Lori was agog watching for the towering icon of Seattle. "Can we go up there?"

"We'll try," Chad said as he fought the traffic while under the instruction of the robotic director on the car radio. Meanwhile, Sierra pointed to help him through traffic to find the necessary 'right' turn.

Sierra sounded happy. Really happy. He could even add content. All that itched. Yes, he wanted her happy, content ... but not there. He should want that for her ... there with her parents. Her parents deserved having the daughter that was stolen from them.

What had hit him when he offered Charlie the house was that selling it to them wasn't because of Margery. It was because of Sierra. Neither of them was there. It was like living in an empty tomb.

Yes, the drive to the airport was a bitch and living closer would be amazing. Gladstone was great for Lori's schools. Maybe north around Smithville. Maybe get some land.

"I can't believe you sold the house to Charlie," Sierra stated as if reading his mind. "Where are you thinking of buying?"

"Smithville, Gladstone, Platte City. Lots of land out there."

He wanted to tell her he had thought of transferring with Southwest to Seattle. He blocked that immediately. He wasn't sure Sierra would even want him moving in on her parent's doorstep. "I just don't know yet."

"You have arrived," announced the voice from the car stereo.

Chad found a parking spot on the street. It was mid-week, but the tourists were still milling about like mosquitoes. He bought tickets as Sierra pointed up at the iconic Space Needle towering overhead. Lori's eyes were ablaze with amazement. The fall day was cool, bright, filled with fresh salty air.

Fortunately, the line to the elevator to the glass floor wasn't exceedingly long. Like the other parents in line with their kids, Sierra held Lori's hand. Chad claimed the other. The closer he came to the elevator, the tighter his inside drew.

Chad forced himself to just listen to the happy chatter around him. Chatter that sounded much like the day at the Farmers' Market. Breathing, forcing each breath, he inched closer to the elevator. *I can do this. I can.* Yet, the instant the elevator doors closed and started upward with the eight others riding with him, Chad felt the panic attack surging through his body like vicious storm.

Breathe, Chad. When you feel this, breathe. Look around you. Find a difference. Dr. Larson's soothing voice whispered over and over. The difference was he was in a box, and he couldn't get out of it. Nor could anyone else. He couldn't get out. He …

"Chad, we are almost at the top. Two floors. One floor."

He sucked in the sound of Sierra's voice. Bing! The doors opened. He shoved his way free. Agitated glances from the others were instantly forgotten by the view.

Chad froze in the elevator hallway as everyone dispersed to their own section of the glass wall to view the vast city dressed in emerald green below. Beyond was the distant Pacific, the bay as azure as the sky. All he saw was the glass. All he saw was how far they all would fall.

"Chad?"

"Uh. Go on. I have to find the bathroom. I'll … uh … join you."

He watched Sierra lead Lori toward an open section of the plate glass window. He saw the crowd *oohing* and *ahhhing* as they too milled about like the people had at the Farmer's Market. He remembered leaving Margery with Lori at the table just as he was leaving Sierra and Lori. He couldn't leave them. He couldn't leave them. He closed his eyes to it all. But the bomber reappeared. He was ready to pull the cord. He was ...

"Sir, are you okay?"

Chad's eyes popped open to the security guard. "Yes. I'm ... fine. I just need to join my family ... over there." He felt the sharp gaze follow him as he forced his footsteps closer, one at a time, closer to Sierra pointing out something to Lori. He saw Margery listening to Lori.

"Sierra, we have to go. I have to get out of here."

Panic flooded her face. "Okay. We can go back down now. Chad. We are leaving. Come on."

"Daddy? Are you okay?"

"No, honey, he's not. We need to get him to the car."

Chad gripped Sierra's arm like a lifeline. The security guard held the elevator open for them to escape. He felt every inch of the elevator dropping. Tremors had claimed him by the time it stopped at the ground.

Sierra clutched his arm stopping him from bolting free of that trap. "Walk, Chad. Don't let this place win. Walk with me, Chad. Walk with me and Lori."

The desire to flee, to run for cover was ready to explode inside him. Chad stopped to study Sierra's green gaze as hard as an emerald could be. Swallowing hard, he claimed Lori's hand, forcing himself to walk with Sierra, stride for quick stride toward the car.

Sierra had to drive. He was in no shape to think. But the moment the car pulled from the parking space, he started breathing.

"What happened, Daddy. Were you scared?"

Chad closed his eyes on the verging tears. They were safe. They were all safe. "Yes, sweetie, I was scared. But I'm proud that you were brave. Did you like the view?"

"Yes. It was beautiful. Did you like it, Sierra?"

"My favorite part was the water. It seemed to go on forever. What was yours?"

"The trees. They were beautiful."

Chad forced his attention to the conversation. Would he ever be able to enjoy going places with Lori? No. He couldn't do it alone. Not alone. Sierra had gotten him out of there. She knew him.

"Can we eat. I'm hungry."

"I know just the place," Sierra announced. "It's not far. In fact, it's new called 'Dog in the Park'."

"Great. We can pretend it's Owen's restaurant. Right Daddy?"

"Sure." In fact, he was starting to get hungry. Not only that, but a sense of victory accompanied that hunger. "In fact, I'm really hungry."

Holding red checkered boxes lined with a huge pieces of wax paper, they carried their fries and hot dogs to a bench inside a park. Their sodas were viciously sweating by the time they put them on the wooden tabletop.

"Can I go play?" Lori asked, eyeing the children racing around the massive playground, swinging on the swings, climbing on the play equipment.

"Sure," Chad answered just as Sierra suddenly froze.

Chad studied her. "Sierra?"

"It happened just over there. The van. Over there." She pointed across the playground. "I was where Lori is." Her gaze rested on Lori now running off with a girl toward the swings. "There were bushes everywhere then. They cut them down."

"Probably because of you, Sierra."

Her gaze shot to him. "Me? Why me?"

Chad shrugged. "Because you were kidnapped right here. That bastard used the bushes as a blind. So, they cut them down to protect the other kids from now on." He smiled at her.

Sierra sipped the iced soda. He could see her stewing on the idea. They both watched Lori laughing with her new friends, playing innocently as if nothing horrible had happened in that exact spot. Sierra scanned the perimeter. He knew she was looking for a white van.

"I don't want any child or parent to go through what I did." She turned toward him. "There is a group here that is helping girls who have escaped trafficking. I met them at church."

"Church? You have a church?"

She smiled softly. "I went to a rally with Susan and Larry, Chad, I asked Jesus to save me. I think he did."

"That's great Sierra. Yes, he did. Nothing is sorta with God."

She smirked. "Okay. Then, yes, I am saved. How about you? Are you back on good terms with Jesus?"

"Me?" Chad studied his fries. They looked better than his thoughts. Eating one, he answered, "I couldn't live with Margery and not be." He ate another. "But yeah, we're on good terms, I guess."

It was his turn to sip the cold soda to gather his thoughts. "I've asked God over and over why? He never answered me. Not once. But I think, maybe, it was for you."

Setting her hot dog down, Sierra stared at him like he'd lost it. "Me. Why me?"

Chad shrugged. "Mom always said, God's into two-fers. You and me." He looked at her seriously. "You mind if I take this thing off so I can eat?"

"Go ahead."

He was about to bite into the most delicious looking hot dog he had ever seen when Lori's new friend screeched. They both shot their attention toward the swings to see the girl pointing at him.

"Oh, that's my daddy. He got burned bad. But he's all better now," Lori said as she swung. "You want to meet him? Come on."

Carefully, the kids followed Lori toward the table. Every nerve in Chad's body wanted to replace the mask to hide behind it.

"Is that really burns?" a boy asked.

Chad nodded. "A very big one." He scanned everyone's wide-eyed gazes. He pointed at his face. "This is why you don't play with fire. It is not only ugly, but it also itches."

The fear evaporated to an onslaught of questions. "What happened? Why? When? Sierra helped answer a few. He just kept warning them. One kid said he looked like Freddy Krueger but without an ear. Chad agreed with him. Finally, they all went back to playing as all kids do.

Sierra studied him. "You are getting better at dealing with everything."

He shrugged. "I didn't tell you, but, last month, the mayor wanted to present me with the key to the city. I wasn't going to go. Really. I wasn't. But Dr. Kendrick talked me into it." He smiled. It felt good without the ever-present reminder of the compression mask.

"I met a few others who were also burned by that bastard. I also found out I wasn't the only one who lost someone that day. There were four other families who lost someone. We're meeting now at the church to talk about dealing with this hell."

"Talking does help," Sierra admitted with a shrug. "I told you I joined a group who helps trafficked victims get a life back. I want to keep helping them."

Chad worked his soda around in its sweat ring. "Do you think you could ever come back to KC?" He looked up as if he had eyebrows.

The flash of excitement faded almost instantly. "Oh, Chad, the nursing school here has no problem with me graduating. And the hospital is great. But mainly, it's my parents. Chad I can't do that to them again … leave them." She rested a hand on his wrist. "Kansas City hasn't offered me anything but you."

"But me?" That did feel good hearing her say that he was something to her. "Did you read those letters I brought."

"No. Did you … read them?"

"No. But Dr. Kendrick told me he wants you working from his office with him, and Jason said he is expecting to see you in the burn unit." Chad studied the shock on Sierra's face. "And, Sierra, I do want you back All of us do. But I mean it. So do I." He did. He had enough holes in his life, and he had discovered that Sierra's now was the largest.

"What?"

"Lori wants you back. Like I said, all the guys do. My folks. We all miss you. Even Owen."

"But my parents?"

She was right. But he had to say it. It had burned in his brain since he left Kansas City. "I get it. But Sierra, I never thought I could want someone in my life again, not after Margery. But I do. Will you marry me, Sierra? Please, let me love you as you deserve to be. Because I already know, I love you, Sierra Ogden."

All Sierra could do was stare at Chad. He wanted her to marry him? Every part of her wanted to say yes, but the word clogged in her throat.

Who would want used trash like you? You're nothin' but ruined goods. Used like yesterday's trash. Were these more lies?

Did Chad really want her to be a part of his life? Not just a caregiver? A Margery replacement?

Then she thought about was the marriage bed, sleeping with him, sharing his bed. Sharing herself with him. Would it be different from a prostitute's bed?

You're a virgin. You've never known the love of a good man.

Chad noticed her hesitation, "I wouldn't blame you if you didn't … I mean, I'm not much to enjoy. I know that. But I really miss you. Maybe more than Lori."

She could see he was hurting. "Chad Michaels, there isn't a better man alive than you. Handsome even. I've known very good-looking men with hearts of beasts. You are not one of them. You are good inside, which makes you even more beautiful," she announced defiantly.

He almost laughed. "Beauty is in the eye of the beholder. But I don't see it."

"Of course, you don't see it. But I do. You are a good man, Chad Michaels. Worthy of everything good in life."

"But not you?"

"Me?" Sierra shook that question off. "You know I'm ruined. I can't have children now. Colton took care of that with the first abortion. And, well... I don't know if..."

A slow smile eased over his lips. "Sierra, you are not ruined. Just damaged by life like I am. So that makes us mirrored reflections of each other. You inside. Me outside. But I know the wonderful person that you really are.

"I understand why you wouldn't want to ... marry me even if you do see past this mess." He waved at his face. "You've got a life here now. I get it. But like Lori, I don't want to lose you. We love you." His gaze darkened. "I love you, Sierra. I want you with me for as long as God will allow."

Chapter 42

Chad stood by the immense front doors, ready to follow Pastor Pete into the sanctuary. Via his connections, his dad had managed to arrange for their wedding to happen at Powell Gardens Chapel. The angular, glass building rose majestically amid the woodland backdrop of the park dressed in green finery.

Since they had return to Kansas City, the world around them had exploded like it was Christmas. After the day in the park in Seattle when Sierra said yes, he had asked her father's permission to marry his daughter. Tears filled the man's gaze. "If that is what Sierra wants, of course."

Even though Sierra appeared thrilled to be back, Chad knew she had brought the baggage of leaving her family with her. Then, the news arrived that her parents had decided they wanted to move to Kansas City. After all, they could live anywhere since they were retired. That was followed with the news that Susan and Larry had decided they could work anywhere. KC would work for them. Mike Jr., surprisingly, was a KC Chiefs fan. He couldn't wait to go to a game with the guys. Now, they were all in the front pew across from his parents.

Chad had to admit the guys were all enjoying Sierra's Scottish attire for the wedding day. Wearing a kilt was rather nice; he liked the feel of a breeze drifting under his green plaid skirt. The loose collar of his white shirt was made more comfortable by the absence of the compression suit. The black leather vest gave it all a manly look. Fortunately, the white wool knee-hi socks covered the burn scars over his legs.

Also wearing kilts, Axel and Owen had escorted the families to the front pews while Ryan, Charlie, and Hunter were busy taunting Mike Jr about how cute he looked in his kilt.

The drums, violins, and bagpipes had those inside the chapel patting their knees, clapping, and dancing in their seats. Dr. Kendrick, Dr. Larson, Jason, and Nicki were seated among what seemed to include his entire church. Not only that, but the media had found out about the wedding, they were snapping pictures faster than the mosquitoes could bite.

After first mentioning eloping, he and Sierra had become under constant guard by both families, especially Lori. Yet, they had dodged all attempts for wedding showers. He was glad they hadn't run off. Sierra deserved this wedding.

Yesterday, he had buried his wedding band with Margery. It seemed to take forever to slide her ring off his finger. He stood there like a guilty boy, waiting to be chastised for doing something wrong.

"Please, understand, Margery. I really do love Sierra. I mean, I love you, too. And I will always. But it's empty without you. Lonely. Sierra fills that. I mean, Margery, I want her in my life. Lori needs her. I ..." Tears clotted in his eyes. "Please understand. I love you. I always will, Margery. But I love Sierra, too."

The bluebird dropped from the nearby tree limb to settle on Margery's head stone. It cocked his head then flew away, taking Chad's guilt with it. "Thank you, my love. Thank you."

"Ready?" Pastor Pete asked with a grin.

Jerked back to the present, Chad answered, "No."

"Too late, my friend," Ryan grumbled. "Time to wear this dress down the aisle. Now move."

The instant Pastor Pete appeared through the massive doors, bagpipers announced their arrival. Bravely, all followed to the raised platform backed with huge panels of glass. Nothing but blue sky and amber sunlight flooded in. As expected, they lined up before the first pew where Owen and Axel now sat.

Seeing the white limo arrive at the side building meant that Chad and the guys had entered the chapel. Sierra's heart stopped. She was really going to do this. Marry Chad.

Constantly fingering Ryan's cross on the chain, once again, around her neck, Sierra felt every adjustment that her mother made to the drape of her gown that poured down her left arm. It was like a long white wing attached to the shoulder of the asymmetrical gown that flowed over her like silken cream.

Meanwhile, Chad's mom continuously poked at her hair wrapped up in a French roll and crowned with large white bow. A crystal medallion, laid like a weight on Sierra's forehead that flowed all the way down the white wedding gown.

It all felt like a lie. Everyone in the church knew her past. They all knew she was no virgin. But there she stood in a white gown as if she were.

Chad's voice kept playing in her mind. *Yes. A virgin. Because you have never known the love of a good man.*

He was that good man. The absolute best. The only one who was capable of claiming her heart. The only man she could ever love. Because of him, her past had healed. Colton, Mario, Levi were all dead. Onyx's tracksuit now lay in ashes in the fire pit. Juliano's earrings had paid for the wedding.

"You look like a princess!" Lori exclaimed, jerking Sierra back to the small dressing room. Chad's daughter danced toward her like a pixie fairy already tossing rose petals to the ceiling like fairy dust.

Rosie, Allyssa, and Cheyenne swept in behind the girl, gathering the petals to return them to Lori's basket for her trek down the aisle. They were all wearing green satin dresses with a matching plaid sash.

"You are beautiful, Princess," Her father's smile radiated with tears as he walked toward her. "I thank God for this day that I never thought I would have."

"Me either," Sierra said as he claimed her hands. Tears threatened her mascara. The sound of Susan bursting into view stopped them.

"The limo is ..." She stared at Sierra like she was a stranger. "Hey Sis, you are going to knock 'em dead." Susan gave her a quick hug. "Your chariot is waiting."

"You ready, Princess?" her father asked as he offered his arm to escort her.

While the bagpipers played jig after jig, the guests were dancing in their seats, clapping to the fun beat, or patting their legs. Even the guys lined up behind Chad were all but dancing. To everyone's amazement, Axel got up to dance a jig. Owen joined him, jumping about like a frog. Chad had to admit, he wanted to, too, but he couldn't breathe.

Fear trickled through him. The last few days felt like a fantasy, but no, this was real. He was getting married ... again.

Through the glass front, he saw the white limo pull up outside the church. The girls climbed out. Mr. Ogden stepped out, offered his arm, which Sierra claimed. Then the small party started up the sidewalk.

Sierra hadn't panicked as he thought she would. There she was, coming to marry him, to promise to spend the rest of her life with him when she deserved someone who wasn't a monster. *God, don't let this one end like before. Please.*

A long silence filled the sanctuary, then the drums thundered. Bagpipes added a long drone cut by the whine of violins, which brought everyone to their feet as the front doors opened wide.

Cheyenne appeared, then Allyssa, then Susan, then Rosie, all carrying white lilies and white roses. The pipers matched Lori's dance down the aisle as she tossed rose petals toward the rafters.

Then, silence. Again, the closed doors opened to the boom of the drums as the pipers presented Sierra, escorting her down the aisle like royalty.

Chad felt her gaze fasten on his, claiming every part of him. It was all he could do to stay put until her father placed her hand in his. It came with the same touch he remembered in the hospital.

Flashes of that nurse in scrubs, hair drawn back, no makeup. Then the image of her sashaying out into the yard came. It all evaporated against the image of the angel smiling at him. He kissed her knuckles and then drew Sierra to his side. Together, they faced Pastor Pete.

He didn't hear anything Pastor Pete said. All Chad knew was Sierra was beside him. She turned, her gaze caressing his face. "Chad Aaron Michaels, you are the most beautiful man I have ever known," she whispered. She pulled her hand away from his grip, to caress the side of his face. "You are the only man I want to share my life with. I will love you forever."

His hand rested on the one cherishing his scars. "Sierra Marie Ogden, you are the most beautiful woman God could ever created, but I know you are even more beautiful for I have seen your soul. I will love you every day of my life."

"You may now kiss the bride."

He did, with every ounce of his soul. But he also felt hers caress his.

The End
Or beginning. Whatever you wish it to be.

Notes

Mirrored Reflections is a *Beauty and the Beast* with a touch of *Phantom of the Operas* story. While Chad was destroyed on the outside, he remained beautiful on the inside. Sierra was destroyed on the inside but remained beautiful on the outside. So, who was the beauty? Who was the beast?

I'll be honest. Writing this story was an emotional journey that, at times, tore me apart. I have shed so many tears of joy and pain while writing about the hell of trauma victims and their family, the hell of PTSD and complex trauma that so many of us never see, never *fortunately* experience. I understand the value of kind hearts and the beauty of God's love in all of it. Hebrews 13:5 "I will never leave you nor forsake you." He never did leave Sierra or Chad. He never will us either.

I believe that Chad and Sierra healed through their own valleys of death, but they did so much faster in this story than is typical. It takes trauma and burn survivors' sometimes years as well as lifetimes to heal.

I watched J.R. Martinez on *Dancing with the Stars* when he danced with Karina Smirnoff. She took J.R., a burn victim, and turned him into one hell of a sexy dancer. I think this story evolved from them. I also remember reading an article about a burn victim dealing with debridement, written by the nurse who had to put

as well as so many more who help us see God working in so many lives. His love is limitless. Churches are partnering around the world, doing all they can to help people realize the danger of pornography. It's not the prostitutes; they are just the victims of this lie.

Of course, I have the best of friends who have put up with me through this book. Angie, Zoe, Karlee, Peggy, Nurse Nicki, Jessica, and Jazzi. Hardee, Brian, Mark, Scott, and Christine. And of course, Mary, Cathy, and Lucy who brought this book to life. It wouldn't have happened without you.

I sincerely hope this story has opened your eyes to all the true angels who help along the way. I see Rosie catching the bouquet and the guys taunting Ryan who can't keep from smiling about it. I see the families melting into one happy clan. I also see Sierra becoming an advocate against human trafficking, helping save children from her hell. I see Chad helping her, doing the same for victims of PTSD caught sometimes in the literal fires of hell.

God works on all of us, and this is for His glory to make this world and everyone in it just a little bit better together. Just ask Him to help you. He wants to. He will never leave you nor forsake you either. But remember, He has eternity on his side. Be patient.

Hugs,

JF Ridgley

About the author

JFRidgley is an award-winning author of historical fiction as well as contemporary romance. What she does know is ... her mother is right. "Times change but people don't." This could not be more true in her stories from ancient Rome up to today. Other than writing, what keeps her sane is God, crocheting, landscaping and messing with wire art. Her home base is Florida, and her real life is about as exciting as watching grass grow. But her books...well ... that's another story.

Be sure to learn more about her books and short stories visit her website

http://www.JFRidgley.com